THE
LEGENDS OF
NOR'AI

WHENCE IT CAME

J.A.GLENN

Contents

DEDICATION

To my extremely loving family who have supported me every step of the way, they are my inspiration and driving force. Without them, this book may not have been possible. To my astonishingly brilliant friendship group who never stopped pushing me. To my beautiful pooches Jess and Luna for keeping me in my place. Also to my proofreader and great friend, who stayed patient, supportive and engaged throughout the entire process (even when events happened in the book that she may not have liked). Finally, to my GoFundMe donators, this novel was made possible by your overwhelming support and wonderful donations. You helped me bring my dreams to life and I can't thank you enough for that.

(This novel was funded partly by GoFundMe).

N
Oktherian
Trivillnae
Unity of Sebliaria
Cyorisian
Kobohrmia
Meranor
Ulnorei
Lehanor
Kingdom of Lochardia
Deythron
Tarlborn
Valanthrea
Uzarian
Isle of Dynestrael
Ores
Filran
Xelkorth
Hluinas
Onaranheas
Klonsalf
Brihand
Handeshona
Ancient Crypts
Paerlowe
Aeldren
Elenanae
Krytiare
Ragrug
Vavarinu
Murimia
Skaalli

1

<u>A LEGIONNAIRE'S</u> <u>DUTY</u>

Ten new moons had passed since the desolation of the Great War, leaving Nor'ai somewhat peaceful as the deep night fell. Since Arcturus could remember, the realm had been locked in an ever-changing ebb and flow as each species found its place. Now, though, even if just for a fleeting moment, Nor'ai's beings could breathe a sigh of hope.

Bright beams of crisp, silver moonlight weaved their way through the clouds to illuminate the dry, arid landscape of Uzarian. As the light crept across the plains, it reflected off a circular, bronze buckler beside a crystalline lake. Its dented and worn dome shone like a torch fighting back the darkness to highlight its wielder. Arcturus carefully slid his short sword from its scabbard and gazed along its blade. Running his sight over the remnants of his past conflicts, kills and victories, he felt a sense of pride. He knew each imperfection held a story, each scratch a conquest and every chip a tale of woe. All of these were worth it to keep Nor'ai safe. With a smirk, he spun the sword and plunged it deep into the dull, sandy soil, leaving it to reverberate like a gleeful flower on a windy day. Plumes of dust rose into the warm night sky and held there, allowing him to trace its path with his hand. He paused momentarily to admire the sweet scent of blossoming water lilies and the distant chirps of small insects trailing over the breeze.

This night seemed milder than usual, almost as if the setting sun had wanted to linger for a moment longer. Embracing the warmth, he gazed over his home and carefully placed down his spherical shield beside an ornate silver kite shield. The angular, white, marble buildings absorbed the dark horizon and sparkled amongst it like stars. Krytiare's outskirts were Arcturus' favourite spot in Uzarian to find a moment of tranquillity; this was where he felt most at home. He and his allies fought for it, for peace and harmony, for the solar gods, but above all, they fought for the realm. Krytiare was but a slight bastion of hope within Nor'ai; its size barely held a candle to the mighty cities like Elenanae and Vavarinu, but this small town did house two valuable assets. One was an almighty band of powerful virago and the other was The Grande Armoury known to house a magical sword of formidable strength.

Short sprouts of dull, green grass interrupted his thoughts as they rustled and clutched to the cracked soil in an attempt to thwart the breeze. He panned his sight over the shrubbery, then to the odd small mounds breaking up the skyline between him and the buildings. Running his hand over his tousled walnut hair, he embraced the feeling of the warm winds and returned his gaze to the town of Krytiare. Faint flickers from the torches danced about like fireflies as his fellow warriors patrolled the streets. Scratching his rough bearded chin, he smiled upon the glorious sight; this was home.

"My love, what are you doing?" Her welcoming voice trailed along the breeze, beckoning him.

Arcturus' brow raised instinctively. "I have never noticed how beautiful our home is until seeing it in this moonlight. It is truly a sight to behold." His deep, flowing accent rolled off his tongue.

The sounds of water lightly trickled behind him. "That's something I adore about you, Arcturus; you always seem to find the beauty in the smallest of things."

He turned to see Maeve resting against the riverbank. Only her forearms could be seen as she lay her head against her palm. Pausing for a moment, he absorbed her breathtaking image. Her astonishing braided auburn hair framed her soft, pale rose skin and lay upon her strong shoulders. Her toned muscles wonderfully complemented her feminine form as they tensed and shifted to reveal her elegant scars that held the secrets of a heroic past.

Arcturus smiled. "Well, one thing I can always find the beauty in is you, Maeve."

She smirked, "how do you always know what to say?"

"Trust me, I don't." He exhaled deeply and removed his cloth shirt. "But how could I not think you are beautiful? All I must do is look over your form and pick any detail to prove that you are the true image of beauty."

"Stop it, you fool. It is you who is the beauty here. I mean just gazing into your chartreuse eyes, I could lose myself." She pushed away from the bank as the glistening moonlight highlighted her runic gold and black tattoos running from her shoulder down to her left hand. "Why don't you join me?"

Arcturus' eyes fixated upon her toned body and pert breasts, refracting within the ripples of the water. "Let there never be a day where I turn that offer down." He unlatched his leather trousers and carelessly tossed them aside.

"I will end you myself before that day!" She chuckled and splashed the water. Absorbing his scarred muscular body as he walked, her gaze locked upon his manhood before his form became distorted within the crystalline water.

The legionnaire tensed at the temperature difference as the cool, crisp water saturated his light brown skin. "The waters are cold tonight." He smiled and wrapped his hands around her waist before pulling her close. "I could gaze into your golden eyes for an eternity, the way they sparkle is just mesmerising." He firmly grasped her neck and kissed her soft lips.

"All virago have golden eyes, my love, you know this," she ran her hands up his back, then pressed her lips against his once more.

Arcturus moved to her neck. "I do know this, but yours always seem to glow brighter than theirs."

"Well, I am a Warden. Maybe that's why?" her words became breathless.

He moved his hands over her body as he mapped each curve with his fingertips, "maybe you're right..." Her body welcomed his touch as her core excited with arousal. Focussing on her sensitivity, he teased and caressed every inch of her to build their pleasure.

She latched onto him, pressing his manhood against her, "I want you, Arcturus Pythare." After the words left her lips, Arcturus felt the animalistic urge burn through him. Locking themselves together, their bodies entwined in a harmony of pleasure. The water rippled around them with each movement as if echoes of their lust. With the sound of their moans calling out into the distance, their euphoria built with every second. Arcturus kissed and teased every inch of her body until she finally released, tightening around him. His jaw clenched and his groans grew deeper until he eventually erupted inside her. Maeve leaned back to catch her breath, her head weightlessly floating upon the water's surface. Arcturus smiled as he watched her float for a moment. Turning, he swam over to the bank to gaze over Krytiare once more.

She grazed the tip of her finger over the scars on his back. "So many battles we have fought together, everything we've done to keep this realm safe. Do you ever wonder if it's all worth it?" Maeve paused, "all these sacrifices we've made to become these respected warriors, yet we will never be able to match what was done in the Great War."

Arcturus glanced back. "What are you trying to say, my love? Do you not believe Nor'ai is worth fighting for?"

"No, of course it is. It's our home. I just fear that one day, it might all be shown that all we have done was for nothing." Her mind wandered. "Trying to live up to the names of the great Wardens before me is hard. Salzalar, Keitera and then there's Tahmaliea..."

"My mother would be proud of the Warden you have become. It is our job to keep this realm safe and you have taken her duties in your stride." Arcturus gazed into her eyes with pride.

"Hmmm, maybe you're right." Her fingers trailed over an arched scar upon his shoulder, "do you remember the battle that gave you this one?"

The legionnaire smirked, "of course I do, I really didn't see that gorltreth coming."

"And do you remember what you said to me when I found you lying there?" A playful joy bounced over Maeve's voice.

"'Worry not, my love! I can barely feel it!'" Arcturus chuckled.

Maeve pressed her forehead against his back as she laughed, "your arm was barely still attached! It was a good thing I found you!"

Arcturus turned with a gleeful smile, "without you, I would have died many battles ago." He kissed her. The lands fell eerily silent for a moment as they embraced. An almighty crack of thunder erupted in the far distance, followed by a sudden bright bolt of crimson light igniting the skies. "By the gods!" He turned Maeve to look upon the phenomenon before the beam swiftly fell silent. The ground rumbled momentarily, corrupting the water's soft surface with violent ripples. "Did you see that?"

Maeve focussed on the distance. "I caught but a glimpse." She looked at Arcturus, "what do you think it was? A storm?"

"No, that was too sudden for a storm and there seems to have been no aftermath." He turned to gaze into Maeve's golden eyes, "maybe it was nothing, but I have not seen anything like that before..."

Her brows raised. "Nor I. My love, what if this is our next purpose?" Swiftly, she pulled herself up the riverbank.

Arcturus watched the water trail down her pert buttocks. "What do you mean?" He followed her out of the water.

Maeve wrapped herself in red cloth ribbons and quickly donned her iconic silver armour. The plate was decorated in ornate engravings of the sun and moon that glistened softly in the moonlight. She lifted her helm and pushed aside its glorious plume of gold before sliding it onto her head, revealing only her golden eyes. "We are Nor'ai's protectors, we are here to keep the realm in balance."

"Correct." Arcturus threw on his leather trousers and cloth shirt then latched his burnished bronze plate and leather pteruges together. He slid his feet into his greaves and sabatons before clamping them shut. "So, you suggest what?" Ripping his sword from the ground, he sheathed it; they both claimed their shields in unison and smiled.

"Come, my love, let's find out what's happening. Once we know the threat, then we can assess how we deal with it." Maeve sheathed her sword and placed her hand against the angular cheek plates of his helmet. "It has been too long since we have fought a good fight for the realm's safety. A battle not of petty squabbles but instead for the good of the realm, for our gods."

Arcturus smiled and pressed his forehead against hers. "Then if this is that fight, let us fight together once more."

They moved quickly over the cracked dirt toward the town. The winds picked up and whipped loose soil from the ground, trailing them as they ran. Arcturus glanced back to the river where they had just swam then back to the town. Pushing themselves as hard as they could, they arrived at the town's border. Fellow legionnaires moved from their homes as they geared up and shifted to find their captain.

"Legionnaires, virago, do not panic. We know nothing of what just happened. Nor'ai is full of magical occurrences, and this may just have been one of them." A shimmering golden warrior moved amongst the crowded streets. "Most likely, it is something we will not have to concern ourselves with." The legionnairion runes and carvings glistened on his ornate breastplate, reflecting an almost blinding light.

Maeve gripped Arcturus' hand, "he is probably right." Arcturus placed his hand on her shoulder. Maeve pulled away and her eyes smiled.

"Arcturus!" A familiar sharp voice called from the crowd, "brother, do you know what is happening?"

Arcturus turned to see a dark-skinned legionnaire approaching him. Each step closer allowed the moonlight to reveal more of his sharp, slender features that flowed to his crescent-tipped ears. He embodied the ael-veth species perfectly with his elegance, height and precise mannerisms. "Sigmund!" Arcturus locked his hand against the warrior's forearm. "I'm afraid I know no more than you. We saw the beam reach into the skies but that's all."

"I see." Sigmund glanced aside. "Let's hope it's nothing more." He looked from Arcturus to Maeve and smirked, "you've been for a swim again, haven't you?"

"Pythare, where have you been?" A booming voice sundered the air as the golden, armoured warrior approached them.

Arcturus turned and slammed his fist to his chest, "I've been... relaxing, Captain Stayle." He slyly looked to Maeve.

Stayle frowned, "I'm sure you were." He rested his spear upon the stone street. "Our scouts have returned with reports of the beam originating within the lands of Deythron." Arcturus tilted his head before the captain retorted, "my response exactly. We all know those lands haven't been inhabited for aeons..."

"Is there not some form of magical permafrost surrounding those lands?" Arcturus looked over the legionnaires of varying races moving amongst the linear streets of Krytiare. "Have you told any of the others within our ranks?"

Sigmund donned his helm, "it was a very distant beam; maybe it was just the elements shifting?"

The captain cocked his head, "I have told no others, they will be addressed shortly." He looked to Sigmund, "let's hope you're right, legionnaire, but as we are so close to Deythron, we must be prepared."

"You are correct, sir," Arcturus agreed.

"Shall I ready the virago, captain?" Maeve spoke up.

"I don't feel we need to raise our defences just yet, no," Stayle smiled. "But we do need to be ready. So only leave the town for good reason." He turned and moved into the crowd before addressing the nearby legionnaires, then glanced over his shoulder, "oh, and no more 'relaxing' until this is sorted." With a chuckle, he left.

Sigmund watched Stayle walk away. "Deythron... Seems strange that something should awaken there after all this time."

"Something does seem off," Arcturus looked to Sigmund, "I will ensure the armoury is well protected, then I shall meet you in the centre." Sigmund nodded then swiftly moved away.

"I shall speak to the other virago and meet you soon, my love." Maeve pressed her lips against his cheek and smiled. Arcturus returned in kind, then walked through the crowds of legionnaires. Moving amongst the children while they were ushered back into their large square two-story marble buildings, Arcturus gazed over their beautifully carved architecture that was symbolic of the legionnairion triumphs. Red and gold drapings flapped against the marble in the warm breeze, as if caressing the smooth ornate windowsills. As he entered the town's centre, he gazed at the great structure of the Grande Armoury. Its vast triangular roof was held aloft by expertly crafted pillars and thick fortified walls. Two towering doors sealed the building shut while the symbol of a burning sun blessed their centre. He gripped the golden, ringed handles and heaved the doors open to reveal the endless racks of legionnairion weapons and armour. Several warriors stood guard with their swords and shields facing the doors while surrounding a large marble trapdoor.

"We have been tasked with guarding Karek'Thur at all costs," A stout dwethren legionnaire called out from behind his shield.

Arcturus nodded. "I know, there has been a happening within the lands of Deythron and I wanted to ensure the sunblade was safe."

The warriors acknowledged him, "Karek'Thur is fine, Pythare." Arcturus begrudgingly nodded.

"Wait, did you say Deythron? What could possibly be happening in that frost-scape?" A silver-tonged reptiare lowered his shield a little to reveal his auburn, scaled snout. Its tall, slender body shifted anxiously as its long, pointed tail curled around its feet.

Arcturus turned to walk away. "We don't know for sure it was there. But from the origin of the beam, it does look as if it was created in Deythron." He glanced over his shoulder, then strolled out of the armoury.

"Arcturus!" Sigmund gestured for him to join him and Maeve. As he walked over, a great thunderous rumble bellowed out from the night sky. The legionnaires and virago gazed up to see subtle orbs of burning crimson flicker into existence as if falling through cracks in the sky. Arcturus ushered Maeve and Sigmund to the outer edge of the town as they watched the cascade. Multiple balls of fiery unknown magic rained down over the surrounding lands and deep into Nor'ai.

"By the light..." Arcturus placed his hand against his chest. A small number of the orbs crashed into the arid plains of Uzarian. The group watched a distant guard tower crumple under the sudden impact, consumed by the crimson explosion.

"Our western guard tower!" Stayle's voice yelled over the destruction, "what in Nor'ai is happening?!" The captain's majestic gold and red accented figure pushed past the group as his plume of pristine white feathers upon his helm wove through the breeze. A few seconds passed until the final visible orb crashed into the distant hill-scape. "Legionnaires, virago, I fear this is related to that damn beam. Ready your weapons, we must fight to defend Krytiare!" The gathered warriors replied with a rousing cry and moved back into the town to ready themselves. "Pythare, gather some legionnaires and investigate the west tower, I need to know what we are up against."

"Yes, captain." Arcturus slammed his hand against his chest.

"Sir, should not a virago join them? We do not know what kind of magic we might be facing." Maeve stepped forward.

"You make a good point, Warden, select your virago and send her along too." Stayle nodded.

"I shall go with them, sir. My virago can stay to protect our town until my return." Maeve's eyes smiled.

Stayle grunted, "fine. But you must return to us, we need our Warden. You are Tahmaliea's chosen, we cannot lose you."

"I shall," Maeve retorted. The group armed themselves and moved to the stables. Several mono-horned keylep of varying browns, blacks and whites tossed their glorious multi-coloured manes while carelessly chewing on a bale of hay. The group swiftly readied them with saddles and leather armour before unlatching the steeds. Arcturus ran his hand down the rough, short hair of the beast as he gazed over its sharp curved horn and point-tipped ears.

The keylep's bright green eyes softened as Arcturus kissed its cheek. "It is good to see you, Lurric." Grunting at Arcturus' words, the beast softly stomped the ground with its hoofed foot. Arcturus smiled and turned to the group. "Sigmund, I would like you to join us." He placed his hand on his brethren's shoulder.

"It would be my honour." Sigmund gripped Arcturus' neck.

"I shall come too!" An eight-foot-tall, rouge, scaled draegorth called out from the street.

"Veyshren? Of course, you are more than welcome!" Arcturus welcomed the legionnaire with arms wide open.

"My sister was in that tower; I need to know her fate." Veyshren donned his helmet, leaving only his great muscular fanged snout protruding out.

He retrieved his keylep and readied it for the journey.

"Don't worry, we will find them," Maeve smiled, "Jaht'el is one of my finest virago."

Arcturus nodded, "then there is no time to waste!" The group commanded their keylep to leave Krytiare and ride out west in search of their lost brethren.

2

<u>INVESTIGATORY</u> MEASURES

Their short ride felt like an eternity as they pondered the fates of their allies. The dull rhythmic thud of the keylep's hooves resounded like a drum in their hearts, beating the anxiety through their veins. Scanning over the landscape, they watched the site of impact grow closer. The riders pushed their steeds with urgency as they galloped through the pluming dust until they finally reached the ruined tower. Arcturus commanded his keylep to slow while he panned over the destruction. Shards of marble lay piled upon themselves in a spherical pattern as if by some sickening design. Cracks of crimson light burned through the ground emitting from the great chasm created by the meteor before piercing through the arid soil. Drawing his sword and shield, Arcturus climbed the rubble.

"Don't get too close," Sigmund pulled Arcturus back, "we know not what's down there."

Arcturus raised his brow, "no we don't, but we need to find out." Sigmund glanced at Veyshren as they both slowly drew their weapons.

Maeve shifted the vast blocks of marble aside, "hello? Is there anyone alive here? Call out if you need our help." Grasping a heavy rock, she heaved as her golden eyes shimmered in the darkness. Glancing back down, she gasped at the sight of a bloodied hand unfurling. "Guys! Here!" Acting quickly, she ripped more of the debris away to reveal the trapped warrior's arm. Sigmund and Veyshren threw their weapons aside and leapt to her aid.

Arcturus climbed higher until he could see into the pit. A great spherical black and crimson meteor lay intact as it thrummed within the centre of the crater. Its unknown magical light seemed to beat brighter and faster the longer he stared. Glancing over to the trio, he felt the meteor beckoning his gaze. It pulled at his heart as he fought the urge to step closer. A thud rumbled through the ground, disturbing the rubble beneath Arcturus' feet. Steadying himself, he looked back to the meteor to see cracks forming along its exterior. He frowned before another thud beat out, shaking the ground once more. Swiftly turning, he sprinted back toward solid ground and shook the image of the meteor from his mind.

Sigmund bowed his head over the uncovered legionnaire's corpse. "He's gone. I think we need to search for the others." He glanced up to see Arcturus sprinting carelessly in his direction. "Arcturus? What's going on?"

"Run!" Arcturus yelled as he grabbed Sigmund and Maeve before urging them away from the rubble.

Veyshren turned as he watched them run past, "guy's what's hap—" A final almighty thud beat out once again. The meteor exploded, sending shards of the broken tower hurtling into the skies. Crimson magic whipped out of the crater, like serpents weaving through the rubble. They lashed at the ground, forcing the marble aside before entwining around the fallen warriors buried in the destruction. Arcturus, Maeve, and Sigmund stood with jaws agape as the crimson ignited the lands around them in sickening light. Tearing the corpses from the ground, the crimson held them aloft. Several dead legionnaires and a singular virago whipped back and forth in the grasp of the dreadful magic.

"Sister!" Veyshren pulled his sword and shield from the ground, "let her go!"

Maeve's eyes widened as she watched the crimson magic pulsing through the bodies of the fallen, "Veyshren no!" Jaht'el's body spasmed before swiftly reanimating. Veyshren charged forth as the tentacle holding Jaht'el dispersed, dropping her to the ground.

She slammed to her knee and opened her now crimson eyes. "Brother, it's so good to see you." The tainted virago smirked and stood, "although it's such a shame to see you under such circumstances." The draegorth's exposed scales were a sickly grey with crimson light pulsing in cracks through them.

Veyshren slowed, "sister? You're alive?" He watched as several legionnaires landed around him, all glowing with crimson light. "What is this?" He readied his sword and shield, "what has that thing done to you?!"

"Oh, hush now. You're wasting your final breaths with petty questions." Jaht'el stepped forward. "Don't try to fight it, just embrace it." Her once vibrant scales were now grey and ashen.

Veyshren frowned, "I don't understand…"

"You will." Jaht'el flicked her wrist to form a crimson blade before lunging forward. She plunged it deep into the draegorth's chest and glared into her brother's eyes. Veyshren dropped his weapons as the burning agony tore through his soul. Glancing down, he looked at his sister's blade and the festering wound surrounding it. Jaht'el gripped his chin, then lifted his head to lock his eyes to hers again, "I will help you understand." A burning crimson light ripped through Veyshren's body as Jaht'el slowly removed her blade. "We will make them all understand!" She tossed her brother aside and shifted her focus to Sigmund, Maeve and Arcturus. "Bring them to me!" The corrupted legionnaires slammed to the ground beside her and nodded, claiming their weapons from the rubble.

"Jaht'el, stop! You don't have to do this!" Maeve readied her sword.

The draegorth raised her head as the cracks in her scales shone with crimson light. "Oh, my sweet Warden. Yes, yes, I do." Without hesitation, the corrupted legionnaires charged at the group.

"Fine! Arcturus, Sigmund, deal with those legionnaires. I will deal with her," Maeve snarled. She clutched her sword and shield, igniting them in golden light.

Arcturus nodded and looked at Sigmund, "where are your weapons?"

"I dropped them back there as we searched the rubble. There was no time to grab them." Concern washed over Sigmund's face.

Arcturus scanned over the assaulting legionnaires, "well, you need something. Here, take my sword."

Sigmund grabbed the weapon, "are you sure?" Arcturus nodded. "Let us fight together then." The pair charged toward the oncoming danger; Arcturus locked his shield against the corrupted legionnaire's blades. While deflecting their attacks he shunted them aside. Each blow beat against his shield, ringing through his muscular form in a symphony of clashing steel. Sigmund watched as one enemy stumbled. He seized the opportunity to plunge his blade through a slat in its bronze armour. Feeling the blade lock against its rib, Sigmund tore sideways and ripped apart its abdomen. The corrupted legionnaire growled in pain before a rush of crimson light burned through its core and out into the atmosphere. It adjusted its stance to counter Sigmund, but Arcturus slammed the rim of his shield into its skull. Its head shattered as the remaining crimson light exploded from its body before it fell to dust.

Arcturus smirked before the slam of a sword against his side broke his stance. Sigmund parried the blade, allowing his ally to recover. Ducking and weaving through the corrupted legionnaire's attacks, Sigmund sliced up removing its forearm. Sprays of blood and shattering bone sparkled in the night as the pair rebuffed the onslaught. Maeve watched the fight continue before beginning her charge. Her sabatons thudded against the dry soil as she exploded into a sprint. Illuminated in the golden glow of her weapons, she saw a rogue legionnaire break rank to attack her. In one glorious flow of movement, she deflected its blade before thrusting forth hers. Propelled by sheer strength, the weapon blessed by solar light burned through the legionnaire's shield before embedding deep in its chest. Maeve smirked as she watched the creature burn with golden light. In one final almighty push, she ripped out her blade, then swung through the legionnaire's abdomen. The sword carved through skin and bone as if it were butter, exploding out of its shoulder and bisecting the soldier. Crimson light plumed in all directions before swiftly falling silent and the husk turned to dust. Maeve's eyes darted from her fallen foe and back to the corrupted virago as she continued her assault.

Jaht'el glanced at her ally then back at Maeve before locking her feet firmly against the ground and summoning a crimson kite shield. She watched Maeve leap into a catastrophic swing. Crouching, she clutched her shield and released a blast of crimson magic from its centre. The impact pelted against Maeve's chest and tossed her aside. Arcturus saw the Warden slam against the dry soil before swiftly recovering. He opened his mouth before the metallic clash of a blade sundered against his shield. Sneering, he expertly slid his shield along the sword to force it away before pulling back and slamming the rim of his buckler into the attacker's chest, forcing it to the ground. Grabbing the legionnaire's wrist, he bent with all his might until he felt its bone snap. He grinned and ripped the blade from its fingers. Blissfully turning the weapon in his hand, he plunged it deep into the legionnaire's abdomen and pinned it to the ground. Smiling, he pulled his shield back then slammed it into the soldier's throat, slicing through its neck, releasing plumes of crimson.

"Nice!" Sigmund called out as he reclaimed his swords from a fallen legionnaire. He turned and slung one into the head of the last standing soldier. "Only that damn virago left!" In the corner of his eye, he watched Veyshren become imbued with corrupted magic from the fallen. Slowly, the draegorth pulled himself to his feet and locked both Arcturus and Sigmund in his sight.

"You both shall pay for eradicating my brethren," Veyshren growled.

Arcturus readied his weapons, "no, not you too!"

"Don't worry, Arcturus, we will make you see. Only then will you understand." Ripping his weapons from the ground, Veyshren charged forth.

Clashes of glorious gold and crimson flashed out into the night sky as

Maeve and Jaht'el traded blows. Maeve's golden blade slammed against the crimson shield before Jaht'el forced her back. Panting for breath, Maeve held for a moment. She watched the angle of her foes swing before calculating her retort. In a sudden spark of genius, she rolled beneath the weapon. Using her shield to push herself back to her feet, she urged her blade clean through Jaht'el's shield arm.

The draegorth screamed out in pain before turning her blade to face Maeve. "I'm fucking sick of your games!" She clenched her fist tighter around the crimson sword, "just die already!" A powerful beam of corrupted magic stormed out from the tip of the weapon. Maeve swiftly pulled up her shield. The almighty force surged her back as crimson light burned in a cone around her.

Holding strong, Maeve bared her teeth while her sabatons scraped along the ground, "whatever this magic is, it is not welcome in my realm!" She slammed her shield into the ground to summon a golden orb of protection around herself, then raised her sword to the skies, "by the light!" Within the clouds above sparked a bright golden beam of pure light. Cascading with glorious speed, the beam streamed through Jaht'el and ignited the land surrounding her. Dry soil kicked out in all directions as the agony of the corrupted virago cried into echoes before finally falling silent as the beam dissipated. Exhausted, Maeve fell to her knee with her weapons barely supporting her.

Veyshren glanced aside after deflecting both Arcturus and Sigmund's attacks to see the burned remnants of where Jaht'el once stood. "Sister?!" Before he could react, Arcturus forced his blade deep into the draegorth's knee. Veyshren collapsed as crimson light burst from his wound.

"I take no joy in this, brother." Arcturus released his blade and stepped aside. Sigmund moved from behind, then sliced his blades through the draegorth's neck, beheading him. Veyshren's lifeless husk fell to the ground before dispersing into crimson dust.

"What was that magic?" Sigmund wiped his blade clean before retrieving a buckler from the ground.

"I don't know, brother. It seems to possess whatever being the magic touches." Arcturus walked over to Maeve, "are you okay, my love?"

"I'm fine, thank you." Maeve pushed herself to her feet. "Are you okay? Did they hurt you at all?"

Arcturus chuckled, "just a few scuffs here and there but I'll live."

"I'm fine too…" Sigmund rolled his eyes.

Maeve laughed. "I was going to check on you, too." As the trio smiled, the debris from the fallen tower exploded into the skies. Diving to the ground for cover, they witnessed a great beast emerge from the centre of the destruction. Its tremendously thick serpentine body raised high above them as it curved back down to face them. Hundreds of bright crimson eyes burned to life and focussed on the trio before its deep brown slime-covered body began to rumble. Crimson tendrils ripped through the arid soil, pulling the fallen warriors around the beast back to life.

"We need to go!" Sigmund dragged Arcturus and Maeve to their feet. As they pulled back, the almighty beast's maw split open into four teethed segments to reveal thousands of razor-sharp teeth and a swirling inner jaw. Globules of saliva poured out as it released an ear-shattering scream before diving towards the party.

"Run!" Arcturus hailed out as he urged them away. They sprinted toward their steeds and flung themselves onto the saddles, forcing them into an almost instantaneous gallop.

3
HOMEWARD DESPERATION

Pushing their keylep with the utmost urgency, the trio stormed to Krytiare. They retraced the pummelled dirt as the hulking beast burrowed deep into the ground forming crimson cracks toward Krytiare.

Arcturus hailed his keylep aside to avoid the sudden bursts of rock and dust. "This is not good!" He glanced at Maeve who replied with a calming smile.

"I hoped that one day I would find myself a partner who smiles at me the way you smile at him, Maeve. But with this damn crimson foe, I might not live to see that day!" Sigmund called out.

Maeve chuckled, "I'm sure you will! Although if you survive, stop boring them with the story of how you single-handedly took down a drake."

Sigmund looked back in shock, "hey! I did do that!"

"Surely now is not the time for this!" Arcturus yelled in disbelief.

"True, my love," Maeve glanced at Arcturus then back at Sigmund, "but, Sigmund, you also don't bother to inform them it was nothing but a juvenile."

"Still counts! I don't need to tell every detail." Sigmund grinned. With their home only a few strides away, the creature burst from the soil at the border of the town. Blazing crimson burned bright in the night sky as the beast blocked out the moonlight. The trio watched on as an army of crimson warriors leapt from its back and raised from the soil beneath it.

Sigmund's brow furrowed, "so, how will we fight this beast?"

"I shall gather my virago then meet you at the front lines. Together we will all be stronger." Maeve turned her keylep toward the centre of the town.

"Be cautious, my love, we know not what this magic can do," Arcturus called out as he watched Maeve nod and pull away to the rear of the town.

Sigmund moved his steed closer to Arcturus. "Caution is overrated." Winking, he drew his sword. Arcturus grinned and drew his sword in return and joined the charge of legionnaires.

Crimson warriors struck down their opponents with reckless abandon before being met with the blades and shields of the great legionnaires. Limbs lay scattered across the battlefield as the clash of sword and magic screamed out into the warm air. Arcturus pushed his keylep into the thick of it, precisely swinging his blade to carve himself a path through the crimson warriors. Turning his sight forward, he saw a wall of foes linking their shields. Urging his mount to leap, Arcturus felt the strong muscular beast propel itself through the air. As they soared over the warriors, the steed released a blood-curdling cry. The impact of the beast slamming into the ground hurled Arcturus into the air. Gripping his sword and shield tight, he tensed before the dry, dense soil burst the air from his lungs. Clawing for air, the legionnaire attempted to compose himself. "Lurric, no!" He watched as his stead plunged its horn through the chest of a crimson warrior before falling to another's blow.

"On your feet, Pythare!" A golden gauntlet grabbed his shoulder and pulled him up, "now is not the time to relax." Stayle's stern gaze was barely visible through his helmet.

"My apologies, Captain!" Arcturus deeply inhaled as he turned away from his fallen keylep. Raising his shield, he slammed it into an oncoming foe, forcing it to the ground. Stayle nodded before gracefully twirling his spear, thrusting it through the downed fighter. Clutching his weapons, Arcturus pushed deeper into the fight. An almighty explosion of legion-nairion soldiers and soil burst before him as the worm-beast annihilat-ed their front lines before diving into the ground again. Blocking then swinging his sword, turning, ducking, weaving before executing one then another as the fight burned deep into the night.

"Arcturus, we can't win this! For every foe we kill, they claim one of us to bolster their ranks!" Sigmund yelled out as he clashed against a crimson foe. Arcturus slid his blade from the throat of a fallen dwethren warrior and gazed over the fight. Crimson seeped into the bodies and souls of his fallen brethren as they clambered back to their feet. A swift flash of gold sliced across his vision. Stayle forcefully struck the warriors, embedding his spear deep into a draegorth's armour. The kin stumbled back, steadying itself before focusing its vision upon the captain. Grasping its blade with both hands, it swung with almighty force. Stayle raised his spear to block its blow, but the sword tore the weapon in two before lodging into the golden captain's skull.

"Captain!" Arcturus pushed through the fight to Stayle's aid. He shunted a warrior aside before leaping onto the corpse of his fallen steed. Cascading onto the draegorth warrior with sundering force, Arcturus plunged his blade deep into its heart. The warrior released its sword as Stayle's lifeless corpse slumped to the ground. Arcturus forced the hulking draegorth to its knee.

"Why continue to fight when you know you've already lost? You are nothing, the crimson will claim all in the name of perfection!" Through gargles of blood, the warrior taunted Arcturus.

"The day I stop fighting is the day I draw my final breath. Until that day comes, I will fight on!" Arcturus ripped his blade from the warrior's chest before slamming his shield into the side of its head, snapping its neck.

"Arcturus, we must retreat!" Panting, Sigmund ran to Arcturus' side. "We need to protect the innocent and the sunblade."

Arcturus grunted as he watched more of his allies fall around him, "maybe you're right. Take some legionnaires back to the town centre, I will grab who I can and meet you there."

Sigmund nodded, "be cautious."

"Caution is overrated." Arcturus winked as Sigmund shook his head and ran into the midst of the battle.

Resounding through the skies, a blinding beam of golden light pierced the darkness above, breaching down toward the horde of crimson fighters. Seconds before the beam made contact, the soil parted, and the great beast screamed into sight. The golden magic tore through the creature, ripping it in half and eviscerating the warriors surrounding it, freezing the battle as the corpses disintegrated.

Arcturus smirked, "my Warden." Almost as soon as the first beam arrived others brightened the night sky. The solar magic resounded from the swords of the virago bolstering the lines. The iconic silver female warriors raised their weapons one by one. Summoning all their might to harness pure solar power, they cast beams of pure light down upon their chosen targets. Locking themselves into battle upon the border of Krytiare, they beckoned the few remaining legionnaires back.

"Retreat! We must defend our home from this madness!" Arcturus yelled over the battle as he gathered as many allies as he could. Fighting off the crimson onslaught, he aided his allies back to their ranks. He watched them as they forced their way behind the virago's lines then gazed over the destruction around him. Fallen legionnaires clambered back to their feet and reclaimed their weapons. Overwhelming sadness and anger befell him as he sneered.

An almighty roar echoed amongst the clouds before a great winged shadow of a gargantuan wyvern soared over the plains. The deep rumble of its flight sliced through the air, shaking the ground below. Gliding over the battle, its vast maw erupted in deep crimson flames, demolishing the remaining legionnaires outside of Krytiare. Guiding its burning destruction, the wyvern rampaged toward Arcturus. Knowing his shield could never block the power of a creature that size, Arcturus exhaled.

"If this is my day, then so be it." He lowered his weapons. The fire drew nearer as he closed his eyes; its heat was unbearable as it lapped against his flesh like hungry hounds. He fell to his knees until a rush of relief poured through his soul. He opened his eyes to see the flames flowing around him instead of through him, beating against a divine golden dome. The glorious magic surrounded him as the glimmering silver Warden held her shield against the flames.

"Today is not the day I let you die, my love." Her voice sang amongst the roaring fire.

"You already claimed my heart, now you claim my life, Maeve." Arcturus smiled.

The flame eased as the wyvern passed overhead. Lowering her shield, Maeve let the golden dome blink out of existence. She turned to Arcturus with her eyes still glowing gold as divine magic coursed through her.

"As I see your eyes, I feel your radiant beauty." Arcturus placed his hand upon the cheek of her helm.

Her eyes smiled. "In this realm, your heart and soul are my radiant beauty." She leaned in to press her helm to his but then jolted forth. Arcturus' eyes widened as he watched her shimmering silver armour rupture to reveal Stayle's golden spear ripping through her abdomen. The light of her eyes flickered as she gazed at Arcturus. She held a moment before slumping into his arms. Stunned in crippling despair, he saw the blood-soaked body of his captain standing in Maeve's place with the sword still lodged within his skull. Fuelled by grief, Arcturus placed her down and threw his shield with thunderous aggression. The bronze buckler swirled through the air, slamming into the hilt of the lodged sword. It split Stayle's head in two and he dispersed into glowing crimson dust. Dropping to his knees, Arcturus tossed his helmet aside and screamed in pain as he held Maeve's body.

"Take my pendant..." The words barely left her lips as she lifted the necklace toward Arcturus.

"My love?" His tears pelted her armour, glistening against the silver details of the sun and moon. He gazed up at the oncoming horde of his fallen allies then claimed the gold and white peony pendant centred with a sparkling gemstone. The gold of her eyes dimmed as her body fell limp. Arcturus gritted his teeth and glanced at the oncoming horde. Falling into the darkness of his mind, he barely acknowledged the continuing battle surrounding him as he moved back to the town. The bellowing roars of the wyvern tore through the skies as its flames lay Krytiare to ruin. His allies faltered as the crimson horde burst through the lines of virago and legionnaires holding the borders of the town. Innocent children and townsfolk were cut down where they stood or burned in the immolation of crimson flames.

"Arcturus!" the voice muttered at the back of his mind, barely able to cut through his subconscious. "Arcturus!" A legionnaire gripped his shoulder and pulled him back to reality, "Arcturus, get to the fucking armoury, we cannot let them claim Karek'Thur!" Sigmund stared into Arcturus' tearful eyes.

"She's gone," Arcturus muttered.

"I know brother, we must save what we can now, we have to survive." Sigmund gripped his head, "Maeve would want you to fight on, do not give up. Please, brother, we cannot lose, not now."

Arcturus turned away, "I don't see how we win this fight, brother."

Sigmund looked over his ruined home, "to be honest, nor do I. But we must try! Let us at least die with honour, together."

Arcturus raised his brow. "Maybe it's not about saving the sunblade, maybe now it is just about keeping it from these abominations."

Sigmund locked eyes with him, "then what must be done, will be done. Find the blade and destroy it." Arcturus and Sigmund locked arms, "die well brother."

"You, too." Arcturus pulled away as Sigmund raised his weapons and stood against the oncoming horde. Twirling his sword in his hand, he analysed his foes and smirked. He charged forth and locked blade against shield. Ducking and weaving between attacks, he elegantly sliced through several crimson warriors' defences. Pushing through the plumes of dust, he fought on. An almighty beam of crimson light burned through his abdomen and into the ruined buildings behind him. Sigmund glanced down to see the burning hole in his armour, then back up to the corrupted virago.

"Your cause is worthless, solarist." She stepped toward him.

Sigmund smirked a bloodied smile, "caution is overrated."

"What?" before she could react, Sigmund leapt forth and sliced his blade through her throat. He fell to his knees as the virago turned to dust and exhaled his final breath.

Arcturus watched his ally fall and clenched his jaw. As the swarm of emotions tore through him, he turned and pushed open the heavy doors of the grand armoury, allowing him to walk inside. Dim torchlight flickered against its pristine marble walls. Gazing around the structure, he searched for any remaining legionnaires. The weapon racks surrounding him lay bare as partially forged swords and shields sat abandoned. He scanned the floors to see the glorious golden latch sparkling within the room's centre.

Arcturus dropped his weapons in awe and walked over. Grabbing the latch, he turned it. Great churning cogs whirred and echoed about the building until veins of gold cracked within the architecture. Arcturus frowned and glanced around as shards of marble began falling from the ceiling and the great pillars crumbled. Suddenly, the trapdoor below him opened to reveal a dark staircase. Without missing a beat, he ran down into the abyss as the stairs shattered beneath his feet. Falling onto his chest, he gasped for air. The cool marble floor blessed his skin as the building shook around him. Glancing up, he saw it. A gloriously crafted blade etched with golden runes flowing down to its hilt. Its guard curved in an almost horn-like fashion, carved from astonishing golds and silvers, and centred with a pristine, sparkling clear gem. The handle was encased in twirled golden metal complimented by blood-red ribbons leading to a diamond-shaped silver pummel.

"Karek'Thur..." Arcturus stood up and walked to the blade. He lifted the spectacular weapon and wrapped his hand around its hilt. Gold ignited the room as the blade sang out at his touch. Waves of happiness and adrenaline poured through the legionnaire's soul as his eyes fixated on the weapon. Marble cascaded down around Arcturus as the armoury crumbled.

He glanced up and smiled, "I suppose today truly *was* my day to die." Kneeling, he rested Karek'Thur upon his thighs and placed Maeve's amulet on top of it. He locked his mind on his fleeting memory of Maeve and closed his eyes as the rubble finally encased him in unyielding darkness.

4
IN SEARCH OF REASON

Now is not your time, this realm needs warriors like you...

The words encased his soul and surrounded him in warmth, washing through him before deafening him with silence. Crackling abyssal darkness clouded his vision before a golden beam formed in the distance to lure him in from his weightless flight. Voyaging closer, he could almost see the image of a virago fighting a great battle within the bright light.

Divine magic empowered his soul, fuelling him with immense energies before transforming his body into the image of a golden phoenix. The darkness began to subside as he found himself guided through the clouds. Pristine blue skies sparkled overhead as he soared above a beautiful green field; on the horizon lay a town with majestic towering white structures that blessed the landscape. Bright pink and violet flowers peppered the familiar fields along his path while legionnaires trained, sparring with one another. A feeling of home comforted his mind as he scanned the plains. His memory attempted to lock together the broken pieces of his soul.

Reaching the town, he felt a sudden sadness as sparks of crimson began tainting the once lush fields. The ground swiftly became arid and lifeless as great crimson bolts cracked and pulsated through the soil.

Two thick, golden winds forced him higher, expanding his aerial view. A singular virago stepped into sight and raised her shield as all the others fled. She formed a golden barrier but as the corruption struck, the barrier shattered, allowing the beam to penetrate her heart. Her golden light became cursed as she raised from the ground. In one cataclysmic motion, she slammed against the ground and sent waves of corrupted magic through the souls of the fleeing. Arcturus hurtled down toward the ruins of the grand armoury as the shockwave struck. The structure lay in rubble as dark clouds swiftly passed overhead. Uncontrollably swirling down evermore into the darkened ruins, his eyes darted in panic before seeing a slight glimmer of golden light.

"I don't know how many times I need to tell you, Maveri, the weapon's gone."

The wizard glanced over his shoulder, "it can't be gone! I still feel its magic resonating here." He turned and pulled back the hood of his pristine white and maroon cloak. His grey-streaked brown hair remained perfectly quaffed as he stepped forward. "Do you understand how much magic this item is said to have? Unfathomable amounts! And if it is all a lie, do you know how much gold an item like that would go for?"

"Alright, alright, don't get your little goatee in a twist. We will keep searching. You and your fucking gold."

Slowly running his hand over his moustache, Maveri frowned, "little goatee? You're a cheeky fucker, Wreyth, you know that?"

"Oh, I know," Wreyth smirked.

"Would you two shut the fuck up?! We have no idea what happened here or if any of these beings survived. Let's try not to piss off anything that might still be alive." The pair glanced over to the demon to see her standing sneering back at them. Her core shimmered with ethereal green magic that gleamed up through her chest. Lowering her great spined scythe to the ground, she whipped her slender pointed tail around her clawed feet.

"Sorry, Aleiá," the pair spoke in unison.

"Thank you," Aleiá grinned to reveal her fanged teeth then closed her green eyes. She turned her angular horned head and sniffed the breeze, "something still lives around here, I can smell its soul."

Wreyth tilted his head, "you know when you say stuff like that you sound quite creepy."

"Oh, shut up and go back to searching for that stupid sword!" The demon's charcoal, scaled flesh shimmered in a ghoulish green. She slammed her tail against the ground and stormed off to search the rubble.

"You're right though, she does sound creepy when she says that." Maveri chuckled. Unlatching a large oak brown and gold accentuated leather book from his hip, he opened its clasp. "Maybe I can't find this sword because I'm not searching properly." He raised his hand over the pages of the book as they fluttered open. Slowly, they began to glow in azure light as symbols and words lifted from the page and surrounded the wizard. He surveyed the area as the pages continued to turn until finally, the ruins of a great building sang back to him. "There!" Swiftly, he snapped the book closed and the azure magic dispersed. Latching the book back to his hip, he adjusted his belts before trudging through the rubble. His boots crunched on the bodies and armour of fallen legionnaires while his blue and white cloth tunic rustled under his cloak.

Wreyth frowned. "Never have I seen a man always stomp with such purpose without concern for where he's treading." He chuckled, adjusting his black leather gloves before following the wizard. Joined by the demon, the trio looked over the rubble of the grand armoury.

Maveri closed his eyes and raised his hands over the fallen debris, "yes, I feel it! The sword is definitely under this."

Aleiá swirled her scythe as it formed into chitin-like armour on her back, "I feel it too. There is magic here with a faint hint of a soul." She crouched.

"Although not quite the soul magic I smelt on the breeze."

"Then what are we waiting for? If it's a solarist, then we can save them and ask what happened here." Wreyth started dislodging the rubble.

Maveri frowned, "what if it's something worse?"

"Then we kill it and I'll claim its soul," Aleiá twitched her brow then helped Wreyth. Maveri's frown switched to concern before nodding and helping to clear the rubble. His pockets jingled with the gleeful chimes of gold with each movement he made. The trio heaved the heavy marble and tossed it aside, piece after piece, as the hot sunlight pelted their backs.

Wreyth stood and stretched, "gods, it seems even in death you can still get a bad back." Aleiá tutted and pulled him back down to help. After a while, the group noticed a subtle golden light shimmering amongst the bricks.

"Wait, is that..." Maveri leaned in closer as Aleiá dislodged more marble, "it is! Solar magic! We found the blade!" Clearing the rubble with more urgency, the trio exposed a glowing dome of golden magic. "Fascinating!" Maveri hovered his hand over the magic, "it seems that Karek'Thur has somehow used its magic to protect itself." He placed his hand against the barrier before suddenly being pelted back across the pathway. Aleiá and Wreyth watched the wizard encase himself in azure magic as he slammed against the ground. They looked at each other before bursting out into uncontrollable laughter.

Maveri stood, swept his hand over his quiff, and dusted down his clothes. "That was not funny!"

Wreyth snorted as he wiped his face and beard, "you're right, it was fucking hilarious!" He glanced down to see Aleiá still rolling on the ground laughing.

Maveri adjusted his tunic as he stomped back to the golden dome, "it seems as if I'll have to dispel this barrier myself then." He whipped his book from his side and began waving his hand over the pages as azure words lifted and surrounded him once more.

There are others here, you must awaken and defend yourself.

The soft voice caressed the legionnaire's mind as Arcturus slowly opened his eyes. He glanced up at the golden barrier encasing him to see its magic weakening. He ran his fingers along his battle-worn breastplate to find Maeve's amulet missing from his neck. Clenching his jaw, he gripped the hilt of Karek'Thur and stood. As the barrier dismissed, he charged forward and shunted the wizard aside before locking his blade against Wreyth's throat. He glared into the calastain's glowing ethereal eyes, then mapped his face. His sharp features led to a wonderfully carved beard. Upon his stern angular brow lay crisp, white waved hair that was shaven at the sides. His scarred skin was a pale lilac, and his ears led to a triple point. Arcturus frowned; his sight scanned over Wreyth's armoured moss-green long coat, latched together by a thick leather belt centred with a demonic buckle.

"I wouldn't try that if I were you..." Wreyth smirked and gestured behind the legionnaire. Arcturus slowly glanced over his shoulder to see Aleiá snarling at him with her scythe primed. Her demonic form trembled with ethereal magic.

"Who are you and why are you here?" Arcturus growled.

Maveri stood, brushing off his sleeves once more, "it's nice to meet you too." He stepped forward, "now, please lower your weapon so we can explain why we are here. It's either that or I will have to kill you."

Arcturus scowled at the wizard, then grunted. "I would like to see you try." He reluctantly lowered his weapon.

Maveri smiled, "brilliant! I'm Maveri Boreas, these two here are Wreythlec and Aleiá. It's good to make your acquaintance." He extended his hand. Arcturus sheathed Karek'Thur and stepped away. "I am a wizard from the lands of Murimia." Pulling his hand back, Maveri paused. "We came as soon as we heard of the destruction and devastation. We really had hoped to find survivors or any evidence to tell us what happened here."

"Pah, no. You came here to look for a magical sword. We came here to look for survivors." Wreyth gestured to himself and Aleiá.

Maveri flashed a furious scowl at Wreyth then turned with a welcoming smile back to Arcturus. Looking over his ruined home, Arcturus' heart wrenched. Dismembered bodies of his fallen brethren lay strewn over the dry ground, discarded without a second thought. "There are no survivors." Slowly, he paced the ruins until the clink of a buckler rang out against his sabaton. He knelt and claimed the shield, then paused for a moment.

Maveri looked to Wreyth and Aleiá, "why would you tell him that, you idiot?"

"Hush, wizard," Aleiá walked to Arcturus, "I'm sorry for your loss. I truly can't imagine the pain you're feeling right now but we really are here to help." She dismissed her scythe and placed a hand on the legionnaire's shoulder. "You're a solarist, right?"

"And you're a demon, what of it?" Arcturus stood and clamped the shield to his back. "It's been a while since I've seen one of your kind and I've only ever heard rumours of his," he gestured to Wreyth.

"Rude." Wreyth rolled his eyes.

"What importance does our race or faith have when all is lost?" Arcturus tensed his jaw.

Aleiá's face grew compassionate. "You may think all is lost but it's not. Your soul is weak; let me help and then we can talk about what happened here."

Arcturus frowned, "why would you help me when you could just try and take the sword?

"I mean, you say try. I could just pull that sword from your cold, dead fingers." Maveri flashed a quick smile then noticed Arcturus glaring at him. "But I won't as I am no savage. I love to collect magical items, but it seems that one is bound to you. It is much more use to us in your hands."

Arcturus wiped his face and looked at Wreyth. "How come you're able to be here alongside your pact?"

Aleiá smiled, "ours is less of a pact and more of a partnership. He swore his soul to me, I saved him and in turn, he's helping to save me."

"Well, they do say calastain are very closely related to demons," Arcturus glanced to Wreyth.

Wreyth's brow furrowed, "uh, that's not true at all. Actually, we are more—"

"Now's not the time, Wreyth." Aleiá glared at him then looked caringly back to Arcturus. Wreyth grunted and strolled off into the ruins. "Don't mind him, he can get stroppy sometimes," she lifted her hands as ethereal magic poured from her soul to Arcturus. "He forgets that his kind was put here to help others as were mine. We have been trying to find a way into Xelkorth."

The legionnaire felt a sudden rush of adrenaline storm through him as his exhaustion quickly evaporated. "Thank you." He cracked a slight smile, "Xelkorth has been shrouded since before the Great War. I can't imagine they would decide to drop their defences for a demon and a calastain."

Aleiá grinned. "We know. But we also know it has some very interesting secrets that could be very useful to us. Trust me when I say there is always a way in, sometimes you just have to look a little harder..."

I trust them, my love. You should too; they seem sincere.

"I see." Arcturus stood tall. "I am sorry for my hostility. Let me try again. I am Arcturus, a legionnaire shield-bearer and this was my home."

Aleiá grinned. "It's nice to meet you, Arcturus. I am a reaper, one of the last remaining, in fact. Can you tell us what happened here?"

"Of course. The day started like any other until we saw a beam of bright crimson light emanate into the skies from the lands of Deythron. Then before we knew it these meteorites came thundering down around us. They seemed to contain some form of corrupted magic that reanimated anything it killed. No matter how hard we tried, we could not fight it back." Arcturus bowed his head. "I lost so much trying to defend my home. Trying to stop it from claiming any more of Nor'ai."

Maveri stepped forward, "did you say the beam came from Deythron?"

"I did," Arcturus glanced up.

"But nothing has inhabited there since the permafrost. No, no this can't be right." Maveri started nervously stroking his goatee. "What colour did you say the beam was?"

"Crimson," Arcturus snarled.

Maveri froze, "but there is no such magic within the whole of Nor'ai! No magic here is crimson!" He scowled. "By the gods, I must speak with the council, they need to hear of this. We shall travel to Vavarinu immediately!" He lifted his finger to the skies.

"Guys, we have company!" Wreyth swiftly strolled back to the group.

Aleiá frowned, "what do you mea—" But before she could finish, an almighty bellowing roar rumbled through the skies as a gargantuan wyvern ripped through the clouds above them. "Fuck's sake."

5
<u>HEATED CHOICES</u>

Wreyth pushed them behind the ruins of a nearby building. ”Get down!“ Almighty torrents of crimson hellfire rained down upon them blasting rubble across Krytiare. “Maveri, do you think we can kill this thing?”

The wizard waited for the flames to ease before glancing over their cover. He gazed over the beast's gargantuan muscular form as it blocked out the sun while gliding through the skies. “I haven't seen a wyvern that big for aeons. Truthfully, I do not know if we can kill such a creature with our magic alone.” He scratched his goatee and glanced at Arcturus, “how much magic do you have? Can you do that shield thingy with the blade again?”

Arcturus frowned. “It is not us that bear the solar magic. I am no virago and I have no knowledge of what that shield was. But, if that beast were to land, I'm sure I could kill it.”

“Brilliant, let's just ask this unfathomably large wyvern to land and sit still while you stab it to death.” Wreyth rolled his eyes.

Aleiá slapped his shoulder. “Hey! He's only trying to help.”

"Why is there a wyvern in these lands anyway? There are so few dragons that leave Dynestrael these days, it makes so little sense for one this large to be patrolling the skies." Maveri watched the shadow of the beast swoop around them. "Although I don't think now is the time we try to answer that question. We can't stay here; we must try and outrun it, hide from it, or kill it."

Arcturus pulled his shield from his back, "if the stables still stand, we may still have a stead or two that can be used here."

"I don't know if outrunning this thing on a keylep will work but I genuinely don't see any other option right now." Wreyth winced.

Aleiá grinned. "Then let's find some keylep." Pulling her scythe from her back, she stood to address the group. "The beast is circling, now's our time to go!" The group leapt to their feet as Arcturus weaved them through his ruined home. They ducked and dived through the plumes of flames as the hot morning sun beat down upon them.

"There! The stable still stands but barely." Arcturus directed them to a crumbling marble and oak building. He grabbed the doors and heaved, "fuck, it won't budge."

Maveri pulled his book from his hip. "I think I can buy you a little time." Raising his hand, the pages flared open as azure words sparked from within. Waiting for the wyvern to turn, the wizard clenched his fist. Seeing his time to strike, he opened it to release an almighty arc of azure lightning.

He tracked the beast's flight before focussing the magic into its chest. The lightning crawled over the wyvern's skin as the creature screeched and pulled away to dodge the magic. Stunned in awe, Arcturus couldn't help but watch. Maveri clenched his fist as the beam dispersed, "there, that should push it away for a second. Did you get that door open?" He turned to see Arcturus staring back at him beside the locked door, "oh for fuck's sake."

"Sorry!" Arcturus took a few steps back and raised his shield. He inhaled and focused on the door before storming forwards, slamming the boss of his buckler against it. In a hail of splinters, the legionnaire breached through, stumbling into the hay to stop himself. Two steads bucked and neighed in shock as they slammed their hooves against the walls of the stable. Maveri, Aleiá and Wreyth rushed in to calm the keylep.

"Woah, woah, woah!" Wreyth gazed into the stead's eyes before slowly reaching to stroke its head as it calmed. He watched the legionnaire clamber out of the hay from the corner of his eye, "that was actually very impressive."

Arcturus smirked, "thank you."

"Only two keylep. It looks like we are riding in tandem," Aleiá grinned.

"Maveri, legionnaire, you two grab that one and get cosy. Aleiá and I will grab this one." Wreyth grabbed a worn leather saddle from the wall and slung it over the keylep.

Maveri assisted Arcturus in prepping the beast. "Do you know how to ride one of these?"

"Of course. Legionnaires are practically taught how to ride from birth." Arcturus frowned, "do you know how?"

Maveri stepped back in shock, "why? Do I look too proper to know how to ride?"

"Oh, quiet you pompous sod, he only asked because you did. Now get your fancy ass on that keylep." Wreyth chuckled as he leapt on the stead behind Aleiá. "If it looks like it's going south out there, I need you to disappear. Remember, I die if you die."

Aleiá rolled her eyes, "don't worry, we will be fine."

Arcturus climbed onto the stead, "I'll direct, you shoot." He lowered his hand to help Maveri, but the wizard promptly slapped it away.

"Get your bloody hand away from me, I'm not a child." Maveri gripped the saddle and inelegantly heaved himself aloft.

"Right, are we re—" As Wreyth addressed the group, a thundering roar bellowed through the skies and interrupted him. They glanced up to see crimson flames storming towards the stables. "Shit, ride!" The group commanded their steads into a gallop, barely making it away from the structure as it collapsed in their wake. Arcturus led Aleiá out of Krytiare toward the river where he and Maeve once lay.

"Hold her steady, legionnaire, Wreyth and I shall do what we can to avert this beast." Maveri turned himself to face the rear of the keylep as Wreyth did the same.

"What's the plan here Maveri? My magic can only go so far." Wreyth yelled over to the dull rhythmic thud of the stead's hooves.

Maveri flicked open his book. "Save your spells until the creature gets close enough and then lay everything you have into it. I'll poke at it while it tries to keep its distance." He looked up to the skies as azure magic surrounded him. Wreyth grinned then flicked open his hands. His forearms became engulfed with ethereal green, and a subtle soul-like glow surrounded his form. Darkness rumbled through the clouds before the wyvern burst through them, it twirled gracefully through the air as it kissed its crimson scarred flesh. Locking its eyes upon the riders, the beast swooned and opened its gaping maw. A crimson flame ignited within its core and exploded out toward the group. The ground churned and rumbled as the flames stuck behind them.

"Oh, that's not good," Maveri glanced down then back to the dragon, he raised his hand as several azure missiles formed above his shoulders. Pointing at the beast, he urged them forth as they sang one after another into the skies. Two pelted against the wyvern's wings as they ripped through its patagium, throwing off the beast's flight path. The creature closed its jaw and locked into a spiral to dodge the other missiles before re-extending its wings and circling the riders. An almighty roar burned above them as the beast stopped ahead of them. Its belly thrummed with crimson light before it opened its gaping maw to rain fireball after fireball upon the riders. It tracked their path as Arcturus and Aleiá weaved through the destruction. The unrivalled heat licked the legionnaire's face as the erratic flames danced upon the arid soil.

"We have to either bring it down or force it away!" Aleiá screamed out as she forced her keylep to leap over a plume of fire.

Wreyth gripped her shoulder as he slung ethereal bolts into the skies, "I need to get closer!" He scanned the landscape ahead of them. "There, take us there!" He gestured to a small hill on the opposite side of the river.

Arcturus glanced over to see Aleiá pull the keylep into the shallows of the river toward a small hill, "where are they going?"

"I don't know, follow them!" Maveri called out without breaking sight of the wyvern. They turned to follow Aleiá and Wreyth but as they reached the river, the keylep ground to a halt and grunted with a splutter of saliva.

"By the fucking gods, we had to have this damn keylep." Arcturus attempted to force the stead forward.

Maveri broke focus, "what's wrong with it?"

"Gerfrus is terrified of water." Arcturus kicked his heels and command-ed the keylep to move but it planted its feet. Before Maveri could respond, an almighty fireball exploded in the river before them. The keylep reared, tossing the riders from its back. Arcturus slammed against the dirt as Maveri rolled beside him. He stood and aided the wizard then drew his shield and sword, "we need to bring that beast down."

Wreyth looked back to see Arcturus and Maveri standing on the opposite side of the river. "Aleiá, the others are down. We need to get atop that hill!" The demon forced the stead to climb faster until finally, they reached the brow of the hill. "Come on you bastard, just a little closer..." He watched as the wyvern readied another fireball. Azure missiles tore through its wings once more, causing the beast to lose altitude as it focussed on Maveri. "Perfect." Wreyth clenched his fist before his entire being burned with ethereal magic. He hurled out a vast bolt of soul magic that pelted against the wyvern's chest before encasing its soul in a vine-like ethereal tether. Wreyth smirked and heaved the beast closer to him with all his might. Lifting his other hand, he clenched his fist and pulled down to summon a strike of soul magic through the beast's core. Screeches echoed amongst the lands as the wyvern tried to break free. Maveri glanced to Wreyth then back to the wyvern. Lifting both his hands, he allowed his spellbook to levitate before him. Holding his palms opposite one another, he forged his azure magic into a bright blue fireball.

"Here's a taste of what you slung at us." He clenched his muscles as the magic grew larger and more erratic. On the brink of losing control, he surged it at the beast. The wyvern flapped and twisted in panic as the fireball sped towards it until finally, it exploded against the creature's chest. The almighty force broke Wreyth's hold as the beast soared back several metres. Screeching and roaring, it tried to disperse the burning azure fire coating its body. Falling into a spiral, it slammed into the arid ground and rolled its massive form against the soil. As the flames died, it dragged itself up. Pushing its great clawed feet against a nearby boulder, it flew off into the horizon.

Maveri exhaled and caught his book before latching it back to his hip. "I won't be able to use magic like that again until I get some rest." Arcturus kept his focus on the silhouette of the wyvern before turning to the wizard and smirking. Maveri frowned, "what is it?"

"Nothing," the legionnaire chuckled.

The wizard's frown grew to a scowl, "no, no, go on."

"If it were me and I could wield like that, I would have aimed for the beast's head." Arcturus grabbed the reigns of their still panicking stead.

"You little shit." Maveri pulled a majestically engraved silver walking cane from his hip and slapped it against Arcturus' breastplate. "I didn't see you whipping out your magic to save us!"

The legionnaire grabbed the cane and pulled the wizard in close to him.

"I do not wield magic as you do. Instead, I was able to keep the keylep steady and you out of danger. Trust me, if I could wield magic such as you, that wyvern would not have flown away." He shunted Maveri away, "oh, and touch me with that cane again and I'll be sure to kill you with it."

"Woah! What's happening here?" Aleiá called out as their stead pulled itself from the shallows of the river.

"Nothing, just a little post-battle tension is all." Maveri adjusted his cloak. "Wreyth, Aleiá, I must say that was very quick thinking to use the high ground."

Aleiá smiled. "It was Wreyth's idea."

"I knew I needed to get close to that damn thing but just had to figure out how," Wreyth glanced to Arcturus. "What's wrong with the keylep?"

Maveri strolled closer to Wreyth, "it seems we managed to find a legionnairion keylep that doesn't like water." He gestured for Wreyth to lean close to him, "I think we need to watch that one, he seems quite volatile."

"Maveri, I don't mean to sound harsh but around you, I've seen the calmest man become volatile," Wreyth raised his brow then pulled away.

Aleiá slid down from her keylep. "Arcturus, may I take a look?"

"Of course, but I think we will have to ride around the river. Gerfrus will not cross water." He handed the reins over.

"Thank you," Aleiá calmed the keylep as she placed her palm against its forehead and stared deeply into its bright blue eyes. The trio watched as the beast's stress seemed to instantly melt away from its body and with a subtle grunt, it nudged against Aleiá. "There, he should cooperate now." She smiled and handed the reins back.

Arcturus frowned, "what did you do?"

"It's much easier to communicate with something when you can talk directly to its soul," she pulled herself back onto her keylep, "now, where did we say we were heading?"

"Vavarinu," Maveri reluctantly heaved himself onto the keylep behind Arcturus, "I need to tell the council of this crimson magic and I need this legionnaire there with me to fill in the details."

Wreyth shuddered. "Ugh Vavarinu," he turned to Maveri, "you know Aleiá and I can't go there."

The wizard frowned, "do I?"

Wreyth gestured to himself and Aleiá as Maveri gazed back in confusion, "our kind is not welcome there. If there's anything the adventurers of this realm don't like it's calastain, drekaiek and undead. She and I are all three!"

"I mean you say undead, but you are really a soul brought back to physicality." He gazed over Wreyth and Aleiá's blank expressions. "Okay, I see your point. I can disguise you with my magic if I need to, just until we can get to a point where we can speak with someone important. They will see the looming threat and they will no longer care about your race."

"Ha, you live in a fantasy land, wizard," Wreyth paused for a second, "and what about Aleiá?"

The demon smiled, "I can shift into the ethereal plain until I'm needed, you know like I normally do when I need to get away from shit."

Wreyth stroked his beard as he glared at Maveri. "Fine. But Aleiá and I will meet you there, we need to gather some supplies first in case things go shits up and we need to leave."

"Should we not travel together?" Arcturus glanced back.

"You'll be fine without us for a little while," Wreyth smirked. "Just look after this old bastard, would you? Oh, and don't let him wander off searching for treasure and shiny things." He winked and then looked at Maveri, "Don't piss off this legionnaire. I don't want to find you half gutted somewhere in the desert, wizard."

Maveri rolled his eyes, "oh, if anything it would be a legionnaire's charred remains you would uncover."

"Behave you two," Aleiá turned her stead. "Stay safe and we shall see you soon." Arcturus and Maveri waved the pair off before carefully crossing the shallows of the river.

"Tell me again why I should come with you?" Arcturus queried the wizard.

Maveri exhaled and lowered his head. "In Vavarinu we can find information and warn people of this dire threat. With it being the adventurer capital we will be able to send out parties to inform and help the surrounding lands. We might even be able to gather an army to find and defeat the source of this magic. Does that sound like a good enough reason to you?"

That sounds like a good plan to me. Although I don't think we needed that snide tone of his. We should go with him and figure out what our next steps are from there, we might even find others willing to fight with us.

Arcturus paused for a moment, considering Maeve's words. "Fine, then we travel to Vavarinu." They rode for hours toward the Uzarian's borders as the midday sun beat down on their backs. The dull sound of hooves rumbled over and over as Arcturus watched the wavering horizon. Dry plumes of grass turned to cracked soil, then to dusty sands as they traversed across the legionnaire's homelands.

6
<u>ROADS</u> <u>UNTRAVELLED</u>

99 I was told land used to be so beautiful. Gorgeous trees, astonishing flora and grazing wildlife. Now it is just baron wastelands. My home was one of the last places within Uzarian that could grow peonies." Arcturus gazed over the arid lands.

Maveri sat still with his arms crossed and his eyes closed, "this land did use to be wonderous; I saw it first-hand many years ago, possibly before you were even born."

"Before my birth?" Arcturus frowned. "You are not that old."

Maveri chuckled, "I appreciate the compliment but yes, I am that old."

"But how? Humans rarely live past seventy new moons, or at least their quality of life vastly deteriorates if they do survive." Arcturus wiped the sweat from his forehead.

"I'm surprised you didn't notice," Maveri pulled back his hood to reveal his crescent-tipped ears, "I am not a true human, part aelveth blood runs through my veins."

Arcturus looked over his shoulder. "I see. That would explain it."

"I visited this land with my father, he always believed a man should know the realm if he means to defend it." Maveri smiled as he touched his signet ring.

"Your father sounds wise." The legionnaire stroked the tiring keylep's colourful mane.

Maveri glanced up. "He was a wealthy man both in his knowledge and his possessions. My mother was a highly renowned wizard too."

"Was?" Arcturus raised his brow.

Maveri looked back down to his ring. "Yes, unfortunately, he and my family were killed a few years back. I got mixed up with a group of adventurers who discovered a roving band of forsaken magic wielders. They torched half of Murimia to the ground in what we thought was some senseless act of aggression. My family and my home were part of that wreckage. I salvaged what I could, but most were lost."

"I'm sorry to hear that," Arcturus looked back to the wizard, "did you ever find out why these mages did what they did?"

"Don't call them that! They do not deserve the title of a mage!" Maveri clenched his fist before slowly running his palm over his goatee, "we managed to capture one as he held us off at the bridge into the city, he spouted out some nonsense about killing the many to save the few. That was all the information we got out of him, but I will search this realm far and wide until I find them."

Arcturus looked to the hilt of Karek'Thur. "They sound like fanatics to me. I have experienced their kind before, and they do nothing but wound this realm."

"I agree." Maveri pulled his hood over his head and crossed his arms once more. "If I ever see them again, I will not be so merciful. This is why I worry so much about this crimson; it might well be their doing."

They travelled for many hours speaking of their pasts and homes. As time went on they passed only the odd keylep and carriage travelling along the trade routes. Arcturus focussed on the road ahead with determination and a heavy, guilt-struck heart. Golden sparks started subtly dancing across his vision. He blinked and shook his head to try and disperse them, but they only grew in numbers.

Remember when I asked you if this was all worth it? Well, I see now that it will be. All the sacrifices, all the choices, all the loss will all be worth it in the end.

Images of a glorious, tiled bathroom began flooding his mind and within its centre lay a great square, marble bath.

Do not worry, my love, I will always be here standing by your side. I will always be here to protect you.

The figure of an auburn-haired woman lay facing away from him. Beads of water danced upon her rose skin as she bathed herself.

I think it's time you trust yourself. Trust your gut; it is normally always right. I trust in you. I always have, and I always will.

The figure slowly began to turn as the gold within her runic tattoos began to glimmer.

"Ah finally! It seems we have reached the border of Valanthrea," Maveri gripped Arcturus' shoulder, forcing the images from the legionnaire's mind. "How are you feeling? We've been riding for a while now."

Arcturus clenched his jaw attempting to reclaim the images of his mind. "I'm fine," his voice croaked as he licked his dry cracked lips, "although maybe we should stop soon. I think this keylep could use a drink and I know I certainly could."

The wizard patted the keylep. "Poor thing is exhausted. It has done great for us especially how it seemed to hold its nerve against that wyvern."

"Hmm, maybe it's best we find a place to rest now then. How far would you say we are from Vavarinu?" Arcturus attempted to blink away his spiking headache.

The wizard licked his finger and raised it to the skies, "I would say we are still a good while away." His eyes glimmered in azure light. "Let's stop at the next piece of shelter we find." Arcturus nodded and pushed the keylep on. More hours passed as they dragged themselves through the deepening sands, it was hard to tell how long it had been since they left Krytiare. Mounds and hills broke up the horizon and crimson cracks distorted the landscape as they avoided the deep dark caverns. Squeals from circling predators called out as they followed them along their journey, holding for their moment to pounce. The legionnaire slumped, leaning on the trudging keylep as it steadily hauled them further and further away from Uzarian.

"Over there," Maveri weakly gestured to a wilting tree in the distance, "we'll stop there." They thumped on for what felt like an eternity until they reached the dying tree. As Arcturus commanded the keylep to stop, the beast lowered its head and planted itself onto the mildly shaded ground. It panted from exhaustion and dehydration whilst trying to tug a plume of dry grass from the sands.

The legionnaire dragged himself off the keylep, "do we have any water with us?" He offered his hand to help the wizard down.

"Don't test me," Maveri slid himself down and thumped onto the sand. He brushed off his cloak then unlatched his silver walking cane and tapped a satchel latched to the saddle. "Try that bag."

Arcturus investigated the satchel, "yeah, here we are." He pulled some water skins from the leather pouch and looked over to the wizard who was intently watching him.

"Oh, good," the figure opened his personal bag and pulled out a rather expensive bottle of red grape wine donned in golden regalia, "drink as much as you like, I'll manage with this."

Arcturus eyed up the wine. "Yes, I'm sure you will." He proceeded to pour some water into his palm and offered it to the keylep. After a moment, the beast steadily lapped up the liquid. "What were you doing in Krytiare? You are not a from around there."

The wizard slyly glanced aside while swigging his wine. He pulled the bottle away and wiped his goatee. "I suppose I should tell you the truth." He pulled back his hood as his hair still lay perfectly quaffed. "As you know, I'm a wizard. I practice the art of azure Nor'ain magic, which if you aren't familiar, is based on knowledge and intellect. I've been trawling these lands in search of ancient artifacts and magical items of substantial worth." He gauged Arcturus' subtle reaction. "Within this world, there are many items that hold substantial power and others that were just crafted with the intent of fashion or display. I had heard from a source that Krytiare may have housed such weaponry or items."

The legionnaire stood for a moment as he gazed over the wizard's well-kept features, "so you were looking for Karek'Thur?"

Maveri smiled, "in a word, yes. Although that was before we knew you were alive and well."

"What would you have done if I wasn't?" Arcturus titled his head.

The wizard slid the bottle of wine back into the unusually small pouch and clasped it shut, "well, I would have examined the weapon to reveal if it were truly magical. If it was, I would add it to my collection; if it wasn't, I would have sold it on for a hefty profit." He stepped over and stroked the recovering keylep, "and to calm that worry I see in your mind, no I don't want to take it from you. You've shown me that Karek'Thur does hold magic, but we do not know how much or how strong that magic truly is."

Arcturus gazed over Karek'Thur and stroked his rough stubble. "I must admit, I still have no knowledge of how I or the weapon did that," he looked up before continuing, "I suppose someday we may find out its secrets. Maybe even your aelveth wisdom could help with that."

Maveri chuckled, "well, yes. My father was aelveth and well versed in magical items, so he passed that knowledge and curiosity down to me." He frowned. "I do hope my aelveth ancestry isn't a problem. I know some aren't keen on hybrids."

"Not at all," Arcturus smiled, "being aelveth or any race in any degree is no issue to me. A great soldier I once knew was aelveth. Unfortunately, he didn't make it out of Krytiare alive." The legionnaire extended his hand. "I know I may not have shown it, but it is good to meet you, Maveri."

Maveri clasped his hand and shook, "as it is to meet you, Arcturus...?"

"Pythare," Arcturus gripped the wizard's hand with great intensity.

"I can definitely tell you have the strength of a warrior," Maveri pulled his hand away and rubbed his palm, "wait, did you say Pythare? As in Tahmaliea Pythare?"

Arcturus took a beat, "how do you know of my mother?"

Maveri's mouth fell agape, "who doesn't know of her?! Your mother is a legend, one of the very first virago! Some were even known to call her the 'Rising Sun'. Her ability to harness solar magic was unmatched." Maveri quivered with excitement. "It was even said that her almighty sword, Beacon, was forged from the Solar gods themselves!"

"You seem to know more of her than I," Arcturus frowned. "All I know is that she was a great warrior and she helped form the virago of today, but I do not know if that is true about her weapon." He scratched his chin. "I didn't hear much of my mother after she left our town. Being but an adolescent when she left, I don't recall much about her."

Maveri watched Arcturus' emotion change, "well it was said that your mother left to fight in the Great War with warriors from all over the realm. Even my father joined her side as they battled to keep the unity of peace between the coasts. Together they fought back Taeylorn, the great king of the vampheare. Without her and the other warrior's bravery and sacrifice, this land would still be at war. Nor'ai would not be the bastion we all know and love." He placed his hand upon the legionnaire's shoulder, "you come from greatness, Arcturus."

"It seems I might not have been abandoned without cause then." Arcturus placed his hand on Karek'Thur and looked to the skies. "Maybe one day I'll learn more of her legends."

"You know, rumour has it she forged an artifact of personal value into a key that could open a well of great power," Maveri paused, "it's a shame no one knows its location or identity as it is unrecognisable from what it once was. I dread to think about all that knowledge and history going to waste."

Arcturus turned to the Wizard with a grin, "thank you, friend. Maybe one day we can find this key and once all this is over, we might be able to uncover that well." He felt the ground shudder slightly under his feet. "We should keep moving, we know not what horrors lurk beneath these sands."

He sure does seem to know a lot about Tahmaliea. I suppose as a High Warden your legend must travel.

Maveri nodded. "Good point. We do not want to be sitting ducks for whatever beast decides it's hungry." He leapt onto the keylep. "This time I'll hold the reins. I know a good route that could cut off some travel time and maybe even a place we can stay the night."

Arcturus smiled, "sounds like a plan." he watched the wizard latch his cane to the steed's saddle then lowered his hand. The legionnaire chuckled and slapped it away before clambering back onto the steed, "how long do you think Wreyth and Aleiá might take?"

"If I have done the math correctly, they will arrive at the gates of Vavarinu at sunup. We should easily make it there by then. Although I never really was any good at math, so it's anyone's guess, really," Maveri chuckled as he urged the keylep forward. "We do need to get a move on though, I hear the dunes are not a friendly place to wander at night. All sorts of beastly creatures are out there to prey on you."

Arcturus smiled. "Are you scared, wizard?"

"Not scared, just regretting the fact that I've used too much magic and can't just portal us to the city." Maveri looked aside. As they moved closer to the desert, their steed became more and more uneasy darting its sight from left to right.

Arcturus gazed over the deathly silent dunes attempting to thwart some form of danger but saw nothing. "I think your concern may be well placed, wizard. Keep your eyes peeled." Maveri nodded in return, and they pushed on with their journey into the night.

7

THE LONGEST RIDE

Riding well into the evening, they pushed deeper into the glistening rolling dunes of Valanthrea. The sun's orange glow was now gone as Arcturus scanned the eerily beautiful lands. A light dusting of sand trailed across the small hills and over the succulent cacti shrubbery. Curled, horned caymelec strolled in herds along the horizon as their long shadows swept out from behind them. Their rough fur cascaded off their humped bodies as their long slender tail whipped away insects. Arcturus lifted his hand to feel the breeze force tiny fragments of stone to clink against his armour.

I wish I was there beside you to experience all of this with you.

He smiled. "I wish you were here with me, my love." As they traversed the land, they could see corpses of unlucky prey that had been picked clean by predators. Small shards of broken wood littered the dunes from old trade carts attempting to make the perilous journey out of the desert. Tiny reptilian creatures scurried over the floor, leaving a subtle trail of footsteps in their wake. Arcturus marvelled over the sights; it had been so long since he had left the familiar sights of Uzarian.

"Do you know why they call this place the creeping desert?" Maveri queried.

"No, I don't," Arcturus held his gaze on the horizon.

The wizard stroked his goatee. "Well, as new moons pass, the deserts of Valanthrea are said to crawl their way deeper inland. It apparently used to be no more than a large beach on the south coast but now it covers a great chunk of the Eastern Isles. The sand here is so dense that it has completely buried old civilisations that once existed here," he paused, "sub-races of reptiare like the siscrati used to reside in these lands but were wiped out due to its harsh conditions."

"Siscrati? The snake-like reptiare?" Arcturus looked intently at the sands, "It is such a shame to hear of races suffering or dying due to such reasons, not of their own doing."

Maveri leaned back. "That, and the fact that many items of their culture are buried deep within this desert along with many other secrets."

Arcturus frowned, "so no sooner than a race dies, you want to dig up its secrets?" He paused, "although, I suppose it would help us to understand their culture better. It sounds to me like you need to employ some adventurers who don't mind doing a bit of digging to help you find these artifacts."

"You joke, but that might just be a plan that works," the wizard's voice hummed with excitement. "Come to think of it, if this desert does keep moving inland, places like Uzarian and Lochardia may very seriously be at risk."

The legionnaire glanced back, "that would explain why my home is no longer the lush plains it was. If this continues, my whole past will be turned to sand. Our whole realm turned to a vast sandy nothingness."

"Well, that is if this crimson doesn't end the realm first." Maveri jeered. Deep in thought, they continued long into the night.

So our home could one day be lost to this desert too? This wizard truly is a fount of knowledge...

As the unyielding darkness engulfed the lands, the crisp white moonlight guided them along their path. Echoes of hoots and howls rolled over the dunes keeping the pair alert. Clearing the brow of a small hill, they finally spotted a small wood-built town beside a deep pit of sunken sand.

"We will stop a little way up here and make camp for the night," Maveri glanced back, "that small village you see is named Ragrug. It's not much, but it will do, and the people are very welcoming." Arcturus nodded in agreement, and they rode on. The night seemed somehow darker here than in Uzarian as it consumed the landscape around them. Maveri slowed the keylep as they entered the village, holding it at a trot while passing the unkempt buildings.

Pulling a torch from his bag, the Wizard ignited it with an azure flame to light their way. "This is oddly quiet."

Arcturus looked around the crudely made wooden buildings. "Maybe it's been abandoned since you were last here?"

Maveri glanced back. "Unlikely, this was once a lively trade hub. For what Ragrug lacked in size, it didn't lack in personality. I bought some fantastic magical items here once." He stopped the keylep beside a small wooden fence and tied it up whilst offering it a pale of warm stale water. Progressing further into the town, Arcturus attempted to make out the details of the old buildings. A sharp strong breeze whipped from behind them urging the shutters to clatter, the structures to creak and the wood to groan. Moving into the centre of the village, they spied an old destroyed well with the signs of a struggle around it. Small holes and sunken dips in the sand surrounded the buildings and along the dusty walkways.

The wizard lifted his torch to inspect closer. "It seems like somebody used to be home."

This is very eerie, please be cautious, my love.

Arcturus drew his sword. "Maybe something decided to claim this as its own." Clenching his grip around Karek'Thur, the blade's golden runes ignited. He looked at the sword and smirked.

"Fascinating..." Maveri moved close to the weapon, almost pressing his nose against it. Arcturus moved it aside and walked toward an old tavern.

The scent of blood grew stronger as it cursed the air.

"Something isn't right here..." Maveri softly muttered the words. A resounding thump emanated from within the structure. The pair shuddered as they jumped back a little. Arcturus primed his sword and stepped closer. Steadily, its golden light revealed the silhouette of a short figure against the wooden door.

"We aren't here for trouble; we just want somewhere to stay the night." Arcturus moved closer until he could clearly see the blood-soaked figure held aloft by needle-like pins.

"Something isn't right here, take this," Maveri handed the torch to Arcturus before slowly opening his palm and placing it against his eyes. As he removed his hand, his eyes were alight with azure magic. "I won't need that anymore."

Confused, Arcturus lifted the torch to examine the corpse of the female dwethren. "Why don't you need the torch anymore?" He poked his sword at the needles within her chest and shoulders.

"Being a wizard, I can gift myself mystic sight in all forms of natural darkness." Maveri glanced around the village.

Arcturus lightly chuckled, "why didn't you just do that in the first place?"

Maveri rolled his glowing eyes. "The ability takes power to cast, a power I'm low on thanks to lack of sleep and minor wyvern encounter..."

"Well, surely lighting this torch took that same power too?" Arcturus smirked.

The Wizard paused and slowly exhaled. "Just be quiet and keep your wits—"

"You should never have come here!" The dwethren's eyes sprung open, ablaze in crimson light. The pair leapt back as they attempted to compose themselves. "This place is ours now." She ripped herself from the door and slammed onto the wooden doorstep.

"This damn magic!" Arcturus swung his blade without hesitation. Its golden light surged through the dwethren's body as it ripped her apart with ease. The legionnaire recoiled in shock as the corpse burned to golden dust, "that's different, the others all turned to crimson."

Maveri looked over his shoulder, "did you kill the others with this blade?"

"No." Arcturus looked aside at the wizard.

"Interesting," Maveri stroked his goatee. The sound of swift chitinous scuttling rang out from the structures and alleys around them. They turned to see nothing, but darkness shrouded in echoes.

"I'm not a fan of this pla—" Before Arcturus could finish, a second almighty thud resonated from inside the tavern. The legionnaire gripped his blade tighter, dropped the torch and pulled his buckler from his back. "That's it!" He stepped back and belted the door open with a powerful kick. The hinges shattered and the door blistered into the alluring darkness. The sounds of the splintering wood echoed out through the village.

"Well, they know we're here now," Maveri sneered whilst recovering from the shock. Karek'Thur's golden glow illuminated the room before the azure torchlight lent its aid.

You always were one to make an entrance. See if you can find any more signs of crimson here.

"I thought you didn't need that," Arcturus glanced aside.

Maveri huffed, "I don't, but I'm not just going to leave it on the ground either." The stench of blood and rotting corpses screamed through the air as Arcturus gagged. Globules of blood dripped from the walls and ceiling down into a deep dark hole. "This is a lot of blood for only one dwethren," Arcturus frowned and looked down to see a subtle crimson hue emitting deep in the pit.

"Look up," Maveri pointed to a great hole in the ceiling. The legionnaire gazed upon the moonlight breaching through the splintered wood. Around fifteen other dwethren corpses hung from the rafters by the same needle-like bolts.

Arcturus clenched his jaw, "this is a massacre."

"Is this the crimson's doing?" Maveri pulled his book from his hip. He scanned the area with his torch as azure letters illuminated his cloaked form, "other than whatever is down that hole, I sense no more magic here."

Panning the room, Arcturus spied a chitinous extremity dangling over the edge of the hole. Lifting it with his sword, he noticed its insectoid structure with a carapace scythe protruding from its wrist.

"It seems they weren't the only ones here," Arcturus moved the extremity to Maveri.

The wizard leaned down, "that's an insetille's arm."

"I see." The legionnaire frowned. "I haven't had the pleasure of fighting those."

Maveri stood, "trust me, there is no pleasure in fighting them. Why would they have surfaced just to fight these dwethren?"

Arcturus gestured down the pit, "I think that uninvited meteorite might have forced them out." The legionnaire moved out of the cabin, "come on, let's leave this place. This isn't somewhere we want to spend the night." He strolled back to the ruined well.

Maveri followed him, "I agree."

Arcturus scanned the surrounding buildings, "let's search for supplies before we leave. Just in case we can't find another safe place before sunup."

"You want to stay here for longer? Did you not see the carnage in there?" Maveri questioned as he paced beside the legionnaire.

He has a point. Are you sure you want to rest here?

"I do and I did, but that's nothing we can't handle." Arcturus tore open the door of an adjacent cabin, "now come on, let's grab what we can."

After reluctantly agreeing, Maveri joined him in gathering what they could from the remaining supplies. "Wait, how did they make wooden cabins here without any trees?" Arcturus stopped as he pondered the thought.

Maveri walked over to the window, "ah, well, you see that great pit out there? That actually used to be a lake. Surrounding it used to be gorgeous plumes of bright green grass and lush tall trees. Dwethrens, being the resourceful creatures they are, decided that the sands weren't strong enough to hold stone. So, they chopped down the trees to make wooden cabins instead." He chuckled. "Little did they know that there was a great drought about the happen and within one new moon, that big lake became the pit you see today."

Arcturus looked over. "I see."

Maveri frowned, "do you really?"

"No, not really, everything you pointed at is all just darkness to me," Arcturus retorted.

Maveri stopped and lowered his hand, "ah, sorry. I forget that when I use this sight, not everyone else around me can see what I see." They moved away from the cabins back to their keylep. Mounting up, they rode against the rising winds closer to the city of Vavarinu.

Arcturus squinted as he noticed a break in the moonlight upon the horizon, "there, we can see if that place is occupied."

They rode a while longer before reaching a cabin much like the ones within Ragrug. Its poorly maintained structure shook as the winds battered against it.

"This place still looks like something from my nightmares," Maveri winced.

"Oh hush," Arcturus slid down from the keylep and latched it against a small post, "hello? Anyone home?" He moved to the door and lifted his hand to knock. Rolling his eyes, he gently pushed the door. It creaked open to reveal a one-roomed dwethren house. A crudely made table and wooden chairs sat at one side of the room beside broken cabinets. On the other side, there sat a small dwethren bed. "Here, we can sleep on this." He dragged it to the centre of the room as Maveri cautiously entered the cabin. "You should rest first; your magic is more valuable than my strength." He moved to grab a small chair to perch in front of the door.

"Isn't that a little small for me?" Maveri walked over to the bed.

Arcturus chuckled, "we must work with what we've got. Get some rest, if anything happens, I'll wake you."

"Well, if you insist. I do need to recover my magic," Maveri placed the torch on the wall. He moved to the bed and ran his hand over the straw-filled burlap mattress. Tutting, he eventually lay down on the bed with his legs hanging over the edge. "Why do dwethren never assume that someone taller may need to use their bed?"

Arcturus laughed, "I don't know, why?"

"It wasn't a joke, it was a genuine question." The wizard chuckled as he turned away and closed his eyes.

Arcturus grunted and placed his chair directly in front of the door and sat down. Leaning forward, he rolled Karek'Thur over his palms watching its golden glyphs shine. Running his hand up the weapon, he inspected its expert craftsmanship as its cool metal graced the tips of his fingers. Each glyph shone brighter the closer he moved to it. "I'll keep you by my side, Karek'Thur, just as I should have kept her." He propped the sword against his chair and sat back, crossing his arms over his chest. Slowly, his heavy eyelids began to close.

And by your side, I'll stay, my love.

Gold sparks danced amongst the darkness of his mind as he spied a beautiful peony.

I wish you could be allowed to rest as I do, but this is not the case.

Arcturus' mind fragmented back to reality as the dying scream of their keylep wrenched him back. He swiftly stood and grabbed Karek'Thur. "Maveri, we have company."

8

<u>A RUDE AWAKENING</u>

The legionnaire moved to the door, sliding open a small crack between the panels. His vision darted from left to right, searching for their keylep. The golden light of Karek'Thur gleamed through the gaps and into the darkness, enabling him to see a hunched silhouette.

"Maveri, are you awake?" He glanced back to see the wizard carelessly slumped over the small bed. "Of course he isn't." Turning back to the crack, he lifted his blade a little higher to gain more vision, but as he did, several sickening crimson eyes ignited in his sightline. "By the gods!" He recoiled in shock and grabbed his buckler from beside his seat. "What in light's name is—" A blood-curdling screech rang out from the creature as it rushed the door. Its hulking carapace smashed against the fragile wood, shuddering the structure of the cabin.

"What's going on out there?" Arcturus looked back to see Maveri clambering up from the collapsed bed.

"I tried to wake you, wizard! Now get up, we have a fight on our hands."

Arcturus primed his weapons.

A massive, razored claw breached through the upper part of the door knocking the legionnaire to the ground. Stunned, Arcturus paused for a moment then dragged himself back to his feet. The crackling gurgle of the creature's mandibles hummed as it whipped its claw back, revealing its orb-like eyes. Seeing this, Maveri leapt up and whipped his book from his hip. He snapped his wrist before launching several azure missiles. They sang swiftly along their path, almost glancing Arcturus as they flew. Pummelling the creature's face, the azure magic dissipated, leaving the beast unharmed. Blinking its horrific eyes, it refocused on Maveri.

"I think you pissed it off," Arcturus raised his shield to the beast, preparing to strike. Reacting with instinct, he dodged its claw as it smashed through the remainder of the door. Spinning past the destruction, Arcturus swung his blade and sliced a chunk from the beast's extremity. Its exposed flesh seared with golden light as it pulled away.

"Watch out for the scorthic's stinger!" Maveri called out over the destruction before a thick needle-tipped tail shattered through the ceiling. The wizard leapt aside and raised his palm to release a torrent of azure missiles. As it saw the incoming danger, the creature ripped itself from the house. The azure magic blasted through the remainder of the wall as the cabin's structure rattled.

Arcturus looked through the ruined wood to see several crimson-eyed dwethren stomping toward them. "It's not alone, Maveri." He clutched his shield as the scothic's hulking claw swept through the darkness. Its carapace grazed against the bronze of his buckler, peeling off fine shards of metal. Following the motion, Arcturus spun and cleaved through the beast's extremity with Karek'Thur. He watched the glowing weapon burn through the shell of the creature tearing through its flesh. Shocked at the ease, he pushed the weapon through and sliced the claw from the beast. Screeching out in pain, the Scorthic drew back as crimson blood poured from the wound. Writhing in pain, the beast twitched its remaining chunk of the claw. The legionnaire smirked, tightening his grip around Karek'Thur. "Maveri, I need you to deal with those!" Pulling his shield to protect his face, Arcturus pointed his sword at the assaulting dwethren.

"With pleasure." The wizard raised his palm as azure symbols swirled around him. He locked his sight onto the dwethren before releasing a focussed beam of azure ice. The chilling magic engulfed the humanoids before freezing them in place. Arcturus turned to the wizard with an amazed grin. Shards of wood cut between them as a second smaller scorthic ripped through the floor. "Maveri!" Debris rained down as the creature leapt at Maveri, dragging him down into the sands below. "No!" Arcturus shifted his feet to run to Maveri's aid but the stinger of the wounded scorthic slammed down beside him blocking his path. "Fine, you first." He slammed his buckler into the extremity digging it deep into its chitin.

Clenching Karek'Thur in his palm, he swept it through the beast's flesh. Crimson blood showered down around him as he turned to the creature, "you should have left when you had the chance!" He pushed into a heroic leap and plunged his blade deep into the larger scorthic's face. Holding for a moment, he watched the sickening crimson glow drain from its eyes as it slumped to the ground.

"Arcturus!" Maveri's muffled voice called out from below the floor. The legionnaire stepped to the ground to see a glowing azure dome protruding from the shallows of the sands. He rushed to the ruined floor beside the magic. Raising his blade, he carved through the wood as he revealed the scorthic attempting to drag the wizard deep into the sand. Its six slender, spiked legs scratched at the dome as it tried to break through. Arcturus turned his blade in his hand before forcing it deep into the beast's abdomen splitting it in two. Its wretched body collapsed in a pool of crimson before turning to dust. Stepping back, he offered his hand to the wizard as the rippling azure magic aura dispersed.

"You took your time!" Maveri gripped Arcturus' hand and allowed him to pull him up.

Ha! He's lucky you were here to save him!

Arcturus smiled. "My deepest apologies, caster, I had a slightly bigger problem to deal with," the legionnaire gestured to the dissipating body of the larger scorthic. "For all I knew, you were either dead or winning the fight, I couldn't tell from up here," Arcturus grinned.

Maveri looked back at the cloud of golden dust. "Well, I felt like I should let you deal with that one since I dealt with the wyvern."

Arcturus chuckled, "you mean you and Wreyth dealt with it?"

Don't upset him, we need him on our side.

"I suppose he helped a little, but it was primarily me," Maveri swept his hand over his quiff and smirked. A hum of clicks and vibrations filled the air behind them forcing them to turn. Two insectoid figures upon the back of a great horned scarek. Its almighty amethyst shell rattled in the moonlight as its bladed extremities dug into the sand. A pair of slender insetille raised their arms as crimson magic poured from them and down into the sands. Arcturus and Maveri steadied themselves as the ground beneath them shifted and contorted.

"Maybe you feel like stopping what they're doing, Maveri?" Arcturus clutched his shield.

Maveri motioned his hands, allowing his spellbook to float before him. His palms ignited in azure magic while he formed a giant fireball between them. The orb grew larger and larger with each passing second forcing the wizard's palms apart. Smiling, he sent the massive sphere of spitting flame hurtling toward the scarek. They watched as the azure magic ignited the dark sky along its flight path. In an almighty blast of glorious fire, it exploded upon the creatures. Sparks of azure flame danced off into the night like shooting stars as they illuminated the shifting sands.

"Well, that was impressive!" The legionnaire smiled. Maveri grinned in return before glancing back to the destruction. His jaw dropped as he watched a crimson barrier shimmer amongst the azure as the creatures remained unscathed. The two figures steadily lowered their hands, causing the cabin to tremble as crimson light breached through the structure. Shards of wood rained down around them as the building began to crumble.

I think it might be time to retreat.

Maveri looked worriedly at Arcturus. "I don't have much magic left within me. That spell they negated was one of my most powerful." Before they could turn to run, the whistle of four needle-like bolts soared toward them.

Arcturus leapt in front of Maveri, and the projectiles embedded within his shield. "We need to go!" He grabbed the wizard and forced him toward the back of the cabin. The legionnaire paused and scanned the fragile wooden wall. Without a second thought, he threw himself shield-first through the wall rupturing it. Breaching out of the falling building in a hail of splintered wood, Arcturus stood and brushed himself off. "This way, Maveri!" He beckoned the wizard to follow. Maveri leapt through the hole landing face-first into the sands. Showers of golden coins poured from the now open pouches on his hip. Seconds after the wizard landed, the structure collapsed into a swirling whirlpool of sand.

"Keep moving!" Arcturus pulled Maveri away as the wizard attempted to recover the gold. They dragged themselves through the deep dunes as the wind whipped ferociously around them. In an almighty explosion of debris, a colossal mammoth Scorthic emerged from the destruction and planted itself on the sands behind them. Releasing a blood-curdling screech, the creature clattered its claws as its massive glowing crimson carapace rattled. Arcturus turned and launched his shield at its glaring eyes. The beast smashed the buckler to the ground with ease, obliterating it. Arcturus watched in shock as the bronze shield shattered into splinters.

"Arcturus, run!" Maveri grabbed him and forced him onward. The pair trudged through the sands as fast as their legs could manage. Slamming its almighty muscular tail down, the monolithic beast lunged toward them. Arcturus felt the swipe of the hulking claw flow past the back of his head. Now on the hunt, the mammoth scorthic burst into the air. Its glowing mass held aloft for a moment before submerging into the sand.

"Where is it?" Maveri scanned the plains for the beast.

"It's gone below," Arcturus ignited the area around them with Karek'Thur. The ground thundered as the sands began to part, allowing the sickening crimson glow to seep through. "Jump!" Before the pair could move, the beast exploded from the ground. The sudden force propelled them aside and slung Karek'Thur from Arcturus' grasp. Its golden glyphs diminished as it fell through the sands. "No!" From the corner of his eye, he saw Maveri crash into the engulfing dunes on the opposite side of the hole.

Arcturus slammed down as the air burst from his lungs. He choked as he clawed back his breath, "Maveri? Where are you?" His words were barely audible as he forced them out and coughed up blood. Arcturus slowly brought himself to his feet. He looked around the darkness mixed with the falling sand and debris. "Maveri?!" A faint crimson glow sparkled through the shadows as a gigantic claw punched through. The impact belted him across the sands. The air burst from his lungs as he tumbled along the desert.

He lay while gasping at the dusty atmosphere to reclaim his breath. Running his hand over his breastplate, he felt a crumpled dent caused by the beast as the splintered metal sliced at his chest. Dragging himself to his feet, he looked around the sands once more. Attempting to locate the scorthic, he raised his hand to his brow. Another crimson glow refracted in the dark. Through the pain, he tucked and rolled under the swipe of the creature, barely dodging its claw. Agony ripped through his chest as the ruptured metal breastplate cut deeper. He unlatched its clasps and slung it to the ground. Searing sensations ignited through him as the sand whipped his open wounds. He fell to his knees before noticing the gaping slice through his forearm. His blood seared with the crimson liquid as it ran down his bracer. Clutching the wound, the legionnaire moved toward the last place he saw Maveri. His vision darted around the falling sands for a glimpse of the wizard. With pain coursing through his body, his eyes grew heavy, and his head fell faint. Stumbling into a lumbered walk, he continued his search. The debris and sand settled around him, revealing a glint of dim, gold light deep in the sands.

"Karek—" As the words left his lips, the scorthic clamped its unbreakable grasp around his core. Lifting him off his feet, the beast pulled him into its sight. Its eyes glared upon him while it snarled, cracking his ribs with its vice-like grip. "GAHH!" He tried to pry the hulking claw open as the creature pulled him closer. Blood trickled from his mouth as he locked sight with the beast. The air burst from his lungs while it tightened its grip around him, and his skeleton quivered under the pressure.

Hold on, my love! We will find a way to fight this!

The creature raised its stinger toward him, holding it inches from his face before whipping it back to strike. Within the depths of the darkness to the rear of the beast blossomed a blinding azure light. Its gorgeous glow exposed the scorthic's vile features as it grew closer. As the bright burning ball of flames crackled, Arcturus smirked a bloodied smile. He watched it explode upon the beast, engulfing the creature in azure flames. Writhing in pain, the creature's claw tossed him high into the air. The scorthic stumbled back as the legionnaire fell into the deep tunnels below.

The unfathomable pain subsided as the soft breeze caressed his skin and the weightlessness eased his mind. His eyes softly closed before he slammed down onto the sand. He howled in pain as his shoulder shattered under the impact. Through watering eyes, he saw the dying glow of Karek'Thur mere centimetres away. His strength wavering, he wearily lifted his hand towards the weapon. Feeling its expertly made hilt in his hand once again, Arcturus closed his grip. The unbearable pain warped his mind as he attempted to hold on. His body shuddered as the cold engulfed him, forcing him to finally surrender to the darkness.

9
THE UNTOLD SAVIOUR

Arcturus' mind faded in and out of consciousness as strong hands tended to his wounds. "Stay still! You're in bad shape," a voice flit between the searing pain. "Fuck, you ain't gunna make it without Anile." He tried to pull himself to his feet. "Sit down you dumb fuck, gah you fuckin' humans!" Using the husky feminine tone as an anchor, he tried to tether himself to reality. "I didn't come here for you, but I can't just fuckin' leave you. No, no, no..." He felt the words fade away as the torrent of pain pulsed through him once more.

Warm, dark liquid rippled against his thighs, forcing his eyes open. He gazed around the pitch-black room for a moment. Running his hands over his body, he felt his naked form. "Wait, where am I?" A small glowing peony unfurled from the water, its petals sparkling its light across the refracting surface. Arcturus leaned to touch the flora; its smooth petals graced his fingertips. Gorgeous, tiny silver stars blinked to life deep within the water around him.

"Gorgeous, isn't it?" Surprised, Arcturus turned. "Don't be alarmed, my love." His eyes locked on Maeve's familiar welcoming form. She stood naked with a glorious golden aura surrounding her. "It seems you're hurt again. Those scorthics really got the better of you, didn't they?"

The legionnaire frowned, "how do you know of the scorthic?"

Maeve smiled. Slowly, she walked into the waters. "I told you I wouldn't leave your side. I've been with you this whole time."

"But I lost you, the crimson took you from me," Arcturus' face became perplexed.

She placed her hand against his cheek and lifted his eyes to meet hers, "nothing will ever take me from you, just as nothing will take you from me." A grin beamed across her face and her eyes glimmered gold. "Could you not sense my voice?"

"Yes, I knew that was you. Although I did worry it might have been grief playing a cruel trick." Arcturus smiled. "I will never stop loving you, Maeve," he leaned in to kiss her.

She held for a moment. "I will strike you down before that day," she chuckled and pressed her lips against his. Pulling him close, their forms embraced.

Arcturus felt the pain subsiding from his soul as his worries melted away. "Where are we?"

"Do you not recognise it?" Maeve smiled as she gazed over his confused face, "hang on." She lifted her hands, and the marble room began forming around them. "We are home, my sweet."

The legionnaire looked over the familiar surroundings. "Our washroom," he smiled, "you are full of surprises, Warden."

She drew him in to kiss her. "You don't even know the half of it. This here was our fortress that fell when the crimson came." Her hands slowly ran over his body, "but you'll learn more of that as you travel across Nor'ai."

"I don't understand," Arcturus tilted his head before he felt the pleasure of her hand surrounding his manhood, "my love?"

"Hush now, your head is clouded with worry. For now, just feel." She knelt before him, welcoming him to her mouth. "I need to taste you just one last time." Pleasures crackled through the legionnaire's soul as Maeve expertly swirled her tongue. She grasped his buttocks as he leaned back feeling the waves of ecstasy pulsing through his core.

"Oh, my..." Every hair on Arcturus' body stood on end while his knees shuddered. Uncontrollably, his eyes flew wide, and he released an echoing groan. Maeve took him deeper, focussing on his pleasure. Shudders rolled through Arcturus' core as his body trembled and his moans filled the silence. Gripping her hair, the legionnaire felt the euphoria explode inside him until he finally released.

Maeve stood as she tasted his essence. "I felt you needed that." She smiled. "I will do my best to guide you and protect you along your journey, my love."

"Can I not bring you back to me?" Arcturus' face saddened.

"I'll always be beside you." Strolling around him, she glanced back with a smile. "I have never known of resurrection within Nor'ai. We would never worry of losing a Warden if that were the case. Your mother might still be with us with resurrection at hand." Lightly stroking her hand over the lily's golden petals, she softly spoke. "Hush your sadness. There is much to be done and a wizard you need to find. Warn the people of Vavarinu and protect this realm as you have sworn to do. Once Nor'ai is safe from this crimson you might finally be able to rest. Now be off with you, back to reality. You have some new people to meet…" She lifted her hand to her lips and blew a soft kiss.

Gorgeous, green magic surrounded them as a shimmering dome formed. Arcturus felt an almighty blast of air expand his lungs. His eyes slammed shut and he was forced back to reality.

"Welcome back, human." The husky female voice resonated from the corner of the room. Arcturus slowly opened his eyes to see a bright green dome around him. He ran his fingers over his chest and paused. Steadily, he glanced down at his healed wounds as the pounding through his soul soothed. "It's impressive," the voice spoke once more.

"Uh, thank you?" Arcturus glanced down at his naked body.

"Not that, you idiot. It's impressive that you thought you could beat that scorthic alone. I've been hunting it for years. I finally find it and your fucking stupidity means I have to leave it and drag your ass back here." Her voice cut the air like a knife.

I think she was talking about that. It is very impressive.

"Idiotic? Alone? I am neither of those things! Maveri was with me, and that beast came out of nowhere. We were resting when they attacked us," he paused, "who am I even speaking to?" Arcturus furiously pulled himself up as he tried to see through the shining magic.

"That's enough, Anile." The nature magic slowly dissipated. Arcturus' vision refocused on his now torch-lit surroundings. He saw a silhouette leaning against the wall holding Karek'Thur. "We save your fuckin' life and you spout out this damn bullshit? There was no other idiot with you down that tunnel. I found you, only you. I tended to your fuckin' wounds and I dragged your lumbering fuckwit of a body back here." She walked forward and pointed the sword toward him. The torchlight flickered against her jade skin, exposing her tall, muscular form covered in roughly stitched leather armour. She snarled a menacing, sharp smile below the beastly furred head of a grelketh as its hide trailed down her back. "Now tell me what the fuck you were doing out there." Her eyes narrowed and her strong jawline tensed.

Come on, play nice. These guys did save your life.

Arcturus looked at the axe hanging from her hip and the short bow strung over her shoulder. He analysed the beast's hide on her back knowing full well a strong, aggressive beast like that takes some skill to kill. Arcturus paused before answering, shifting a little as he analysed the pure power of the or'kerec before him. "Okay, fine. I am Arcturus Pythare, a legionnaire from a small town in Uzarian. We... I was travelling here after my home and my people were slaughtered by the crimson."

The or'kerec's eyes scowled. "The what? Crimson? What the fuck are you on about?"

Arcturus scanned over her intimidating form before locking onto her rouge eyes. "If I'm honest, I don't truly know what it is. All I really know is it's powerful and will wipe out this realm if we leave it unattended."

Her expression softened as she tilted her head. "If it's so bad then how did you survive?"

He looked to Karek'Thur. "I barely did, that blade saved me."

She smirked, exposing more of her elongated canines that protruded over her top lip. "I see." She pressed the blade against his chin. "If it was my tribe of or'kerec who fought that crimson, we would beat it without a single loss."

"Gathera! Put down that blade! This is no way to welcome our new guest!" The door slammed against the stone wall as a hulking draegorth stood in its wake, holding a tray of various coloured mugs.

The or'kerec grunted. "Oh Trey, I'm only having a bit of fun. We don't really know who this bloke is."

"That is not the point. He is weak and he is our guest and if he did try anything, I would flatten him!" The draegorth strolled over to Arcturus and slammed down the tray before extending his hand. "Hello friend, I am Treyoth Jaruun. Please do ignore her aggression, she does not know how to make friends."

Arcturus smiled nervously and met Treyoth's hand with his, "I'm Arcturus."

"It is fantastic to meet you, friend!" The draegorth clamped his hand shut and shook vigorously.

"Well, I'm Gathera. As I'm sure you can probably tell, I'm an or'kerec. A huntress from Unorei, to be exact. This skinny reptiare is Anile Naquilla, a druid from Leltanor. He's not the biggest talker."

Arcturus looked over to Anile while trying to pry his hand from

Treyoth's vice-like grip. His slim aqua-blue scales were mostly hidden behind his bright green leather armour and niqab. "It's nice to meet you all. Thank you for helping me." Anile nodded as his eyes smiled.

"You were in very bad shape, little one!" Treyoth's deep bellowing voice rumbled around the room. "I'm glad to see you recovering so well! I didn't think a being as tiny as you would come back from that! Ha! You're so puny! Ha-ha!" He looked down at Arcturus' hand still locked in his grip, "oh, sorry!" The draegorth unfurled his hand and patted the back of Arcturus' wrist.

This one seems very friendly.

The legionnaire steadily rolled his fingers. "That's not a problem."

"Now, little one, tell us more of this 'crimson'." Treyoth dragged a small wooden chair from the side of the room and lowered his muscular form onto it. The chair creaked and groaned as its legs bowed. Treyoth smiled, his sharp teeth gleaming from beneath his horned scales. His ginger eyes sparkled in the torchlight. He grabbed a mug and passed it to the legionnaire.

"Thank you." Arcturus took a sip. The intensely strong yet bitter flavours scraped along his tongue. A mix of sharp and smooth textures entwined with an almost dirt-like scent. He forced it down as he attempted to hide his disgust. "Well, I don't know much but around a day ago, a beam resonated from the lands of Deythron. A matter of moments later, these boulder-like projectiles fell from the skies before crashing over the lands of this realm. We investigated one of the crash sites to find all the beings killed by this magic resurrected and hostile. Friends, allies and lovers we all once knew were turned and anything they killed seemed to turn too." He instinctively took another sip of his drink before being filled with regret. "It was like something I have never seen; I'm surprised you didn't see anything around here. I am sure they must have landed within these lands too. We even encountered some insetille on our journey over to Vavarinu that seemed to have been turned. I might have lost the wizard I was travelling with during a scorthic fight."

Treyoth sat for a while as he pondered the words. He took a long sip of his drink and swallowed. "This does sound very worrying, little one. I have heard reports of odd things falling from the skies, but you hear so much in this city from its adventurers that you don't know what to believe." He turned to Gathera and Anile, "it sounds like the insetille finally got what they wanted. With the numbers of the scorthic at their side, it won't be long before they try to take this place again."

Arcturus placed his mug on the tray. "This city? Did we make it to Vavarinu? We were coming here to tell some sort of council about it all."

"You have arrived in Vavarinu, yes," the draegorth smiled. "What did you say this wizard's name was?" Treyoth cocked his head.

Arcturus frowned. "Maveri Boreas or something like that, why?"

The draegorth's eyes widened. "Ah, no matter. You should rest, we will talk more in the morning." Treyoth pulled the covers over the legionnaire. Gathera propped Karek'Thur against the side of the bed.

"I think maybe you're right, I haven't really slept since all of this began." Arcturus leaned back and placed his head on the pillow.

Treyoth nodded. "I understand. Anile can help you with that." The reptiare looked toward Treyoth and nodded. He glanced at Arcturus and waved his hands as nature magic swirled around his fingertips.

"Wait, what are you doi—" Arcturus dropped into a deep slumber.

"Anny, come, we need to talk." Treyoth turned to Gathera, "stay with the little one and make sure he's okay. I think there's more to this story that we need to hear."

Gathera nodded. "If that's the Maveri I think it is, we might finally have some fuckin' luck!"

10
A WELCOMING ARRIVAL

Arcturus stirred, rolling from one side to the other. Opening his heavy eyes, it took a while to focus on his dimly lit surroundings.

Good morning, my love.

"You're finally awake. I was worried Anile accidentally killed you." Her raspy voice filled the room as she perched on the side of the bed facing away from him.

"How long have I been out?" Arcturus sat up as his tired words left his lips.

"I'd say just over a week in total. We just kind of left you to it in the end." She stood, her body distorted by the flickering torchlight. "Took me fuckin' ages to drag your unconscious ass back to the city."

"Oh, that's not too bad then." He threw the covers off himself. "Wait, A week? I cannot rest while this crimson is still such a threat!" Leaping from the bed, the cool air whipped against his naked body. He looked down. "Where is my armour?"

"Hmm, you are large for a human. I can imagine you can handle yourself quite well." She walked towards him. He gazed at her powerful muscular form and large, toned chest. "Enjoying the view, Aranctus?"

I told you she was looking! Worry not, my love, her figure is gorgeous, and I am enjoying it too.

Arcturus snapped his sight to her face, shaking himself out of the trance. "It's Arcturus," he released a sly grin. "Sorry, I haven't ever seen a naked or'kerec before."

Gathera smirked. "Well, I would tell you to keep it in your pants, but you aren't wearing any." She chuckled. "You look at me like you've never seen tits this big. Trust me, you wouldn't be admirin' 'em so much if you were the one who had to fight with 'em. That's why I lock 'em away with this." Gathera grabbed her fur-lined leather chest armour and wrapped it over her toned chest.

I can imagine. Fighting with breasts as large as those would be a real feat!

"I'm very sure you can hold your own in a fight. I apologise for staring." Arcturus turned away and searched again for his clothes.

"Nah, it's fine. Just don't try and touch or I will kill you." Gathera donned the rest of her attire, "oh, who's Maeve?" She tossed him a pair of basic leather trousers and a drab cloth shirt.

"Thank you. I would never dream of touching another without consent." Arcturus began to clothe himself. "Maeve is... was my love and a Warden within the virago. I have known her since I was a child and we fought together for years. Unfortunately, she fell when the crimson destroyed our home." He slowly fastened the last button on his shirt.

Gathera nodded in understanding and latched her axe to her belt. "So she's dead then? I'm sorry to hear that." She pulled on her brown leather gloves and clamped her horned bracers to her wrists before throwing her grelketh pelt over her head.

Maybe dead, maybe not dead. More like I'm in limbo, bound to you and your soul.

"I'm not sure that she really is gone. We solarists believe that even in death, our souls are bound." Arcturus gazed over Karek'Thur.

Oh yeah, she can't hear me.

Gathera smirked as she laced up her boots. "You solarists are all about your soul bonds." She stood and walked past him, placing a hand on his shoulder, "let's get some food."

Arcturus latched Karek'Thur to his hip, "where did you say my armour was?"

Gathera stopped at the door. "It's fucked. We will get you somethin', but right now, I'm fuckin' starvin'!"

They strolled down a dark corridor leading to a steep flight of stairs. Damp uneven stones lined the walkway and dim torchlight danced along the wood-supported dirt walls. As they moved up, a faint light crept through the cracks within the door ahead. The distant sound of music blessed the air. Twangs of a light-hearted instrument harmonising with a gruff voice echoed around them. Gathera pushed open the heavy wooden door and stepped into the room. Arcturus followed closely behind. Large tables and chairs were scattered about the room as if placed in a careless fashion. Beings of various races sat around each table, tapping their feet as they listened to the music. To their right sat a vast bar spanning across the wall, with stools full of beings drinking their morning away. At the far end of the tavern upon a table stood a muscular, hickory-skinned dwethren playing an oak lute. He skipped around as the wood creaked and groaned below him to the beat. Gathera strolled to an empty table in the corner of the room and gestured for him to sit. Arcturus paused for a moment as he admired the dwethren's talent.

"And as the day grew long, I burst out in song and cracked their heads for doing me wrong!"

Gathera rolled her eyes and moved back to drag him to the table. "Right, watcha' want?"

Arcturus looked about the room for some sign of a menu. "What is there? Also, I don't have any coin."

The or'kerec grabbed her coin purse from her hip. "Don't worry, you can owe me for this one. It's not a choice of what there is, it's more of a choice of what you want." He looked at her blankly. "Right, I'll just fuckin' order you somethin'." She turned toward the dwethren standing on the table, "Hank! Stop fuckin' around!"

"I took they're worth and spared the tip, for this is mi bar I can't let that slip!"

The dwethren held his final note as his eyes flicked to Gathera from beneath his leather hat. He strummed a few more times before silencing the lute, "look who finally decided to show up!" The twang of the dwethren's voice echoed across the room. "Better late than never, eh?" He leapt from the table as he flung his lute over his shoulder. The drop would have been minute for a human, but for the short height of a dwethren, it was a little greater. His stout body slammed to the floor in a symphony of creaking wood. Adjusting his suede waistcoat and black, buckled trousers, he strode over to the table. "Hmm, I ain't seen your face around here before. You one of her new conquests?"

Woah, where is that accent from?

Gathera laughed. "Ha! No, he wishes. I saved his sorry ass from being devoured by that fuckin' scorthic I've been huntin'!"

Hank turned to Gathera and frowned. "You ain't killed that thing yet? And you call yourself a huntress! What a load of shite!" Arcturus watched the interaction between the two with amazement. The dwethren turned back to face him, extending his hand, "I'm sorry brother, how rude of me! I ain't introduced miself. The name's Haeckel Wilson but you can call me Hank, everyone else does. I am the owner of this here establishment and an unfortunate friend of Gathera."

Arcturus grasped his hand, "I'm Arcturus Pythare, it's good to meet you. Your music is fantastic!"

Hank pulled back and tipped his hat. "Well thanks, lad, you truly are a foreigner! I ain't heard an accent like that for a long time."

Arcturus raised a brow. "I was thinking the same about you. I haven't heard a voice like yours before."

Gathera chuckled, "He's from the dirty northern lands of Lochardia! They barely speak the proper tongue up there." The or'kerec poorly attempted to recreate the dwethren's twang.

Hank rolled his eyes. "At least I'm actually from 'round these parts! You've come across the vast sea! From the ass-swamp lands of Unorei." He chortled and grinned at Arcturus, "anyway! Let me grab you folks, some grub! I'll be right back. Gotta see if the chef is still awake."

Arcturus watched the dwethren stride behind the bar into the kitchen. "Well, he's definitely a character. Did he state that he owns this tavern?"

Gathera leaned back and rested her boots atop the cherry wood table, "he likes to think so, yeah. A while ago he bet the owner that if he could beat her in a game of shilcheck draw, then she'd give it to him. As you can guess, Hank lost. Then 'cause he's a hot-headed bard, he grabbed his lute and burst into song. Blades were drawn as he kicked up a fuckin' ruckus, that's where I came in."

Arcturus sat back in his chair. "You don't seem like the singing type."

Gathera glared blankly at him, "fuckin' hilarious. No, I had to save his sorry ass from gettin' absolutely creamed by the owner and her lackeys! I mean, who picks a fight with twenty idiots all by themself? Fuckin' Hank does!"

Arcturus smirked, running his hand over his unkempt stubble. "Sometimes hot-headed choices can lead to great outcomes! And to be honest, he does have a fantastic beard so I can see why he's so confident."

It was a fantastic beard! Maybe you should grow yours out?

Gathera smiled, sliding her slim bone dagger from her hip. "If we are ever out in the field together and you pull any shit like that with me," she slammed the dagger deep into the thick table, "I'll leave you there to die!" Her snarling grin changed as a confused look washed over her face. "Also, what the fuck does his beard have to do with it?"

Gosh, she is feisty.

"Woah, woah, woah! I told you not to stab my new tables! Do you know how many people I had to cheat to get 'em to make tables this size for free!? At least seven!" The dwethren strolled back toward the table with piles of bread and meat. "Next time, I'll make you pay for your damn food!" He lay the plates before Arcturus and Gathera. The expertly cooked meats still sizzling piled on top of one another. Their mouth-watering smell coated the room in a delicious aroma. "Now shut up and eat this. It's the chef's special of wolvren thigh and aelken steak topped with succulent cactus broth. Oh, and some fresh bread." Without missing a beat, Arcturus grasped his fork and began devouring the feast. The otherworldly flavours coated his pallet in a glorious swirl of ecstasy. "Damn son! When was the last time you ate?!" Hank watched in shock as the legionnaire carelessly tore into the meat and bread.

That looks delicious and it should fuel you for the adventures ahead. I have a feeling you'll need it.

"It has been at least three days since I have eaten. Please excuse my manners," Arcturus barely swallowed his food before the words left his mouth.

Hank raised his brow, "well, I'll be! You carry on fella. When you're ready, come up and grab a drink from me." Arcturus nodded and continued. Gathera observed for a moment watching the legionnaire engulf his food before tucking into her own.

"You say you're from Unorei? I have never ventured over the vast sea," ecstatic flavours blessed Arcturus' tongue as he spoke, "what made you sail over here?"

Gathera glanced up from a crudely made sandwich. "I'm a huntress, so I follow wherever the trophy huntin' takes me."

Arcturus furrowed his brow, "so you're a trophy hunter?"

Exhaling deeply, she pulled the sandwich away from her open mouth, "yes. And since I've been here, I've been huntin' that scorthic. The same scorthic I had to let leave my grasp because you fuckin' fell down the hole in front of me."

A look of concern swept across Arcturus' face. "Maveri!" He waved his meat juice-covered hand at Gathera, "you said it was only me in that hole, right?"

Gathera lowered her head. "Yes! You were the only idiot in the fuckin' hole! Don't worry about this damn Maverick chap, we will go save his dumb ass too."

Arcturus stopped eating, "his name is Maveri, I think. But surely a wizard as powerful as him is a great threat if the crimson gets him? Treyoth said himself that the insetille will be looking to assault this city again now that they have the numbers of the scorthic."

Gathera's eyes locked straight onto Arcturus, "for fuck's sake, you do make a good point. Yeah, maybe we should be a little more urgent in our rescue attempt." She tore apart her sandwich with reckless abandon. "Where did you say you lost your wizard buddy?"

Arcturus cocked his brow. "It was near Ragrug if I remember correctly."

"Right, and it was just the two of you?" She wiped the saliva from her chin.

The legionnaire ripped apart the soft crusted bread. "Yes, the other two that found me in Krytiare didn't follow us to Ragrug."

"Other two?" Gathera watched Arcturus mopping his plate with the bread. "Ugh doesn't matter, how much do you know about this wizard?"

Arcturus glanced up. "Not a great deal. I know he's a strong wizard, I know his family died in some fires or something in Murimia and that he must have connections here to a council of sorts. He also helped me fight a wyvern."

Gathera smirked, "that's good enough for me." She urged Arcturus up and forced him away from the food. "Wait, helped you fight a wyvern?"

"Woah! Where you two goin'?" Hank stepped in front of them with two tankards filled to the brim with ale.

"We need to find Treyoth, we have a wizard to save," Gathera's voice crackled with excitement. Hank returned with a perplexed frown. "Ya know... the wizard." She raised her eyebrows suggestively.

The dwethren's eyes widened, "oh, of course! Well, before ya go there's a fella at the bar asking to speak to ya, Arcturus."

Arcturus looked over to the bar. A familiar cloaked figure sat nursing a brown liqueur on ice. "Maveri?!" He brushed passed Gathera and moved toward the figure.

"Took you long enough. Where have you been?" Maveri turned to look at Arcturus.

"How did you get here?" The legionnaire stepped back in shock.

"I didn't. I mean, I'm not. This is a manifestation of myself, an 'image' of me, if you will." Maveri took a sip of his drink.

"Then where are you, wizard?" Arcturus went to place a hand on Maveri's shoulder, phasing through his now azure form.

"I fell through the sands. I don't know how far down I am or what's around me, but I'm locked in a stone room." Maveri placed his drink down and stood.

"Can you not just leave?" Arcturus ran his hand over his rough hair.

"Oh, what a fantastic idea, why didn't I think of that?" Maveri rolled his eyes, "there's no door you fool, and my magic doesn't seem to be working here correctly." He paused, "there's something outside. I can hear it. I need you to come and find me, I shall make it worth your while."

"If your magic isn't working there then how are you doing this spell?" Arcturus tilted his head.

Maveri's shoulders slumped. "It is but a simple swift spell, a child could do it!" The image stuttered and distorted, fading into a faint azure glow, "these are not the questions you should be asking! Quickly, Arcturus, I sense I don't have much time here. Gather some sort of party and come save me..." Maveri's voice faded away as the magic dispersed. Arcturus waived his hands through the magic then slowly moved back to Gathera and Hank.

"Maveri?" Arcturus scanned the room.

He really needs our help, just like he helped you. I think that's where you need to go next.

"Was that him?" Gathera asked quizzically.

Arcturus' jaw tensed. "Yes, that was Maveri. Or at least his image or something, it seems he's stuck in a stone room underground."

Hank stood staring at the bar, "why doesn't he just open the door?"

"That's what I said!" Arcturus chuckled. "Apparently there is no door. It does seem like he is in danger, though."

The dwethren frowned, "wait, he didn't pay for that drink."

Gathera slapped the back of Hank's head, "it wasn't really him, you idiot! We need to find Treyoth and Anile and find this wizard." Arcturus and Gathera moved to the large arched doorway to leave.

"Well, I'll stay here and man the bar, come get me if you need me! Keep ya heads down, they're still looking for ya, Gathera," Hank called after them before moving to wipe down the bar where Maveri's image once was. "I'll make him pay for that drink."

11
<u>INTO THE CITY</u>

Bursting through the heavy wooden doors, they stepped onto the streets of Vavarinu. Arcturus shielded his eyes as the blinding desert sunlight beamed down upon them.

"This way, stay close." Gathera lifted her grelketh hood and moved down onto the rough sandstone road. Quickly following, Arcturus gazed about the stone-built buildings. Beautiful cacti and palms decorated the houses and walkways. While city folk went on with their day, the two of them weaved and manoeuvred through the bustling streets.

"Why are you wanted here then?" Arcturus slipped between a pair of aelveth as he spoke.

"Keep ya fuckin' voice down," Gathera glared back at him. They swiftly turned down a new street, narrowly avoiding a slobbering, humped caym-elec and trailer.

"Hey, I'm walkin' here!" The g'anomi rider looked glaringly at Arcturus. It turned back as the horned head of the beast he rode slammed into the rear of a cart. "Ah, balls!"

"This city ain't the most easy-goin' place in Nor'ai. The folks here are mainly adventurers between quests or traders lookin' to make quick coin. The trophy huntin' business ain't what it was, no one wants to buy pelts or carapace for good money anymore. So, I've had to move onto bigger kills."

"Like that scorthic?" Arcturus questioned.

"Exactly, that fucker would get me a lot of gold. Unfortunately, a kill like that takes a lot of resources and sometimes, I need a companion to help me hunt." Gathera navigated the swarming market stalls, "sometimes them companions don't return with me. It's normally due to them being little bitches who die too damn easy. Well, it turns out my last companion might have been someone important's kid and they ain't happy that he got ate," she sneered as a dwethren stepped in front of her. Shoving him aside, she flashed a crude gesture while moving forward. Sellers of all races yelled into the street, attempting to catch buyers for their produce. Arcturus looked around at the worn structures behind the stalls. The further down the street they travelled, the worse kept it seemed to become.

"Hey, you! Want some of these fresh melons?"

Arcturus turned to see a small grolt holding some browning square fruit. His mud-brown skin was exposed beneath his torn leather vest. Two narrow eyes sat beside his wide, stubby nose. His head twitched while awaiting a response causing his two large, folded ears to flap against the sides of his head. Arcturus' brow furrowed, "no, sorry. Also, those definitely aren't fresh, I'm not even sure they are melons."

The grolt dropped the strange fruit back into his trailer and glared at Arcturus, "what did you just say? Of course they are melons!" He raised his bony finger and paused, "that's an odd accent, you ain't from round these parts. Where are you from?" Arcturus watched as the grolt slowly moved toward him with his left eye twitching.

"Arcturus! We don't have time for this! Come on!" Gathera's voice called out over the noise of the crowd.

"Yeah, go on, run on!" The grolt placed his hand on the small leather holster attached to his belt.

"Haha don't try me. Good luck selling those odd melons!" Arcturus turned to walk away as a hulking fire golem towered over him. Pools of dripping magma seemed to somehow glue its obsidian form together.

"Don't try me either!" The grolt yelled. Crowds of people began slowly dispersing away from Arcturus. The legionnaire slumped his shoulders in exasperation. "Your kind always thinks you're better than us, don't you?"

Arcturus placed his hand on the hilt of his blade, "Not at all, I just think you're trying to trick these lovely people into buying shit."

The grolt gritted his teeth. Magic coursed through the elm-wood wand within his hand. "Shit?! They are fucking melons!"

Arcturus rolled his eyes, "Fine, I'm sorry." Unsheathing Karek'Thur, he briskly slammed the side of the blade against the grolt's head. Its small body rolled across the road. Arcturus chuckled. Without a second thought, he looked down at the wand and crushed it beneath his foot. He glanced up to see the fire golem crumble to the ground. "Interesting."

Oh, that was mean! What could that little guy really have done?

"Arcturus! Fuckin' hurry up!" The or'kerec yelled out from a nearby alley. Sheathing his sword, he mulled over Maeve's words and jogged toward Gathera. "What the fuck were you doin'?" Arcturus grinned and shrugged. "Fuck it. Don't tell me. We need to move." Gathera grabbed his shoulder and forced him further down the road.

Pushing through the crowds and market stalls, they eventually turned onto a quiet alleyway. "Now, stick with me. We're in the back alleys of this dusty shit city." Arcturus glanced over the damaged housing and uprooted sandstone slabs. The noise of the street seemed to drown out as the wind tore amongst it. Wooden shutters rattled against the sides of buildings echoing down the narrow lane ahead.

"How can we go from such busy streets to this in such a short amount of time?" He crossed the empty lifeless road.

"It's something that the outsiders of this city never hear about. Since the eternal drought that has run rife within these lands for years, the city of Vavarinu just hasn't had enough food or water to keep the city alive. As more adventurers stop here between quests, more and more of the city's residents must leave. They form a new life in better lands. This is what's left behind. The closer to the city centre you travel, the better it's kept. But on the outer edge where the working class used to live, it's a shit show. That's where the poor folk try to make ends meet."

This looks nothing like the adventurer city from before the war.

Arcturus shook his head in disbelief. "From the stories you hear about this place, you wouldn't think that to be true."

Gathera shrugged as a voice squealed behind them. "Oi, you there! Stop!" They turned to see the small grolt standing rubbing his head beside two city guards.

"Oh, for fuck's sake Arcturus! We don't have time to pick petty fights with the bastard grolt!" She placed her hand upon the top of her axe. "Fuck off! We've got bigger problems than you! You can deal with this later!"

The guards drew their swords. "That's fuckin Gathera! Grab her!"

Arcturus grasped the hilt of his sword. "Back off!"

The guards gestured to Arcturus. "Draw that weapon and we will take you down!"

"Fuck's sake." Gathera grabbed Arcturus, "this way, quickly!" She drew her bow and launched a bright jade arrow into the skies. "Don't look back."

The arrow exploded releasing a blinding light that dazzled the guards.

A frown slid across Rickrum's face, "you win this time, Arcturus!" He tightened his grip around his broken wand and raised it to the skies. "But I will find you!"

"You're kiddin' me." Gathera placed her head in her hands as they ran through the alleyways. "He knows your fuckin' name too."

Arcturus looked over to Gathera, "you told him my name!"

"Well, let's not point fingers." Gathera smiled.

Yours is a name and a face that is hard to forget.

Arcturus smirked at the compliment.

"Get in here!" Treyoth leapt before the pair of them and dragged them into a nearby house.

"Gah! You really shit me up then!" Gathera dusted herself off and turned to see Anile attempting to comfort a scared female kenket in the corner of the room. "We are sorry to intrude."

"Give us a moment and we will be out of your hair, little one." Treyoth shifted past Arcturus. "We need to lay low for a little while, so the guards don't find us." He closed the door and battened the shutters.

"Good idea." Arcturus placed his hand on his scabbard, "where's my blade?"

"Catch!" Gathera called out.

The glimmer of his Karek'Thur span toward him, firmly lodging itself in the sandstone beneath his feet. He looked up to Gathera in shock, "you just threw a sword at me!"

Gathera shrugged, "gotta keep a close eye on your shit in this city, mate." Arcturus shook his head in disbelief as he dislodged the blade.

I really do like her...

"Stop it, you two. Come, my friend, take a seat." Treyoth pulled out a chair and gestured for Arcturus to sit. The group sat around a small wooden table in the dim, torch-lit kitchen. The room's stone walls were bare with only kitchen utensils hanging above a poorly maintained stove. "Sorry we commandeered your house like this, but you understand, right?" The female figure nodded and then slid down the wall to sit on the floor.

"She's terrified, Trey." Anile shifted over to the table and sat.

Treyoth smiled and walked to the figure, his hulking form towering over her. "No need to fear us, little one. We might be wanted but we are not wanted for murder!"

Gathera rolled her eyes, "yeah, that's gunna calm her."

"Just sit with us, Trey." Anile pulled out the chair beside him and looked at the female. "We will leave as soon as we can, and we won't break anything." Treyoth smiled at the figure then slammed his massive shield down and leaned it against the wall. He squinted a little at the sound then carefully moved to the chair. Anile rolled his eyes, "just sit." Treyoth eased around the chair and lowered himself onto the aging wood with an almighty creak.

Arcturus smiled, "it must be hard being a draegorth in a city that wasn't built for your kind."

"No, the hard part is being an oaf without realising how big you are." Anile's quiet voice grew a little more confident. "Remember when we first got here?" He looked to Treyoth.

"Yes! How could I forget!" Treyoth turned to Gathera, "that was the day I met you!"

Gathera chuckled. "Fuckin' met me? You trampled me!" She leaned over to Arcturus, "this big prick comes storming down the street with his eyes locked on this one's arse, didn't even see me standin' there."

"Haha! But you're so small! How was I meant to see you? You were being sneaky if I remember." Treyoth grinned.

"Small?!" Gathera stood and punched the table.

Arcturus slammed Karek'Thur on the table, "you are going to get us caught."

Gathera grunted and looked down at him, "fine. Sorry."

That was brave of you. Ask them why they need to find Maveri so badly.

Arcturus raised his brow at the comment. "So, why is it you all need this wizard?"

"We need to save him so he can pardon us. The crimes we have supposedly committed were not done by us," Anile looked aside, "well not all of them…"

"I see." Arcturus stroked his rough, stubbled chin. "And why were you so eager to help me?"

"It's what we do." Treyoth smiled. "This world is full of ugliness, so we do what we can to make it a little more pleasant."

Anile locked eyes with Treyoth and kissed him on the cheek. "Well put."

"Get a room." Gathera rolled her eyes and winked at the pair. "Maveri is very important in this city, if you want influence here you need him."

I did think he was rather fancy.

"I see you have a soulstone in your blade. Did a calastain gift you that?" Anile gestured to the sliver gem within Karek'Thur's guard.

The legionnaire lifted the weapon, "a soulstone?"

Anile stood. "Yes, they are so incredibly rare." He walked around to Arcturus. "May I?"

"What is it you want to do?" Arcturus pulled back a little.

Anile paused, "I just want to check if there is a soul within it."

Arcturus nodded, "how will you know?" He lifted the blade to Anile. A small blossom of mint green magic poured out from the reptiare's fingertips as he closed his eyes. Arcturus noticed a small patch of flora growing on the stone floor around his feet.

"Her soul breaths life." Anile rolled the pendant in his hand. "It seems the wizard could be of great use to you too then."

He could see me, I felt it. He seems like a kind-hearted being.

Arcturus felt a small rush of happiness pour into his heart. "How so?"

Anile released the sword. "Wizards along with other azure magic and ether magic wielders are some of the only ones able to commune with and find the aetherwells located within Nor'ai."

"Aetherwells? What is that?" Arcturus frowned.

Walking back to his chair, Anile placed his hands on Treyoth's shoulders and leaned down. "It is believed in ancient calastain lore that Nor'ai houses the power of resurrection. If a soul contained within a soulstone is brought to an aetherwell, it can be brought back to life."

Arcturus swiftly stood. "You mean, she could come back to me?" He sheathed Karek'Thur. "Where are these wells?"

Does that mean we could be together once again?

"Seems we best go find this wizard." Gathera moved to Arcturus. "He could help you with that, help gather an army to fight this crimson and help get me off!" Treyoth, Anile, Arcturus, and the female figure all slyly looked at Gathera. "I didn't mean like that!" They all burst out in fits of laughter as the chair beneath Treyoth groaned and cracked before giving way and dropping him and Anile to the ground. "Come on you fuckin' idiots, let's get this guy some armour and go find this wizard!"

12
A COMMON GOAL

The group stood, thanked the female kenket for her hospitality and cautiously walked on the streets once more.

"That looks cool, does it normally glow like that?" Gathera looked over Arcturus' shoulder.

Arcturus lifted Karek'Thur toward the sunlight. "No, this is new."

Gathera shrugged, "strange, maybe it's the soul inside smilin' or somthin'." She strolled along the street behind Treyoth and Anile.

That's odd, I am smiling.

"This way." Treyoth tried to move a crudely made barricade. "Did you not want to lend a hand? This...is...heavy!"

Gathera smirked, "nah, you're both big boys. You and your lover can handle it!" Anile's vines whipped around the sandstone and forced it aside as they emerged onto the main streets. Treyoth turned to Anile, "stay close to me, okay?"

Anile rolled his eyes. "I'll be fine Trey, I have you to protect me." His soft voice was barely audible over the bustling city streets.

"Gah! Just get a room you two!" Gathera grinned and winked.

Treyoth ignored her and softly kissed Anile's forehead. "I'll never let harm befall you."

Arcturus strolled over to the three of them, "did I hear that you are a blacksmith, Treyoth?"

The draegorth turned. "Yes, a blacksmith by night and a guardian by day! Uh...yes, we need to get you some armour, I can almost see your bits in this sunlight!"

Arcturus looked down, "ah, sorry, this clothing really isn't my size."

Treyoth chuckled. "Well, it's a good thing I've been working on some armour for you. Oh, and a little surprise that Anny found amongst the clutter within my workshop. I have another tiny friend who's tuning it for you."

Gathera pushed her way between them. "Aww, ain't that great guys, eh? Let's stand here and chat all day, shall we? It will be really fuckin' cute. No! We have a bigger fish to fry! We can't talk about this on the streets. Just in case this fuckwit pisses off any more fruit sellers."

Treyoth's joyful smile slid into a look of concern, "you actually seem worried, Gathera? Okay, let us go." They sprinted deeper into the city until its drab ruined structures changed to gloriously well-kept, curved, sandstone buildings. Beings of all races moved aside as the group pushed through. Gathera kept her head low while covering her face. City guards glared from their posts while a few moved toward the slums.

"I heard something about a council here," Arcturus spoke while absorbing the sights.

Treyoth looked back. "Yes, the council of the seven. They are magic wielders from all around the realm. It is them that uphold the magical barrier that surrounds this city."

The legionnaire looked up to see the gleaming turquoise dome that covered the city. "That must take a lot of magic to keep active." He looked back to Treyoth, "any ideas on where they might be?"

So, with that barrier active, this city remains fairly safe. Let's hope it holds.

"My guess would be the big fuckin' tower where the magic comes, you idiot." Gathera snarled and rolled her eyes. Arcturus shook his head and glanced at the almighty spiralling tower within the centre of the city. Its structure was hundreds of metres tall with decorative spines leading to its domed roof. The streets opened into a vast square with glimmers of magic sparkling throughout. Children of all ages and races sat before a mage as she taught them basic cantrips. One created a plate of warm sweet buns, and another, a small glimmering image of a floppy-eared haystek. He watched as warriors trained by hitting targets stuffed with straw and sparred with one another. Adventurers restocked at the local market stalls as berserkers and knights strolled past in hulking plate armour. Ferocious snarls and cheerful neighs called out from a nearby stable. Arcturus gazed over the aelk, wolvren, keylep and caymelec all grazing in harmony.

Arcturus gasped. "This place is amazing! I've seen nothing like it!"

Gathera looked back to see his childlike glee. "Well, apparently all shit-heads come here when they want some sort of adventure. It's a hub for anyone looking for quests or supplies or even just somewhere to stay," she sneered a little. "I hate the fact this place is so fuckin' busy..."

Treyoth patted her shoulder, "cheer up! You're always out hunting. I love seeing all these beings living and working together!" They slowed while approaching a junction of lanes, "my smithy is just down here!"

"Treyoth, I hope you don't mind me asking," Arcturus stepped aside to narrowly avoid a pair of mages, "what is a guardian?"

The draegorth smiled. "It is something only known to the draegorth. A form of magic-wielding combat that sees you focus only on using a shield to protect your fellow warriors. My shield and I are perfectly in tune with one another so I can use it as a focus to cast my magic through."

"Well, I look forward to seeing you in combat." Arcturus smiled.

As do I. Guardians are highly respected protectors.

"Alright you two, let's just not, eh?" Gathera rolled her eyes as the group continued further into the city.

"Trey, we're here, aren't we?" Anile spoke up halting the group. Treyoth guided them down a small staircase toward a massive metal door. He pressed his shield against it for a second. Great locks and cogs could be heard churning away as they unlatched before finally, the vast door slowly swung open. As the sunlight crept in, it revealed a narrow hallway leading to a chain curtain.

"Through here," Treyoth pushed through the curtain. A large iron forge could be seen burning away next to a great forge hammer and anvil. "Here, sit at my workbench, I'll prepare your armour," he grinned at Arcturus. "Gathera, come over here a second. Anile, can you find him some clothes?" The large workbench spanned from one end of the room to the other. Arcturus looked about the workshop to see racks of expertly forged weapons and armour. Tools hung from the lower brickwork of the iron forge. Deep in the corner sat a little candle-lit table with a small figure working away with tiny tools and bottles of glowing liquid in all shades of colours.

"Ah! Ve have ze guests! Let me come see!" The small figure hopped off his seat onto all fours and scurried his way to the table. The click of his claws rang out across the stone flooring, "hallo! Ah! Uh... on no! Vhy can bazically I zee your genitalz?!" Adjusting his goggles, the small rat-like creature stood back in shock as he looked over Arcturus.

Attempting to cover himself, Arcturus grinned. "I'm sorry. My clothing really isn't very covering." Anile patted Arcturus on his shoulder as he handed him a new cloth shirt and leather trousers. "Thank you, Anile." Arcturus clothed himself as the rattren covered his eyes.

"Vell...zat vaz a shock! Let me try ziz again! Hallo! I am Klauz ze mouze," he shuffled closer to Arcturus and gestured for him to bend down. "Even zo I am a rattren!" His hot breath whispered in the legionnaire's ear. Klaus chuckled, "zey call me ziz az it vaz a nicked name zat I have been gifted vith."

Aww, I really like this one too! Look at him!

Arcturus took a step back. "It's good to meet you, Klaus. I am Arcturus."

Klaus tilted his head as Arcturus extended his hand. "I zee... vell izn't zis fantastic! My muzer alvayz uzed to tell me zat vhen a human offerz you a handy, you must never decline!" He met Arcturus' grasp with his small paw and began to shake.

"Why is your paw so sticky?" Arcturus attempted to break the hand-shake.

Klaus pulled away. "Ah! Ziz iz the trick kvestion! You do not vant to know ze anza." Arcturus frowned as he looked at his own hand to see a greenish liquid stained on his palm.

"Klaus! Have you finished that project yet?" Treyoth called out from beside Gathera.

The rattren gazed into the darkness as he adjusted his goggles. "Ah, Treyoth! Ze big basher! I didn't zee you zer! I am nearly done! Just give me a teeny ticktockz worth of ze time you have, and I'll be reaching completion!" Klaus looked back to Arcturus and smiled. His dark blond fur exposed his pointed teeth as he whipped up his hood and scuttled back to his desk.

Treyoth stepped beside Arcturus and chuckled, "he gets me every time. Here little one, take these." Arcturus watched the rattren. Pulling out his tools from his satchel, Klaus began tinkering. "Arcturus? I said take these."

He looked up at Treyoth to see him holding an armful of armour. "Oh sorry. I thought you were talking to Klaus."

Treyoth tilted his head in confusion, "why did you? This armour is much too large for him."

Arcturus frowned then shook his head, "no, no, never mind, my mistake." He grabbed the armour from the draegorth and lay it on the table. Gazing over the beauty of the silver textured armour, Arcturus noticed the majestic, golden, engraved outlining. The design imitated the classic legionnaire shield bearer with an iconic draegorth twist. Leather and chainmail pteruges fanned out from the lower part of the breastplate. The pauldrons and gauntlets were crafted by layering gold and silver armour plates upon one another, almost like the scales of a dragon. An astonishing scarlet cape flowed down from leather straps fixed to the cuirass by sun-shaped pins. "Treyoth, you have left me speechless. This armour is outstanding, some of the best blacksmithing I think I have ever seen!"

Treyoth released a coy smile. "I thank you for your compliments, Arcturus. Although I am no Skarforge. Their work is perfection!" Arcturus grinned as he lifted the gauntlets, turning them in the dim light, he assessed their hardy structure. The cuirass was solid but at the same time flexible, as if able to take a hit without restricting movement. "I have adapted your people's design a little with the addition of pauldrons. I've also added plated, yet mobile leg armour to fit beneath the pteruges."

Arcturus ran his hand over the bright scarlet leather pteruges. "How can I repay you for this?"

Treyoth chuckled. "Don't thank me yet, little one." The draegorth strolled over to the corner behind the furnace. He lifted the final piece of armour, "I had to guess on head size, but I measured the rest as you slept. But I'm sure this will fit." He wandered back, holding a gold and silver helm. Its pointed lower shape resembled the design of the Corinthian helmet style worn by the legionnaires. Its lower points curved from base to tip. Treyoth moved further into the light. Gorgeous bright scarlet plumes of almost feather-like material blossomed from the peak of the helm. Arcturus froze, astonished by the pure beauty of this armoured composition. "I've done this for you to show you that you can trust us. To aid you through your adventures and to help you find the reason behind all of this madness."

That is absolutely gorgeous, my love. Wear it with pride!

A tear crept into Arcturus' sight as the draegorth spoke. "You do not understand how much this means to me. Thank you so very much, Treyoth Jaruun." The pair locked into a look of admiration and respect.

"Izn't ziz a gloriouz moment! Ah yez, foobulouz!" They both glanced down to a grinning Klaus standing beside Gathera. "I'm here to make ziz eeeven better! Arcturus, ziz iz for you!" Klaus held a golden-rimmed silver buckler as high as his arms would let him. Gathera grabbed the shield and passed it to Arcturus. He grasped the cool metal as he looked over its design. "Zis iz called ze Aegis of Solarity! It iz attuned to ze solar magic!" Klaus smiled and squeezed his paws together whilst staring up at him. Arcturus gazed over the golden sun expertly crafted into the centre of the shield. Interwoven were multiple solar symbols and runes. "I hope ziz bringz you much protection!"

"How do you know how to do this?" Arcturus looked to Klaus.

"I am an Artificer. A tinkerer if you vill! I make things achieve zer full magical potential!" Klaus smiled.

Gathera lifted her axe from her hip. "Well, lil' rat, you got another fuckin' job to do then."

Klaus' eyes fixed on the weapon before he grinned. He grasped it and ran back over to his desk. "Zis shall only take me a teeny ticktokz!"

Arcturus chuckled. "I best don my armour." Treyoth aided as Arcturus slipped into his bespoke fitting gear. He felt the smooth leather lining of each piece as it latched together. The silvers and golds shimmered and refracted in the dim light. The legionnaire marvelled over its majesty as each piece clicked together perfectly.

"Arcturus, I see zat you already have a soulstone, zis is vunderful!" Arcturus turned to Klaus. As the rattren uttered the words, a bellowing crash resounded around the room.

Hank stormed in, almost tripping over, "what the fuck have you guys done? The whole damn city is in flux!" He looked to Gathera, "hun, ya may wanna hide."

Gathera's jaw dropped, "what? Why?"

"That bastard Greystone is on his way here!" Hank moved to peak through the doorway.

Treyoth threw the rest of the gear onto Arcturus, "you two need to leave."

Gathera turned to the draegorth, "Trey, we will find him and come straight back."

Treyoth paused for a second. "Do what you can, I'll hold them off. When they see what you've done, they will do nothing but thank us!" Rushing over to a hidden trap door, he flung it open, "through here. They won't find you if you go this way, it should lead directly under the city. Bring that wizard home and let us finally live our lives again. Klaus, get as far away from here as possible. Head to the coast and find a man named Finley

Rogers. Tell him Treyoth sent you." Treyoth forced all of them to their feet as they geared up.

We must find that wizard and return to help these guys out. They need you, Arcturus.

"Gathera, you vill need to keep ziz in your hand for a while for it to attune to you, but it iz ready!" Klaus dragged the axe off the table and handed it to the or'kerec.

"Thank you, lil' rat. Now solar boy, get your ass in that hole. We've got a wizard to find!" Gathera pushed the legionnaire to the trap door. Arcturus latched Karek'Thur to his hip and clamped his shield to his back. Descending into the darkness, he gazed up to see the or'kerec exchange glances with Treyoth, Anile and Hank before closing the hatch. "We have to save him, or it will be our heads. Maybe down there we can learn more about this fuckin' crimson shit too."

"I might finally be able to answer some questions and save Maeve." Arcturus glanced up.

Gathera smiled a sarcastic smile. "Maybe. Now get fuckin' down there!"

13
DIGGING FOR GOLD

The moist mud squelched under Arcturus' sabatons as he stepped off the ladder. Drawing his sword and shield, he let Karek'Thur illuminate the way ahead.

"I gotta say, that sword is fuckin' cool," Gathera looked quizzically over the blade, "although, I don't need your light. I have excellent vision in darkness. So, maybe I should lead the way." She winked and pushed past him. Arcturus rolled his eyes. He quickly became distracted by the absolute ease of movement within this new plate armour. The expert craftsmanship kept to his form even down to each roll of his fingers. His shield slightly cupped his forearm as it sat snugly against him. Finally, he felt complete again. They walked for hours through the narrow tunnels, weaving through the twists and turns of the intricate system.

Arcturus glanced over his surroundings. "I can't see any signs of in-setille." He scanned his palm over the walls.

"Trust me, they're down here somewhere," Gathera trudged on.

"How do we know if we are even heading in the right direction?" Arcturus knocked his fist against the damp stone.

Gathera stopped. "Are you questioning my trackin' skills?" The or'kerec turned, "because I'm sorry, but without me, your friend will probably die. Then the whole city of Vavarinu will fall and me and my friends will be on the run, and you won't get to that aetherwell. Is that what you want?" She paced closer as her voice became more hostile.

"No, of course not. I was just making conversation." Arcturus looked aside and shrugged. "How did Maveri become so important to Vavarinu?"

Gathera snarled, "he's one of the seven and a member of the Boreas family. That name is crazily famous across the realm, I'm shocked you haven't heard of them. Basically, saving him would mean the city is in our debt."

"Thus, saving you all from whatever nonsense you've done wrong. I see what you mean now." Arcturus smiled. "I guess his fancy clothing really was purposeful then."

Trekking deeper into the tunnels, Arcturus rolled Karek'Thur over his hands. Its handle sent sparks of ecstasy up his forearm while solidifying his connection to the weapon.

Feels good, doesn't it? Almost as if it were I touching you.

Arcturus grinned.

"Why the fuck's that stupid smile for?" Gathera grunted.

"Just the majesty of this weapon is all," the legionnaire kept his focus on the blade. Subtle scratching noises resonated through the musty air. "Or'kerec, can you hear that?" Arcturus paused. The sounds of shifting soil slowly surrounded them. "Is that—" Gathera gestured for him to be quiet. After a few moments, the scurrying subsided. Arcturus exchanged glances with Gathera before carrying on through the tunnels. He felt his sabatons sinking deeper into the soil. "Does the ground seem softer here to you?"

The or'kerec stopped and looked back at him, squishing the dirt around his boots. "The dirt is soft everywhere, especially for an oaf like you." He looked up and shrugged. Suddenly, the ground crumbled beneath him. Instinctively he braced himself for the impact until he slammed against a stone structure. He sheathed Karek'Thur before standing.

Be careful, my love!

"Fuck, are you okay?" Gathera's voice resonated from above.

He glanced around. "I'm fine, are there meant to be stone buildings down here?"

"Stone what? Move your ass, I'm comin' down!" Arcturus moved aside.

He heard the or'kerec crash through the stone into a splash of water. "Oh, It's real wet down here." Arcturus slyly glanced aside. "Yeah, I know what I said…"

The legionnaire drew his blade, its golden light humming over the stone to reveal a hole created by the or'kerec, "is it a far drop?"

Gathera pulled her axe from her side, "nothing your fat ass can't manage." Arcturus rolled his eyes and leapt down. The waters splashed up his armour as he landed. Gathera frowned as she held her weapon in her palm; its engraved runic blade began shimmering in a glossy jade glimmer. "Oh damn! What did that rat do to my axe?"

Arcturus smirked, "looks like it's not only my blade that's cool."

Gathera shunted past him, "come on you smug bastard, we've gotta find this dim-witted wizard."

Arcturus chuckled. "Oh, you and Maveri are going to get along so well." They forged on down the wide stone corridors. As they walked, they passed burnt-out torches protruding from the walls. "It looks like something used to live down here." Arcturus ran his hand over the crumbling structure until they reached a crossroads. "Right then, hunter, which way now?" Gathera raised her palm to halt Arcturus. "What is it?" His voice was now almost a whisper.

"I felt like I heard something." She pushed her hand to his lips.

Arcturus clenched his grip on his shield as he scanned over the darkness.

"I can't see anything."

Gathera squinted. "Let's keep moving, but we need to stay quiet." The pair trudged forward cautiously toward the centre of the intersection. Karek'Thur's golden glow surrounded them, fighting back the darkness.

I don't like this place.

Arcturus bolstered his shield as he saw a figure lying in the distance. "Do you see that?"

Gathera's eyes narrowed. "I do." Arcturus clenched his grasp on Karek'Thur as the shallow waters echoed along the stone walls. Slowly, the figure slithered up in front of them, its body weaving in a snake-like fashion.

Gathera readied her axe. "Who the fuck are you?" She glared at the creature. "Right, have it your way," she flipped her axe in her palm and then slung it at the figure. In a swift snap, it lifted its arm and caught the weapon.

Two crimson, orb-like eyes sparked to life within the figure's head. "You are not welcome down here. Turn back or die."

Arcturus shrugged. "I'm afraid we can't do that."

"I guess death it is then." Without missing a beat, the figure tossed the axe back at Gathera. The or'kerec stepped aside as the weapon lodged into the stone beside her.

"That was a mistake, you slithery fuck," Gathera whipped her bow from her back and released three jade arrows at the creature. It weaved amongst the projectiles with ease as it pulled two scimitars from its back. Its tail-like body slithered along the ground while holding its armed torso aloft. Arcturus stepped in front of Gathera as the creature lunged forth. Echoes of clashing metal called out as Aegis blocked its sweeping attacks. As they locked in combat, the legionnaire saw its slim reptilian face sitting within its flared neck.

"Let us show you the truth of this realm," the creature's forked tongue whipped back and forth as it spoke.

Arcturus shunted the beast back. "There is no truth in the crimson, only corruption." He swung Karek'Thur as two jade arrows sang past his head and through the creature's face. Its body writhed before turning to crimson dust floating on the waters.

"Was that what I think it was?" Gathera gripped her axe and heaved.

Arcturus knelt to look over the dust. "I think so, but I was certain the siscrati died out a long time ago."

How are there siscrati still alive down here? Something really doesn't add up.

The or'kerec clenched her jaw as she heaved harder, "maybe that crimson shit brought 'em back." Tensing her muscular arms, she finally ripped her axe from the wall. Thuds rang out down the tunnels as shards of rock followed the weapon. "What's that noise?" Rushing waters echoed from down the walkway. "Oh, for fuck's sa—" A torrent of water forced them down the tunnels. Arcturus clutched his weapons as he frantically gasped for air. The waters pushed them deeper around the corners of the walkways until opening out into a sudden drop. Gathera and Arcturus braced themselves as they were tossed from the edge of the waterfall. The musty air kissed their skin until finally, they plunged into a large warm pool. Arcturus dragged himself ashore and gazed around the torchlit room. Statues of siscrati warriors dressed in majestic armour stood before them. They held glaives and scimitars as they lined the walls leading to a narrow doorway opposite the pool.

Are you okay? That could have been a deadly fall!

"Where the fuck are we now?" Gathera dragged herself onto the bank as she panted.

"I have no idea, but it looks like our only way out is through that," Arcturus pointed at a well-kept wooden door. They stood and moved to the exit, avoiding the statues as they walked.

Gathera reached down to grip its handle before pulling away, "ugh I fuckin' hate snakes."

Arcturus looked over the ornate handle; it was designed to mimic the image of a hissing cobra. He gripped and lifted it. "Not much of a huntress, are you?" Gathera sneered as the door creaked open to reveal a great open room with a pathway through its centre. A large statue stood illuminated before them as the path split and surrounded it. A great siscrati queen clad in astonishing draped chainmail wielding two glaives fought back an assaulting scorthic. Arcturus walked into the room toward the statue and attempted to read its plinth, "selscare tuk froun bel sul't mire." He turned to Gathera, "any idea what that means?"

"Yeah, it means let's fucking leave this bastard snake pit," she growled while scanning her surroundings. Her eyes panned over the stone-built houses and trade posts surrounding the area. Their structure was pyramidic in shape, each built in a spherical fashion surrounding the statue.

"Wait, is this the siscrati city centre?" Arcturus turned to see thousands of crimson eyes igniting around them as chattering mandibles rang throughout the musty air.

"Oh, of course the fuckin' bugs are down this deep too." Beads of anxious sweat rolled down Gathera's skin. An almighty insectoid screech convulsed from above as the insetille leapt down upon them. The fighters dashed aside, narrowly avoiding the creatures. Gathera swung her axe, tearing through the onslaught. She hacked apart limbs and shards of chitin whilst standing her ground. "They're fuckin' everywhere!"

Arcturus watched as their mantis-like features leapt towards him. Skilfully, he deflected them with his buckler to gain a better angle for his sword. The swift breeze of a claw sang past his helm. He swung Karek'Thur into the dimly lit fight, as the blade contacted the numerous attackers it burned them with gold light. The bodies swiftly turned to glowing crimson ash before falling to the ground. His eyes focused as he forced down each foe ahead of him, blocking then pushing the blade through while the onslaught continued.

"Arcturus! We need to bottleneck 'em!" Gathera snarled out from a pile of dismembered insetille.

The legionnaire glanced up. "I'll follow your lead!"

Gathera turned. "Fuck's sake!" The swarm of insetille forced her to the ground and piled on top of her.

"Gathera!" Arcturus spun and burned apart his surrounding foes. Following through with Aegis in one swift surge of force, he hurled the buckler toward where the or'kerec last stood. A golden copy of his shield spun from his wrist, ricocheting amongst the horde, igniting a dancing path of bright light. He glanced to the buckler still fixed to his wrist and smirked before the mandibles of an insetille clamped down upon his pauldron. Forcing the creature away, he compelled his blade through its head. He raised his shield and pushed through the gap between him and Gathera. The buckler beamed in beautiful golden light much like Karek'Thur as it slammed against the bugs. The clang of the image rang out as it boomeranged it's way back to Arcturus and settled against Aegis. He smiled and gripped the weapon whilst exploding through the horde.

"Gathera!" Suddenly, her runic axe burst through the head of an insetille followed by the or'kerec. She scaled up the back of another creature and spun herself to face the crowd. Flowing through the air she released six jade arrows, sending them piercing through multiple foes. Combat rolling as she landed, she drew her bowstring as far back as her strength would allow her. Between her hands formed a beautiful bright jade bolt. She released the arrow, decimating deep into the horde before clashing against Arcturus' shield. The projectile split into multiple smaller projectiles, embedding within the surrounding insetille.

"This way!" Her voice pierced the darkness. Arcturus forged on as he burned through the oncoming creatures, blazing a path toward the or'kerec. The searing scent of the fight cursed the air as the fallen foes writhed on the ground.

"You should use your bow more often!" The legionnaire panted.

"Well, the fuckers landed on us, I didn't have a chance to whip it out," Gathera smiled and pelted arrows to cover their flank.

"At least we haven't seen any scorthic yet," Arcturus threw the image of his buckler. It homed in on the Insetille before clashing amongst them. He swung his blade whilst watching Aegis' golden light sing into the distance.

"Seems like you have some new tricks." Gathera watched the shield create its glorious golden path of death.

The pair moved along the walkway before seeing the edge of the vast pentagonal room approaching. Masses of insetille scurried toward them, crawling along the floor, walls, and ceiling. Gathera picked them off one by one as they approached, her jade arrows spiralling toward them with ease. The image of Aegis rose toward the highest part of the room, exposing the charred face of a gargantuan Scorthic. The shield clouted the beast's hulking mandibles, then began its return to Arcturus.

"Oh, fuck," his eyes widened. The beast released a bellowing scream before bounding its way through the horde of insetille. Flailing bodies of the creatures in its path flung effortlessly aside as the stone rumbled under its weight.

Gathera focused her arrows upon the towering monstrosity. "You kill the lil' ones and I'll take on the big fucker!" She watched her jade projectiles glance off the creature's chitin. Each shot only seemed to anger it. Streaks of azure light beamed across the tunnel. A catlike beast's roar rang out as the scorthic broke its charge to change its focus.

"Run to the stairs!" The command echoed around them. Arcturus scanned over the area as he held back the oncoming foe.

Gathera examined the ceiling. "There, if we can rupture that, we can shower debris on them! That should give us some time to find this damn wizard." Gathera began hailing her arrows at a crack within the stone.

"I can't see in this damn darkness." Arcturus kept sprinting as he glanced around.

"Just aim where my arrows land!" The or'kerec yelled without breaking focus. Arcturus pulled back as he caught the copy of Aegis. Leaping, he launched the golden image toward Gathera's arrows. Planting on his back, he felt the full weight of several insetille crashing on top of him. He bolstered his shield, bracing to force them back. Miraculously, he felt the pure energy of Aegis burn through his wrist as his buckler ignited in golden light. The creatures eviscerated before his eyes. He instinctively scrambled to his feet before seeing shards of stone and soil plummeting toward the ground. "Move!" Gathera dragged him away as they fled into the tunnel. "Ah, shit! My fuckin' axe!" She glanced back as she reached out in a poor attempt to retrieve it, "that strange, lil' rattren just made it better!" Just as she pulled her hand away, she saw its jade runes spinning toward her. Before her axe arrived in her grasp, her jaw fell agape. "That clever lil' bastard."

Arcturus pulled her closer to keep up. The insetille clawed and screamed behind them. Just as one lunged forth, the image of Aegis decimated its skull before returning to the buckler. Finally reaching the stairs at the edge of the room, they began to climb. They stomped higher and higher as the musty air seared their lungs.

"Fuck! Arcturus, jump!" Gathera urged him as she leapt over a gap within the staircase. The step broke beneath the legionnaire's feet as he pushed with the tip of his sabatons. Gathera turned to see him drop below the ledge. "Arcturus!" The collapsing rubble stormed towards them, crushing the insetille, bursting forth in clouds of dust and acidic blood before slowly settling. Gathera fell back to avoid the debris and peered into the darkness. The hallowed screeches of the dying creatures snuffed into the depths of the crumbling structure.

14
UNLIKELY COMPANIONS

Shuffling back, Gathera grabbed her axe from beside her. "Ah, fuck. Don't tell me I've lost another one." She stood up and moved to look over the edge. "Don't cross the vast sea, Gathera. You won't find what you're looking for, Gathera. Ha! Fuck off, brothers!" The or'kerec scratched her head. "I found what I was looking for, but the damn thing has nearly killed me every time I've seen it. It was the fucker that ate Partuluk, although he was shite anyway," Gathera stopped, "I guess if Partuluk hadn't come here with me that once, I wouldn't be in such deep shit right now." She scanned over the rubble as the insetille tried to claw free. "I guess I've gotta find this fuckin' wizard by myself now then."

"Ugh, fuck."

Gathera paused for a moment as the clank of metal rang out against the stone.

"A little help here."

She glanced over the edge of the broken staircase to see Arcturus clutching onto Karek'Thur as its blade slid from within the stone. "Oh shit, you made it?!" The or'kerec knelt and offered her hand.

"Looks that way, doesn't it," Arcturus grunted as she dragged him up.

"I guess jumping in that armour ain't easy," she grinned as he pulled himself to his feet.

Arcturus sheathed Karek'Thur. "No, it's not easy."

It will always amaze me how your strength and determination keep you alive.

She smiled, "you're stronger than you look."

"Thanks." He rolled his eyes. "So, am I right in guessing Partuluk was the son of that important person?"

Gathera stepped back, "oh, you heard me say that?"

"I did," he grinned.

She slyly looked aside, "ah, well, he was the son of Ilmeyous, a g'anomi member of the council. Used to be my lil' mate who followed me around on my hunts. That was until he was—"

"Eaten?" Arcturus interrupted her.

Gathera innocently smirked, "yeah. I did tell him not to come on that last one, but he insisted."

"He was eaten by the scorthic?" Arcturus adjusted his helm.

She pointed into the darkness, "you mean that big one?" The legionnaire nodded. Smiling in an attempt of innocence, she exposed her canines, "yeah, that one ate him."

Arcturus chuckled. "I thought you said you hadn't been able to find that scorthic before?"

She shrugged, "well, technically I didn't find it. It's more like it keeps finding me."

Shaking his head, Arcturus patted her on the shoulder, "Don't worry, I don't go down that easy."

"Nah, you're much fatter than a g'anomi," Gathera winked. The pair exchanged smiles as the screeches of insetille echoed around them. "Right, yeah, we should go." They cautiously scaled higher up the seemingly never-ending staircase.

Arcturus huffed as he climbed the final steps, "did you hear someone tell us to run earlier?"

"Yes, it was just after that streak of blue light," Gathera muttered.

"Did it sound feminine to you?" He slowed down a little.

Gathera followed closely behind. "It was definitely a female's voice."

"I wonder why she's down here," Arcturus paused, "and why save us?"

"No fuckin' clue," Gathera shrugged.

What if that person is in trouble too? We need to find them.

Finally reaching the top of the stairs they were met by an ancient wooden door. Arcturus turned the rusted handle and pushed against the wood, "it's stuck." He stepped back and raised his shield, "hang on." Slamming the buckler against the door with almighty force, it swung open and shattered against the wall. A long dark corridor extended before them with multiple wooden doors on either side. Arcturus lifted Karek'Thur. "Great, more long, narrow tunnels."

Gathera pushed past him. "I guess we check each door for magic boy." She strolled along the walkway before stopping at the first door. She glanced over to Arcturus and proceeded to boot the door down. Scanning the room, she saw a small bed-like object and multiple broken cabinets. "Nothing in here." Arcturus moved to the next door and pushed it open to reveal an extremely similar room. He frowned and they moved on to the next two doors. Gathera booted hers down once again to reveal another empty room. Pausing for a moment, the legionnaire noticed a slight shimmer running along the door in front of him.

"Gathera, do you see this?" He called over to the or'kerec.

She frowned, "see what?"

"It's almost like a glyph or barrier or something on this door." He hovered his hand over the wood.

"Oh yeah." She lifted her leg and slammed her boot against the door, but it held strong. Snarling, she retreated into the opposite room. "Move." The or'kerec charged at full speed, pelting her shoulder against the wood only to be repelled backwards. Arcturus grinned as he tried to stifle his laughter.

"I mean, that was a good effort," a voice chuckled from the darkness. Arcturus primed his shield as he investigated his surroundings only to see azure claw marks etched into the walls. "Ah yeah, that was Bleu. He likes a good scratching post." Gathera stood in the doorway, clutching her axe. "No need for that! Scooch aside and I'll introduce myself." Arcturus frowned then backed away from the locked door. "That'll do. You two stay there. Oh, and don't shit ya'selves." After a few moments, the door swung open. The image of a human female crept into reality within the centre of the room like a shadow highlighted by light. Her almost ice-white hair roughly thrown into a bun appeared first whilst her agile form followed. A brown leather tunic cascaded down to her thighs, sitting over studded trousers that extended into her knee-high boots. Kunai decorated her belt as it lay across her waist supporting the hilts of two sheathed swords angling out from her hips. Her arms sat crossed against her chest. Long, fine, leather, fingerless gloves ran up her biceps, greeted by a singular pauldron strapped to her right shoulder.

"So, you're the one who helped us?" Arcturus removed his helm.

"Well, I can't take all the credit. Bleu helped too." The figure smiled.

"Right, I gotta ask, who the fuck is Bleu?" Gathera jolted her arms in despair. A bellowing roar of a large tigaris erupted from beside them. Arcturus jumped as he fumbled his helmet, dropping it to the ground.

"I told you not to shit ya'selves!" The female chuckled as Bleu scaled the walls and leapt back to her, his tousled fur rustled as he landed with a light thud. Swirling black and white detailing majestically fell in a mane-like fashion around his face. The crisp azure colour of his eyes glimmered as he looked down at the female. He lowered his long, pointed ears in an act of submission.

"So, that's Bleu?" Arcturus locked eyes with the beast, "I'm more of a wolvren man myself." He scanned the tigaris' muscular form as it growled. "But, uh, he is fine too. Why did you name him Bleu?"

My gosh, look at that beast! He is fantastic!

The female smirked, "you'll figure it out." Bleu licked his paw.

"Very well. I am Arcturus and this friendly or'kerec here is Gathera." Arcturus gestured to a snarling Gathera then looked back to the figure, "and you might be?"

The woman squinted at the or'kerec before adjusting her hair a little. "I'm Seraphina Gealfen."

Gathera cracked her neck and sheathed her hand axe. "You live down here?"

Seraphina laughed. "Gods no! It's just a little camp I made. I got trapped down here looking for my father."

Arcturus furrowed his brow. "Your father is down here?"

Seraphina looked aside. "I mean, he could be, yeah. He was banished when they found out about me."

Gathera looked at Arcturus, then back to Seraphina. "Banished? Found out about you? What do you mean by that?"

Seraphina glared at Bleu. "Forget I said that. So, why're you down here?" She began to gather up her bedroll and supplies left in the room.

Interesting. I think this one might have some secrets that could be of great use to us.

"We are looking for this one's wizard pal, Maverus," Gathera shrugged.

Bleu and Seraphina tilted their heads, "a fancy-looking bloke? Little beard? Looks almost half aelveth?"

Arcturus' brow tilted, "yes, that's the one. Have you seen him?"

Seraphina nodded, "yep, he fell down a hole and is stuck in a room with a stone door." She chuckled, "a couple of those insetille prophets tried to get at him but gave up in the end."

Gathera frowned. "There are prophets here?"

Arcturus stood in confusion, "what are prophets?"

I was just about to ask you that.

"There are like three forms to the insetille," Gathera scratched her head, "depending on how long they live, they go through phases. Drones are the start; those are what we fought in the tunnels. Carabus are the second form;

these can negate magic but not create magic of their own. Then you have the Prophets. These are the last form and need to have lived for over forty new moons. Prophets can both steal and create magic once they have found a source to fuel them." She locked eyes with Arcturus. "Basically, the city might be fucked if those things have been got by the crimson."

"Wait, crimson? Is that like from a rock thingy?" Seraphina glanced at Arcturus. The legionnaire nodded. "That's why their eyes are red!" Bleu cocked his head.

Arcturus grasped his sword. "We really need to find Maveri and get back to the city."

Gathera snarled as she drew her axe. "He better still be alive."

Seraphina smirked. "I'll show you where he is, come on!"

The Tigaris and the warrior led the way through the dull and damp tunnels, turning left and right until finally, daylight lit up their path. The stone crumbled away to reveal a great crater centred with a glowing crimson meteor. High above them, the sunlight sparkled through the opening of the hole. Two Prophets stood before the meteor as they raised their arms toward the blossoming magic. Their blue and brown chitin became engulfed in crimson light as they syphoned the power. The larger of the two held its wide head high as its antenna twitched and trailed almost to its feet. The smaller kept its head low, clenching its claws. Its arm seemed to house a partly healed wound where a second bladed extremity should have been. Bleu growled as Seraphina urged them all back.

"We should strike now. They have no idea we are here." Arcturus readied his weapons.

Gathera snarled, "are you crazy?! We barely escaped the last horde of those fuckers."

"She's right, you know; without us, you would have died," Seraphina grinned.

I'm sure you could have handled it.

The or'kerec grunted, "she's annoyingly right. We have no idea what kind of an army these things have, especially if the siscrati are back too."

"Oh, there's loads of those, right Bleu?" The tigaris snarled at Seraphina.

"Skell! Our armies gather topside. With this, we will finally show them the true way of the insetille." The prophet turned as a chattering horde erupted from the tunnels. Hundreds of scorthic and insetille alike scurried up the walls onto the sands.

Gathera recoiled. "We need to warn the city." A chitinous echo rumbled through the tunnels behind them. "Oh, fuck."

"Skell, deal with these intruders. We shall proceed to the gates." The smaller prophet nodded before the pair scurried away.

Save Maveri and get out of here. If these creatures reach the city and breach that barrier, Vavarinu will fall.

Arcturus nodded and readied his blade and buckler. "Looks like we will have to fight our way out." Gathera and Seraphina stepped beside him with weapons ready as they focused on the oncoming horde. He spun Karek'Thur and smirked at his fellow warriors, letting the glorious gold glow illuminate his armour.

15
LOST AND FOUND

Arcturus slung the image of Aegis at the horde as Seraphina and Bleu dispersed into the shadows. The golden light swirled through the creatures, dispersing them one by one. Glorious jade arrows sang through the tunnels, picking off each drone able to avoid Aegis. As the horde grew closer, Arcturus raised his shield.

Crush them, my love.

Streaks of sparkling azure magic danced amongst the creatures like erratic lightning before Seraphina appeared. Drawing her two short swords, she expertly carved through the onslaught. The ceiling cracked above as a carabus slammed to the ground beside her. Towering over her, it readied its chitinous extremities. It unfurled its four scythed arms before the shell on its shoulders slid aside to reveal several primed bolts. Seraphina sheathed her sword and slung three kunai from her belt. The blades soared through the air, igniting in azure flames, and plunged into the beast. Engulfed in flames, the carabus writhed. Suddenly a jade arrow burst through its head. Seraphina exhaled and redrew her sword to repel the other drones. Bleu blossomed to life beside her, ripping and tearing his claws through the creatures. The shrill screams of dying insetille grew louder and louder to an almost unbearable level as the tunnels shook.

"What the fuck is happenin'?" Gathera glanced over to Arcturus.

The legionnaire caught the image of Aegis. "I don't know, but I can't imagine it's good." Plumes of dust burst from the rupturing ceiling. "We need to leave these tunnels." He searched the horde for Seraphina. "It's time to go! Seraphina, we need to find Maveri and get out of here!" The walls beside them cracked as scorthic breached through the stone. Arcturus slammed his shield against one and then carved apart another.

Gathera rolled around him while loosing multiple jade arrows. "Seraphina, we have to go now!" A scorthic clamped her bow in its claw and ripped it from her hand. "Ah, you fucker!" She whipped her axe from her side and slammed it into the creature's face. Carving perfectly betwixt its eyes, she sliced the scorthic's face apart before grabbing her bow and tearing it back from the creature. She slipped the weapon onto her back as Arcturus shunted an insetille into the wall beside her. He embedded Karek'Thur into its abdomen.

"Where is she? We need to go!" As he turned to Gathera, he saw a crimson shimmer behind her, "watch out!" Before he could push her aside, the prophet buried its scythed arm deep into the or'kerec's shoulder. It pulled her away and shunted against Arcturus, urging him to the ledge over the crimson meteor.

"Skell, your kind have inhabited this land for too long. Now it is time for us to take it back!" The prophet pelted him off the ledge.

Gathera clutched her shoulder in agony while looking up at the prophet's twitching mandibles, "you fuckin' shit!"

"You thought I left too, skell? Jatahh will destroy your precious city. I will be the one to devour you, skell," the eyes of the prophet narrowed.

Gathera smirked, "looks like you're wounded. I guess that makes this a fair fight." The prophet's face twitched in confusion as it glanced over its part-healed scythe. It snarled and leapt at Gathera. The or'kerec unlatched her hand axe and deflected its attack before shunting the insetille against the wall.

Seraphina flashed into sight. "You called?"

"You took your fuckin' time. We need to leave, hold off them bugs while I crush this one," Gathera sneered. Seraphina nodded and turned to the horde. Wielding her swords with speed and grace, she carved apart the assaulting creatures. The whistle of chitinous bolts echoed down the tunnel. Locking her blades together, she deflected the projectiles and melded into the shadows. Bleu leapt from the darkness as if replacing Seraphina. He breached through the horde, stomping the scorthic to the ground.

Hearing the destruction above him, Arcturus pulled himself back to his feet. The meteor thrummed with chaotic energy as sparks of crimson magic whipped across its surface. He stepped back, shifting the ground below his feet. "Oh, come on." Clutching his shield and sword, he plummeted through the soil into a dark stone room. Karek'Thur's light revealed a pile of dying insetille shrivelling in azure flames before dispersing to crimson dust.

"Stay back or I'll be forced to kill you too!" Two small balls of azure flame formed in the darkness.

The legionnaire smirked, "snap out of it, wizard, you couldn't kill me if you tried."

"Want to bet?" Maveri stepped into the golden light of Karek'Thur.

It's good to see he hasn't lost that attitude since being down here.

Arcturus chuckled, "there's no time for this. We're in the centre of an insetille army that has managed to use the crimson to resurrect the siscrati. Do you have any magic in that little book of yours that can take us back to Vavarinu? Then we can leave this place and warn them of this threat."

Maveri gazed back deadpan, "that's a lot of information to take in all at once. Yes, I might just have enough magic left in me to open a portal to the city, but I won't be able to hold it for long." He pulled his book from his side. "Small problem though, you'll need to find a way of stopping that crimson from negating my more costly spells."

Arcturus stroked his rough beard, "I have an idea." He moved to the hole in the wall caused by the insetille and clambered through.

Don't stab the meteor, my love.

Arcturus released a manic smirk.

Maveri closed his eyes in frustration, "he's just going to stab it, isn't he? Brute force is that man's answer to everything."

Arcturus pulled himself out of the small tunnel. "Or'kerec, I found the wizard, get down here when you can!" He called out through the destruction.

Gathera glanced back as she clutched the dirt, "yeah gimme a fuckin' minute!" Heaving herself back to her feet, she gripped her hand axe and swiped up, locking against the scythe of the prophet. "I don't know your name, bug. How will I tell this story of an easy fight without reciting your dumb title?" The or'kerec sneered, the pain burning through her shoulder.

The Prophet forced her back, "Zatel will be the name of the one to kill you, skell!" It swung its bladed extremity toward her.

Gathera spun away to leave the creature unbalanced, then cleaved her axe into its leg. "What a fuckin' stupid name and stop saying 'skell'!" She smirked.

Zatel dropped to their knee, "you are skell! Nothing but a stain on our lands! No matter, for now, is your end, green skin." A shock of crimson light burned through its chitin, almost ripping it apart. Now quivering with corrupted magic, the insetille pulled itself to its feet. Swiftly, it crossed its arms against its chest to form razor-sharp spines across its back. Zatel exploded in crimson light tossing Gathera back along the ledge. The prophet paced towards her. "We harness their magic, skell. You can't defeat us." It raised its scythe.

Gathera used her wavering strength to pull herself up as Zatel swung. She gripped the creature's forearm and bellowed, "I," the or'kerec punched through its abdomen, "fuckin'," grasping its other arm, she spread them aside, "hate," her knee slammed against Zatel's crotch, "bugs!" Pulling with all her might, she tore the limbs from the creature and threw them aside. As Zatel screamed out in pain, Gathera gripped its head in her palm. "Just fuckin' die." Her hand clamped around the insetille's skull and squeezed until it caved under her strength. Watching the crimson burst into the air, she dropped Zatel's lifeless body to the ground.

Seraphina pulsed into existence beside her, "ooh, damn! Nice one!"

Before Gathera could respond, Seraphina leapt into a cascading backflip narrowly avoiding a scorthic's claw. The bright azure streak of Bleu radiated through the beast as he skidded to a halt before the or'kerec. Seraphina twirled her swords and planted them deep into a carabus' back before ripping it apart. An almighty quake shook the tunnel as rocks and debris cascaded around them. Gathera shambled to the ledge to see Arcturus fighting back several crimson tentacles. With each swipe from Karek'Thur and each clash against Aegis, they recoiled, allowing the legionnaire closer to its core.

"What the fuck are you doing?" The or'kerec called out through her searing pain.

Do not stab the meteor!

Arcturus slyly glanced back, "I'm giving the wizard some room to work!" He sliced apart the incoming tentacle and deflected another before leaping onto the meteor. "I hope this works," he muttered to himself. With his almighty strength, he plunged Karek'Thur deep into the meteor's structure. Gold light crackled through it as it trembled with immense power as its tentacles writhed and slammed against the surrounding tunnels.

You actually stabbed it.

Arcturus recoiled in shock, "oh, shit." He ripped out his blade and leapt to the ground. "I think now's our time to leave!"

"Ya think?!" Gathera attempted to drop off the ledge, but Bleu leapt beneath her and carried her down into the stone room. Arcturus followed with Seraphina appearing beside him. Azure runes circled Maveri while he tore open the plains of reality.

Seraphina smirked, "the wizard guy!"

Maveri glanced over his shoulder, "who the hell are you?"

"No time to explain. We need to leave now!" Arcturus steadied Gathera as she climbed from Bleu's back.

"Fine." Maveri clapped his hands together as a glorious oval azure portal formed in front of him. "Quickly, I can't hold it long!" Seraphina and Bleu sprinted through the portal as Arcturus walked Gathera closer.

"What are you waiting for?" The or'kerec growled.

Arcturus frowned. "I've never used a portal before." He looked over the swirling magic, "I don't know if I trust it."

You'll be fine, my love, I'm sure it's safe.

"Oh, fuck off," Gathera used the last of her strength to shunt the legionnaire through. Maveri chuckled as blood trailed from his nose and the final essence of his magic burned through his soul. He jumped into the portal as the meteor behind him exploded in glorious, golden light, sealing the tunnels shut.

16
A TRIUMPHANT RETURN

Glistening shades of blue, white, and turquoise swirled and entwined as Arcturus' weightless body passed through the portal. For a moment, he could stare into the abyss while watching the city of Vavarinu speed closer to him. Sparkling magic ran through his hand until finally, his sabatons slammed against the familiar sandstone streets.

Well, that was interesting...

He looked back to see Maveri fall to his knees. "How do you feel, wizard?"

Maveri wiped the blood from his face. "As if I've finally stopped drinking after a four-week bonanza."

Gathera unlatched a vial from her hip, "here, drink this." She tossed it over to Maveri.

He fumbled, barely catching it before inspecting the vial. "Where did you get a potion of mana?" The wizard gazed over the textured aqua liquid.

Gathera smirked. "Eh, found it somewhere." She clutched her shoulder as her muscles spasmed. Maveri inspected the vial as he uncorked it. Sniffing the liquid, he pursed his lips and chugged the shimmering solution. Within seconds, the wizard's skin became flush with colour.

Arcturus looked at Gathera and asked, "why didn't you just drink that to heal yourself?"

She lifted her brow. "That doesn't heal you, that only gives a portion of your magical ability back without havin' to rest."

"That's a basic explanation but yes, that is correct, or'kerec." Standing, he tossed the vial aside, shattering it on the ground. "I feel much better." He opened a pouch on his hip then looked to Gathera, "oh, here, have this." Pulling a similar vial from his pouch filled with shimmering maroon liquid, he handed it to the or'kerec. "This should help with the pain."

Gathera looked at the shards of the vial and then back at the wizard's extended hand. "Hmm, thank you." She ripped the vial from his grip and chugged it.

"I'm Maveri Boreas, it's good to meet you," he extended his hand once more.

The or'kerec raised her brow, slung the empty vial aside then clamped her hand around his, "I'm Gathera. I know who you are, Maveri."

Maveri's eyes widened as he tried to pull his hand away. "You do?"

"I'm Seraphina and this is Bleu." Bleu stamped his feet as he proudly posed. Confused, Gathera, Arcturus and Maveri all turned to look. "Oh, we thought we were doing introductions and stuff." The tigaris growled and gazed at Seraphina who responded with a shrug.

Gathera finally released Maveri's hand. "Yes, I do and you're gonna help me and my mates."

The wizard nervously smiled. "Ah, I see." He turned to Arcturus, "what does she mean by that?"

Arcturus raised his brow. "You'll find out soon enough." He glanced up to see a couple of silhouettes strolling towards them.

"Gafera Kinjale, yous are placed undarrest." The group was met by a pair of unusual adventurers aiming their weaponry toward them. A pink-haired g'anomi mage in black and silver robes held its fire magic primed. Forcefully, a hulking chainmail-wearing reptiare warrior thrust two almighty halberds at Seraphina and Maveri's throats.

I guess it was only a matter of time until they found them.

"Who the fuck are you two?" Gathera snarled.

The reptiare licked his tongue along his chipped teeth. "Wes the ones gunna cash in yous bounty. Greystone wants ya 'ed."

Maveri frowned as the words clashed in his mind, "sorry?"

"I says, wes the ones gonna cash in yous bounty. Greystone wants er 'ed!" The reptiare's red and green crest rattled in anger.

Gathera leaned over to Maveri. "I think he's sayin' something about takin' us to Greystone to cash in my bounty, mate."

"Oh! Thank you. I honestly had no clue what he was trying to say." Maveri smiled and looked back to the warrior. "Umm, hello friend. The name's Maveri Boreas, you may have heard of me?" The reptiare stared blankly back at Maveri. "I see. Well, I'm a wizard and part of the council of seven. If you would kindly take us to Greystone so I can explain this whole situation, that would be splendid." The reptiare snarled at Maveri's response.

"Oh, for fuck's sake, I got this." Gathera pushed Maveri aside and squared up to the reptiare. "Look here you big fucker, we have some grave news concerning the fate of this city that the council needs to hear."

"I wouldn't threaten him if I were you," a well-spoken kenket yelled from the rooftop above. "He could crush you in seconds." She leapt into a flowing backflip and landed elegantly behind the reptiare. "Excuse me, Yowtel, let me speak with these criminals." Yowtel snarled then stepped aside and lowered his blood-stained weapons. "What's this big news then?" She removed the hood of her black leather studded tunic to reveal her ginger feline face. Her arched ears were battered and torn; her face was scarred but her eyes still shone a hopeful bright, sky blue.

Gathera smiled an impressed smile. "You're that rogue that people keep goin' on about, aren't ya? The one that took down the bandits that tried to steal a ship from Murimia?"

Oh, that sounds like an interesting story! So many of these adventurers could be useful to us.

"I'm glad you asked," Eshspen lowered her head into a dramatic smirk toward Gathera.

Yowtel picked his teeth with his halberd. "fuckin' sakes."

Eshspen rolled her eyes. "Fine! I won't say anything about it! So going back to what I said earlier, what's this news?"

"Look, I don't mean to be rude and it's nice to meet you and all, but we don't have much time." Seraphina stepped forward attempting an aggressive snarl. Bleu's bared teeth turned to a purr as Eshspen smiled and winked at him.

"Fine, we will take you to Greystone but, we will be getting our bounty." Eshspen turned and pulled her ornate, bladed disks from her hips. "If you try anything, I will gladly kill you all." She looked at Gathera, "especially you, or'kerec."

Gathera smirked. "I'd like to see you try." Eshspen hissed and lifted her hood. Jealte rolled her eyes while Yowtel shunted the group forward.

"I really don't know what to make of that interaction," Maveri scratched his goatee.

Arcturus stepped close to the wizard. "Nor do I. Maveri, I hear you are some sort of well-known wizard?"

"He sure fuckin' is," Gathera slapped his back, "he's my group's ticket to a pardon, aren't ya bud?"

Arcturus smirked, "he just loves being useful." Gathera winked at Arcturus as he spoke. "And you'll be my guide to an aetherwell."

Maveri scowled. "How do you know of aetherwells? And why would I be your guide?"

"I hear things also because I saved you." Arcturus turned away. They moved through the busy streets towards the city centre. Seraphina's face ignited with glee as she watched adventurers of all different races stroll past. Tempting aromas blessed the air as market stalls prepared all kinds of exotic foods. Patrons flocked to weapon stalls as they traded items and coins for wares.

Maveri looks confused and angry, and I love it!

"Seem's like you grabbed a couple of low lives too!" A proud-looking aelveth adventurer clad in leather armour strolled through the crowd. Steel plates were buckled over his chest and shoulders, seemingly more for decoration than protection. A long tan scarf wrapped around his neck and flapped in the breeze as it whipped at the long sword sheathed on his back. "Yeah, Gwen and I helped round a couple of them up too." He stopped and placed a hand on an archaic-looking cogwork revolver latched to his belt. "He ain't from round here," he gestured at Arcturus. "Nor's she, or that." He pointed at Seraphina and Bleu.

He's rude.

Gathera halted in place, "fuck off, Kolfren."

"Oh, watch your tongue, or'kerec. I can't imagine you're going to come out on top this time," Kolfren crossed his arms and smirked.

"I would appreciate it if you didn't address my guests in such a way, Jeake. Have you brought me that relic yet?" Maveri stroked his goatee.

Kolfren stepped back, "Maveri? Oh my, I do apologise. No, I haven't found it yet."

"Well keep searching. With each passing day, your payment drops," the wizard raised his eyebrow. Kolfren nodded and then swiftly moved off into the crowd.

"You know him?" Gathera glanced at Maveri.

"I do. Jeake Kolfren is on a quest to find something that doesn't exist. Don't tell him that though." The wizard chuckled. "Tossers like that deserve to be put in their place." The group moved deeper into the city passing bands of adventurers sitting at tables reciting tales of past battles. Gamblers bet money over games and feats of strength. Through the open windows, the group watched families of city folk sit down to dine in their homes.

If only we could have a family, my love.

Arcturus smiled as her soft tones caressed his soul. He looked over the well-armed city guards as they glared at the group. Abruptly, they reached the edge of the crowd. A warrior stood upon a vast three-tiered staircase leading to a great four-towered bastion. Its almighty sandstone structure was connected with the great wall surrounding the city.

"Adventurers of Nor'ai, it has come to my attention that one of you has captured another of my bounties. Bring forth Gathera and you shall be granted your reward." The warrior's pitch-black plate armour almost absorbed the deep sunlight before refracting it with precise yellow accents. Upon his pauldrons sat rows of crisp white candles flickering with magical flames. He shifted his almighty two-handed mace ignited in the same white flames onto his shoulder.

"We have her, sire!" Eshspen urged the group through the crowd.

Yowtel forced Gathera into the centre, "yous kneel now."

"Make me," Gathera snarled.

The great warrior slammed his mace to the ground. "I need only her, who are these others you bring to me?"

Eshspen opened her mouth to speak but Maveri shunted past her. "King Greystone, please allow me to apologise for the stupidity of these capturers. You see, Gathera may have committed crimes unbeknown to me, but these three have not." He gestured to Arcturus, Seraphina, and Bleu. "Heck, one of them is but a tigaris." The crowd chuckled as Greystone smirked. "You are the king of this city and welcomer of adventurers, so you must surely welcome three new?"

"Maveri, wizard of the seven, I am sorry you had to be escorted by such poor company." Greystone's voice softened, "come, let us welcome these new adventurers. Although Gathera and her lackeys must still answer for their crimes."

Maveri smiled, "of course, sire! There is urgency though, this legionnaire and I bring some dire news. I feel it is imperative to the safety of this city and the beings within its walls."

"Then this is not a joyous occasion? Come, we must discuss this at once! Guards, bring me Gathera and welcome in our new guests." Greystone turned to walk inside and grasped the shoulder of a nearby guard, "gather the seven and find me the archmage, he may well need to hear this too."

"Yes, my king," the guard nodded and swiftly moved down the stairs.

Arcturus frowned as he turned to Maveri. "That seemed too easy."

They did say he was important.

"Not at all, I have a lot of influence here. Let me talk to the guards, I'll make sure they don't rough up Gathera too much." Maveri winked at the or'kerec and walked off.

Gathera flashed a sarcastic smile, "yeah thanks, mate."

"I don't like this at all. Make sure we stick together; they need to learn the severity of this crimson situation." Arcturus patted Seraphina on the back.

"Right, you lot follow me. And you," the guard turned to Gathera, "come here, I've gotta put these on you." She pulled cuffs attached to a chain from her belt and latched them around the or'kerec's wrists. "Try anything and I get the fun of whacking you with this," she waved a small, spiked mace in her face. Gathera snarled as the guard guided them up the steps towards the large arched iron doors.

"Oh boy, I hope we don't fuck this up," Seraphina smiled nervously.

Arcturus glanced back, "we won't."

17
BATTLE PLANS

The guards dragged open the heavy doors, scraping them along the sandstone floor. Their shadows extended deep into the room ahead as the low sunlight crept in behind them. As the groups' eyes adjusted, they were met with dim torchlight emitting from mounted torches along the slim corridor. Arcturus glanced upon the statues lined along the walls depicting the majestic warriors of the siscrati. Their aged and crumbling appearance still resonated with the species' slender, snake-like form blessed in draping chainmail armour.

"Glorious, aren't they? It's a shame they are no longer alive to tell their tales of love and war. The siscrati's history is practically lost to this creeping desert, but we still try to preserve what we can." Greystone stood beside a great, circular sandstone door centred with a golden sun. "I'm surprised the legionnaires didn't adopt more from these beings, you both worship the same gods." He placed the head of his mace against the centre of the door. Veins of gold light streamed like cracks through the walls as the stone rolled aside to reveal a vast circular room. Almighty pillars led skyward, supporting a regal sandstone staircase that led to the peak of the bastion. Within the centre of the room sat a spherical rustic wooden table surrounded by seven leather-padded wooden chairs. At the far end of the table, a great serpentine throne crafted of sandstone and gold towered over the room. Greystone gestured for the group to enter as he strolled over to the throne and slammed his mace down beside it. "Please do come in, the council will be arriving shortly. Do behave yourselves though, I don't want to have to start adding to the list of criminals I already need to reprimand." He unlatched and lifted his long layered plate helm then placed it upon the arm of his throne. "Maveri, I do believe you had something you needed to tell me." Greystone turned. The group locked sight upon his white, speckled, charcoal-grey fur. His aelk-like features twitched as he smiled, and he rubbed his gauntleted hand over his scarred muzzle.

"You're a drudanea?" Arcturus pulled his helmet off and placed it under his arm.

Gosh, I haven't seen one of his kind in person for so long.

Greystone chuckled. "Well observed, legionnaire."

Maveri looked to Arcturus and tutted. He stepped forward, "King Greystone, first let me apologise for my company. Although I must admit, without them I may not still be here."

Greystone raised his eyebrow. "What do you mean by that?"

"Well," Maveri strolled over to a chair and leaned against it dramatically, "upon my travels to Krytiare, I met this legionnaire. He was buried beneath a pile of rubble. With my aid and the protection of the blade known as Karek'Thur, he thankfully survived." Greystone's sight turned to Arcturus as the legionnaire rolled his eyes. "He told me of a great loss that befell his people prior to my arrival. If only we had arrived sooner, it may have changed the tide of battle." Maveri lowered his head in distress.

Arcturus frowned, "wizard, why are you talking like some damn bard?"

Greystone chuckled, "you make a good point, legionnaire. Sorry, I didn't catch your name."

"Arcturus, King Greystone," the legionnaire grinned.

"Then, Arcturus, please, can you continue this story instead?" Greystone eased onto his throne.

This is your time to shine.

"Of course," Arcturus smiled as Maveri glanced back in disgust. "We witnessed a bright beam burn into the skies from the lands of Deythron. Not long after, meteors encased in crimson flames tore through the skies and into the lands of Nor'ai. We investigated one of the crash sites and it seemed that anything killed by the crimson magic was resurrected. Fighting to save our home, we lost everything to this magic. After this wizard and his companions saved me from the rubble, we had to fight a wyvern. This struck me as odd as they haven't ventured away from Dynestrael for centuries. Maveri and I continued alone but on our journey through the desert, we encountered a force of insetille that almost bested us. If it wasn't for Gathera and her allies, I would be dead. Once I recovered, we ventured into the tunnels beneath the desert to find Maveri, but we discovered more than we anticipated. It seems the insetille have been able to harness the magic from one of the crimson meteorites and use it as their own." Arcturus strolled over to one of the siscrati statues beside him and gazed at its chipped fangs, "we also encountered some siscrati. We assume they were awoken by the crimson down in those tunnels. From what we could tell, they plan to siege this city in force."

Well said.

"I see," Greystone stroked his chin, "and you witnessed this too, Maveri?"

Maveri looked up. "I did. This crimson magic is not like anything I have encountered before. It also pains me to admit it but, without Arcturus, Gathera and those other two, I wouldn't be here."

"Well, it seems we have much to discuss," Greystone stood as the great iron doors behind the group opened and several guards dragged in Treyoth, Hank and Anile.

"Gathera, you're alive!" Treyoth's face softened as he saw the or'kerec, "and the little one made it back too!"

"Oi! Pipe down, scum!" A guard shunted against Treyoth to silence him but the draegorth barely moved.

"Father?" Seraphina cocked her head as she looked at the towering drae-gorth.

Treyoth's eyes sprung wide as he looked over Seraphina and Bleu, "Daughter? Daughter!" He shunted the guards to the ground and wrapped his arms around the pair.

The group collectively looked at one another, "wait, he's your father?"

Treyoth chuckled, "yes friends, I'm her father."

"Fuckin' how are you?" Gathera's face lay awash in confusion.

Seraphina pulled away as tears ran down her cheeks. "I've been looking everywhere for you."

"I know, Seph, but I am here now, and I shall not be leaving again." Treyoth wiped the tears from Seraphina's eyes. Portals of differing elements blossomed to life around the table as several robed mages of various races stepped through them.

"Welcome council," Greystone reluctantly broke his puzzled gaze and glanced about the room. "Guards, take our guests away, there is much to discuss here, and I don't want them interrupting." The guards nodded and moved the group to one of the outer doors. "Leave Arcturus here, he has more to tell us; I'm sure of it." Greystone smiled at the legionnaire. The mages pulled out their chairs as they sat around the table. Greystone looked at the empty seat opposite Maveri. "Where is the archmage?" The mages looked around the room and murmured.

An ice portal swirled to life and a hooded figure dragged Wreyth through. "Sorry my liege, I was dealing with this calastain lurking around the city borders." His voice seemed to resonate within Arcturus' mind as if not spoken but instead just a mere thought. Maveri's eyes widened as he stroked his beard in embarrassment. Wreyth's hands and mouth were clamped shut with magical ice as his sight scanned around the room before locking onto Arcturus.

"A calastain, you say? That is a rare find these days." Greystone stood and strolled over to Wreyth. "What crimes has this man committed, arch-mage?"

The hooded figure looked over to Greystone. "Rare indeed. No crimes as such but he did look very shady. Keep an eye on that one as I haven't seen him around this city before."

Greystone chuckled. "I see. Guards, take him to the others."

"Don't try anything." The archmage clutched Wreyth's arm tighter. "I've seen skulkers like you before."

"Throw him in the cells with the others." Greystone moved Wreyth over to the guards. "Now take a seat so we can begin." The archmage reluctantly nodded and sat at the table. "Before we begin, I would like to introduce Arcturus. He could be one of the last known legionnaires alive." A collective gasp resonated from the mages. "He has shared with me some information relating to those mysterious meteors that fell onto our lands."

The council all turned to face Arcturus. "Go on, legionnaire, tell them." Arcturus raised his brow and placed a hand on the hilt of Karek'Thur.

Go on, my love, tell them.

He smiled, "I believe it was the crimson beam which resonated from Deythron that summoned these meteors here."

"Deythron? No beings can survive the harsh climates there." A g'anomi mage leaned back in his chair, "your story is already full of holes, legionnaire."

Arcturus flit his sight to the mage, "I didn't specify that the beam was conjured by a being, it may have been a natural occurrence."

"Let Arcturus finish, archmage," Greystone gestured to the legionnaire. "Continue."

"Thank you. Each being killed by the meteor, or a creature cursed with the crimson magic these meteors contain will return to life. Empowered by the crimson, they are but a shell of their former self," Arcturus paused.

"You mean to say its necromancy?" The g'anomi mage spoke up again.

Arcturus stroked his beard, "it does seem to have necromantic properties but almost more like it corrupts the being's soul rather than its body. The more urgent issue at hand is one of the corrupted insetille joining forces with both scorthic and siscrati to siege this city."

"What utter tosh! Where is your proof of any of this? The siscrati are extinct!" As the archmage yelled, a murmur of disapproval resounded around the table. They chuntered for a while speaking of war, defence and rumour, talking louder and louder with each spoken word.

"I can back up the legionnaire's story!" Maveri stood up. "Back in Krytiare, we fought a wyvern corrupted by this magic. Upon the sands of Valanthrea, we fought scorthic and dwethren cursed by it and below the sands we found the meteor fuelling it all," he slammed his hand down on the table, "our enemies march here to ruin our home and we squabble like children over proof? Every day we harness magic beyond our own knowledge yet when an outsider comes to tell us of this new dark threat, you need some sort of evidence?" The wizard locked eyes with Greystone. "My king, you must believe us and trust me when I say we are going to need all the help we can get to fight back."

Greystone leaned back into his throne. "I have already heard reports similar to this from my scouts, but I needed to hear it from someone unbiased. The council does make a valid point, without evidence, we don't truly know what we face. I will place my guards on high alert and our guests shall be placed into a holding cell until we can figure out what is truly happening." He lifted his hand and gestured at the legionnaire, "guards, please escort Arcturus to our other guests, we can finish this meeting without him." The guards nodded and grabbed the legionnaire, pushing him to the door.

Arcturus resisted and turned to Greystone, "with all due respect, king,

I fear when you finally make up your mind, it shall be too late." Greystone grunted and commanded the guards to leave. They dragged Arcturus out of the room and sealed the door behind him.

18
SO CLOSE, YET SO FAR

The guards pushed Arcturus toward a bench. ”Sit there.“ Seraphina, Bleu, Treyoth, Hank, Anile and Gathera all sat glaring at the legionnaire.

“Go well then, did it mate?” Gathera snarled.

Treyoth chuckled. “Leave him be. He is trying his best to make some very small-minded mages see something in a way they can’t imagine to be true.” He clenched his fists and ripped open the steel cuffs surrounding his wrists with ease.

“Thank you, Treyoth,” Arcturus smiled. “I have to ask, and I don’t mean to intrude, but how are you Seraphina’s father?”

Seraphina looked up at Treyoth. “I mean, technically he’s not my real dad.” She glanced at Arcturus. “My family used to live in a small town in Meranor, but it turned out the locals there don’t approve of my kind. So, they slaughtered my family and banished me from the land. Treyoth found me and took me in; he practically raised me. When they figured out what he did, they banished him too. We took a boat over to Tarlgoan and took up haven there. After a while, they discovered what had happened and who we were. They split us up and rode me into the woods to kill me. I managed to escape, and I've been searching for my father since."

"I'm so very glad you finally found me," Treyoth released a tearful smile. He wiped his eyes and looked to Arcturus, "now, little one, how long do you think we have until that force shows up here?"

"They're already here." The group turned to see Wreyth sitting on the far side of the bench.

"What, they've reached the city already?" Seraphina raised her brow as her face fell to shock. "Why wait until now to tell us, creepy person in the corner that I haven't met yet!"

"At most, they're an hour's ride away but, that was before I got caught," Wreyth stood and cracked his neck.

Arcturus' brows raised in astonishment. "Already? Why are you so calm about all of this?"

Wreyth shrugged, "no sense in panicking when we are in one of the best cities to hold off a siege."

"He's correct, this city can withstand a lot of punishment!" Treyoth glanced around. "Although we should probably still act now, little ones!"

"Then we have no time to waste!" Arcturus stood and addressed the group. "We need to get out of here and aid with the fight."

"Why the fuck would we help to save a city that wants to lock us away or behead us?" Gathera stood and ripped apart her restraints. "A city that has kept a father from his daughter."

The legionnaire stroked his stubbled chin. "Don't look at it that way. Instead, look at it more like if we save this city and stop the crimson in its tracks, you will all be hailed as heroes."

That's it, get her inspired. We need to keep her morale up!

Gathera released an aroused growl, "oh, I like that. Then I could finally prove to my brothers that I'm worthy of being the next chieftain! Yeah, make me a fuckin' hero!"

"Keep it in ya pants or'kerec," Hank stood and tried to pry open his cuffs. He strained until his face turned blue then sat back down. "Fuck me, they obviously put the strong ones on my arms." Treyoth chuckled then effortlessly pried the cuffs off the dwethren's wrists. "Ah, I see now, I musta weakened 'em."

Wreyth moved to Arcturus. "I'm glad to see you and Maveri survived."

"I'm glad to see you alive too," Arcturus looked around the room. "Where is Aleiá?"

Wreyth smiled. "She's here," he gestured to his chest, "just doesn't wanna show herself." They clamped into a handshake.

A resounding slam echoed around the room as Maveri burst through the door. "Quickly, we don't have much time!"

"Whatcha mean, wizard?" Gathera grunted in confusion.

Maveri moved toward the locked door on the opposite side of the room, "they are here." He fiddled with the handle before finally just hurling an azure missile at the lock and booting it open. "Grab your weapons, we need to leave before the guards show up. It's time to defend this city." They gathered their equipment and rushed to the door.

"Oi, where the fuck do you think you're going?!" A small group of guards blocked the doorway. "Maveri, these prisoners are to stay here while we hold off this threat."

"Sorry chaps, but there's no time for that." In a swift elegant flick of his wrist, Maveri released a plume of azure magic. The guards slumped to their knees before falling into a deep slumber.

"Quickly now!" The group sprinted out of the bastion and back onto the streets of the city. Crowds of civilians screamed in panic as they returned to their homes. The group watched as guards and adventurers climbed the outer walls of the city. "We need to see what's happening."

We need to ready ourselves for what may come, my love. This crimson can't be allowed to claim this city.

Wreyth pulled Maveri aside, "I need a weapon, I can't be seen using my magic here."

"We will need all the magic we can get my friend," Maveri patted him on the shoulder then moved to the wall.

"For fuck's sake." Wreyth rolled his eyes. "Sometimes he just doesn't fucking listen."

Arcturus chuckled, "I'll agree with you there." He glanced over to a bow and quiver leaned against a table, "how about that?"

"It's been a while but fuck it, it's better than nothing." Wreyth grabbed the bow and then followed Maveri up the stairs to the top of the battlements. Moving to the edge of the wall, they saw the great expanse of endless desert roll out like a carpet before them. A glorious azure dome shimmered over the city as its border seared a line into the sands. Beyond it sat an almighty army of insetille and siscrati warriors primed for war. The distinct glow of crimson light burned through their bodies as they readied their weapons.

Arcturus glanced to his left, then to his right to see hundreds of adventurers and guards. "There isn't enough of us."

Together you are strong, but if the legionnaires couldn't hold Krytiare then I don't know if this force can hold Vavarinu.

"They may outnumber us, legionnaire, but these are powerful warriors and mages. We can hold our own against these bugs." Maveri glanced over his shoulder, "as long as this barrier holds, we win this fight."

Arcturus looked to the mage tower as the barrier shimmered in the dying sunlight. He frowned as movement caught his eye in the streets below. Walking to the edge of the wall, he watched a cloaked figure move into a dark side alley. He squinted. "Maveri, how easy would it be for the scorthic to dig up through the city floor?"

"Impossible; the barrier goes underground too." Maveri frowned, "why do you ask?"

Arcturus pointed at the streets, "because a cloaked being just very suspiciously moved into that alleyway."

Maveri moved to the legionnaire. "It will be nothing, probably just someone returning home or a lowlife stealing what they can." A distinct azure light shimmered in the darkness of the alley. "Odd, there isn't another azure mage in this city." The group moved over to join them.

"What're we lookin' at?" Gathera leaned carelessly against the battlements.

Arcturus pointed to the alley, "that light."

"Maveri, there isn't another azure mage here is there?" Treyoth slammed his shield down as he gazed over the group's heads.

Maveri scowled, "no, there isn't. We should probably investigate that." The wizard swiftly moved down the stairs into the city. After an exchange of glances, the group urgently followed him. Walking quickly through the deserted streets, they focussed on the alleyway while drawing their weapons. Turning the corner, the azure magic burned brighter and brighter. As the group walked closer, the silhouette of a cloaked figure stood between them and the magic. "Stop what you're doing!" Maveri yelled out.

The figure paused and glanced over its shoulder, "you're too late." It whipped a crimson crystal from its hip and crushed it against the azure crystal already in its palm. The corrupted magic poured into the portal. Slim crimson beams burned up from multiple alleyways across the city toward the domed barrier. As the crimson clashed against it, slowly, it began ripping apart the protective spell. "Embrace Nor'ai's fate, for there is no stopping perfection." The cloaked being stepped through the portal before the rumbling screams of scorthic burst into the atmosphere.

What or who the hell was that?!

"You're fuckin' kiddin' me," Gathera pulled her bow from her back.

Maveri levitated his spellbook before surging his azure magic into the portal. "Protect me while I seal this damn thing shut!" Arcturus and Treyoth nodded then leapt in front of the wizard before igniting their shields to create a barrier against the oncoming horde. The gold and ginger magic gracefully entwined together before forming a protective arc around them. Wreyth and Gathera readied their bows and Seraphina and Bleu dispersed into the shadows. Scorthic ripped through the crimson portal, screaming and chattering toward the group. The sandstone ripped apart and vines lashed out to bind them in place. Gorgeous plant life bloomed around Anile's feet as he cast his magic. Gathera released her jade arrows with reckless abandon into the horde. The projectiles ripped through the beasts with ease, tearing limbs and chitin from their bodies. Knocking his arrows, Wreyth loosed them past the creatures. One after another, glancing or missing the scorthic horde.

"Ah, fuck me, lad, what're ya doin'?" Hank frowned as he watched Wreyth miss almost every shot he took.

Wreyth glanced over, "this isn't my weapon of choice. It's been many moons since I've used a bow."

"Then why the fuck you usin' it?" Gathera sneered.

Maveri held strong as his azure magic purged the portal. "Just. Keep. Shooting!" More creatures burst through as they piled on top of one another. Tearing apart Anile's vines with their powerful claws, they freed their trapped brethren. Leaping forth from the carnage, a scorthic clashed against Treyoth's and Arcturus' shields.

"Hold strong, little one!" Treyoth yelled to Arcturus as more and more of the creatures slammed against their shields. The legionnaire felt his sabatons grinding across the sandstone as the scorthic forced them back.

Keep your strength, my love, you can do this.

"Faster, wizard!" Gathera released flurry after flurry of arrows into the horde.

Maveri gritted his teeth. "I'm going...as fast as...I can!" Before their eyes, twin bolts of azure light sparked from opposite sides of the alleyway. The magic ripped through the horde, clearing them from the shields and sending dismembered claws and chitin into the skies before it turned to crimson dust. With one final push, Maveri sealed the portal shut before exhaling and catching his book.

Seraphina and Bleu appeared at either side of the alley. "Phew! That was a close one."

"Why the fuck did you wait until then to do that?" Gathera snarled as she dismissed her arrows.

Sheathing her swords, Seraphina looked to the or'kerec, "that takes a lot of charge time to do, we can't do it willy-nilly, my dude."

Treyoth gripped Gathera's shoulder, "leave them be, they did good." He winked at Seraphina.

Seraphina seems very powerful. Keep her close.

"Either way, good job all." Arcturus lowered his shield. The screams of scorthic resonated through the streets of Vavarinu as they poured through the city.

"It seems we have more portals to close before it's too late." Maveri placed his fingers against his head and released a wave of azure magic. "Mages of Vavarinu, the city has been breached. Follow the crimson beams of light and close the portals!"

Wreyth counted his remaining arrows, "sorry for my performance there."

"Too fuckin' right ya are, lad," Hank shook his head in disgust.

Arcturus pulled Karek'Thur from his hip. "There's no time for this, we need to get moving." The group agreed and stormed out of the alleyway. Multiple adventurers ran into the streets to join them as they readied their magic.

"Mages, seal the portals and protect that barrier! If that falls, so does our city." Maveri addressed them as they acknowledged his commands and dispersed into the alleyways. The wizard turned to the group, "come, that barrier is the only thing keeping this city standing."

19
UNWELCOME GUESTS

The group moved through the streets to see the bodies of dismembered civilians cluttering the sandstone. The once solid stone buildings and beautiful cacti were trampled and laid to ruin. Half-eaten bodies of dying fighters screamed out in pain as the crimson magic tore through their bodies. Arcturus clenched his jaw as flashbacks from his home cursed his mind. Chattering mandibles rang out from the collapsing rooftops and several scorthic crept over the edges. Gathera readied her bow and without a moment of hesitation, slung jade arrows through each of the creature's heads. The lifeless bodies flopped to the ground around the group.

Keep it up, you can't let the crimson claim this city!

"Impressive, but we can't be blasé about this. We should conserve our energy until we really need to use it, so nothing fancy unless it's warranted." Maveri ran his hand through his still perfectly quaffed hair.

Gathera smirked, "yeah, that weren't anythin' fancy." She winked and continued down the street.

"Right, you are a difficult one to read." Maveri pointed gingerly at Gathera. The group moved through the streets toward the closest portal.

"A more organised version of what we did with the last portal is probably best," Arcturus readied his shield.

Seraphina tightened her bun. "I mean, we can do that again, but it does take time. Bleu, you think you can do that again?" Bleu bared his teeth and growled. "I'll take that as a yes."

As the group started to move, a small swarm of scorthic stormed toward them. Their claws ripped into the sandstone as they began climbing the buildings. Arcturus clutched his shield and flung the swirling image of Aegis. Its golden light rebounded amongst the creatures as it burned them from existence. Hearing the commotion, more scorthic charged from the other end of the street. Gathera turned and launched flurries of jade arrows into the fray while Maveri lifted his book and cast several azure magic missiles. The projectiles weakened the lines, but the creatures still charged. In an almighty explosion of sandstone, a great horned scarek burst into sight.

"Take cover!" Arcturus leapt shield-first in front of Maveri and Gathera as the rubble slammed against his shield. Seraphina and Bleu swiftly melded away into the shadows. The creature's glistening amber shell split open as it raised its back toward the group. Piercing spines launched from the creature's flesh and rained down from the skies. Treyoth scooped Hank and Anile close and slammed his shield down. The chitinous bolts clashed against Arcturus and Treyoth's shields before ricocheting into the surrounding buildings. Beaming lines of azure magic burst from the shadows through the scarek's legs. Before the creature could react, Seraphina and Bleu crossed paths and tore the bug's limbs apart. Seraphina landed and swirled her glowing swords then ran at the beast. She sliced apart its horn with ease as Bleu tore open its abdomen. Gathera slid out from behind Arcturus and released a large glowing jade arrow. The projectile burned through the creature's back and out into the rubble behind it.

"Phew, I thought I might fuck that up," the or'kerec smiled as she slammed against the street.

"Thank you for that, Arcturus," Maveri patted the legionnaire's back.

Arcturus nodded, "you would do the same for me."

Maveri stroked his goatee. "Of course." He turned to Seraphina and Bleu as they re-joined the group, "you two seem to harness some extremely powerful magic."

Seraphina looked to Bleu, "just some stuff we've been able to pick up over the years, right buddy?" Bleu purred and licked his paw.

"Mummy, mummy where are you?" The voice of a little kenket child called out from the rubble.

Seraphina looked over to see the child clutching a crudely made bear.

"Hey, be careful!" a large shard of sandstone dislodged above the child. Bleu leapt forward and lightly grasped her in his jaw, pulling her away from the danger. After the stone slammed into the ground, several scorthic clambered through the rubble. Seraphina jumped into the air and released a flurry of azure kunai upon the attackers, killing three of them. Maveri surged a beam of pure energy through the remaining beasts, vaporising both them and the rubble.

"Nice one!" A city guard dressed in royal blue leather armour sprinted up to the group, "here, I'll take the girl to the safehouse." She wiped the blood from her blade on a nearby corpse and sheathed her weapon.

"Gwen, have you seen my mummy?" The child ran to the guard.

The guard knelt and removed her winged, silver helm, allowing her jet-black hair to fall onto her shoulders. "Don't worry, Taylie, she's safe and sound." Gwen looked at the group; her soft round face and pronounced cheekbones seemed to shine in the deep orange sunlight. "We need you guys in the city centre; these damn bugs are surrounding the mage tower." Her cocoa eyes narrowed as she looked at Gathera, "I've seen you round this city before, ain't I?"

"Uh, no. Maybe, probably not," Gathera frowned.

Gwen bit her lip in thought, "nah, I definitely have." She stared for a moment then blushed, "oh nope, I don't know you." Quickly looking away, she gripped the child's hand, "come on, let's get you somewhere safe."

Arcturus stepped forward, "did you need us to help escort you?"

Gwen looked back and smirked. "Nah, you're alright. Just help save this city, yeah?" The pair swiftly disappeared down the street.

Seraphina looked over the group. "What was that about?"

Gathera shrugged, "no idea. I have no clue who the hell that was."

They've slept together, I can tell.

Arcturus smirked. Bleu growled and Seraphina nervously looked at Gathera, "uh, yeah you're right Bleu, she did seem cool."

Gathera gripped Seraphina's shoulder and winked. "I've fucked her." She chuckled. Arcturus and Maveri's eyes widened. The group shrugged off the fight and moved to the city centre. Before them stood a horde of scorthic screaming at a nearby structure.

Told you!

"What the fuck are they doin'?" Gathera looked about the group. "Wait, where's Hank?"

Treyoth checked under his shield, "he was just next to me."

Suddenly, a figure lunged from the structure and slammed his elemental hammers to the floor. The sandstone cracked and a river of lava surged at the creatures. Attempting to react, the scorthic clawed at the floor before slipping as the burning liquid consumed them. More creatures stormed out from behind the figure as he turned and raised his hammers. Shards of pointed stone flew up from the ground behind him. He thrust his weapons forth and commanded the debris forward. The rocks plunged into the beasts, killing them instantly. He turned and scratched his beard with his weapons while admiring his work.

"Ye little shites chose the wrong dwethren to piss off!" The familiar figure kicked a scorthic's head across the street.

"Hank?" Gathera yelled out in confusion. "How the fuck did you do all that?"

The dwethren looked up, "do what?" Hank looked over to the group and grinned, "oh that? I've always been able to do that! You've just never given me the chance." He lowered his hands and the magma subsided. "I'm a geomancer; always have been, always will be! It runs in mi blood!"

Arcturus scratched his head, "what in Nor'ai is a geomancer?!"

Hank strolled over to the group, "means I can manipulate the earth around me." He winked, forming his two earthen hammers into axes. "Right then, to the tower!" Arcturus glanced to Maveri who responded with a shrug. The group sprinted through alleys and narrow streets until finally reaching the mage tower.

"Ha! You're too late, skell! Come here to save the city? We will end you all, skell!"

Maveri glared at the prophet as azure electricity sparked within his hands. "This one is mine!" He forced a beam of erratic lightning toward the creature. Clenching its claws against its chest, the beast formed a crimson glowing field. The magical torrent impacted against the barrier and refracted toward the sky. The prophet tensed as it turned the beam, carving it through the upper half of the Mage Tower. The group watched as shards of the great tower crumbled to the ground while its protective barrier flickered out of existence.

"Yes, skell!" The prophet's mandibles chattered as it laughed, "you've done exactly as planned, skell! Now you cannot keep us out!" It sneered. Gathera stood frozen in shock.

Arcturus gripped the or'kerec's shoulder. "We can do this."

"No, Arcturus, we can't," Gathera's words were engulfed in worry.

You have to do this.

Maveri gazed into the skies, "what have I done?" An almighty bellow echoed out across Vavarinu as the forces guarding the walls witnessed the barrier fall. The rumble of the insetille and siscrati forces thundered through the sands as they charged at the city walls.

"Attack!" Greystone's voice pierced through the carnage. Explosions rang out as cannons fired upon the horde. Arrows hailed through the beams of dying sunlight before planting into their foe.

Seraphina drew her swords. "Looks like this might be our final stand." Several portals sprung to life around the group, allowing multiple prophets through. The sandstone streets cracked and split as scorthic and scarek poured out of their tunnels. Groups of guards and adventures ran into the centre to fight back the horde. They looked over the impending danger as the city walls began to splinter around them. Mages slung magic into the fray, archers pelted the beasts and warriors locked into combat.

"Witness as this city falls, skell! All thanks to your foolish acts. You all worship false gods, they will never be able to defeat the great crimson! We shall take this city and all other skell lands surrounding it!" The prophet reverberated in crimson magic as it spoke. In an almighty ground-shattering explosion, a behemoth gorthrel sundered the streets. Its quad-jawed gaping maw split open, revealing tens of thousands of serrated teeth. Swirling high into the skies, its multiple sickening crimson eyes focussed on the battle below. Curving its great pulsating body, it crashed down into the fight consuming every warrior in its path. Guards and adventures fled as the beast tore through their ranks. The ground rumbled as the beast tunnelled below before emerging once again.

"You see now, skell? All is lost, our kind is superior. We shall prove the power of the great crimson!" The prophet's mandibles chattered in glee.

"This corruption rewards no one! It is not a forgiving or kind-natured entity, all it desires is to ruin Nor'ai and all life within this realm!" Arcturus yelled out as he hurled Aegis into the horde.

The prophet tilted its head, "pitiful wasteful skell. It is your kind that does not understand, skell. Therefore, you must be destroyed; you ruin this land." Raising its hands, it released a burst of crimson light. The magic screamed through the air before plunging into Treyoth's skull. The draegorth's body trembled as he tried to resist until finally, he fell to his knee.

"Trey?" Anile stepped over to the draegorth and placed a hand on his shoulder, "Trey, you must resist." The draegorth swiftly glanced up before clamping Anile's throat in his grasp.

"We will make you see," Treyoth tensed his wrist before effortlessly snapping the reptiare's neck. He carelessly tossed him aside and turned to Seraphina, "such a waste of great power."

Gathera's jaw fell agape. "Anile, no!" She charged at the draegorth and shunted him to the ground. His head slammed against the sandstone as Gathera pummelled him with tears streaming down her face.

"Father, no!" Seraphina grabbed the or'kerec's shoulders and tried to pry her from Treyoth. Gathera turned and pushed her away. The or'kerec glanced back to see a horde of scorthic storming toward her. Treyoth thumped his hulking fist into her stomach and threw her onto the sandstone.

"Enough!" Wreyth snapped his bow as his hands tensed. A surge of soul magic burned through Treyoth's mind as he screamed out and fled in terror. The calastain, now burning with soul flame, turned to the horde. "We can deal with the draegorth later, right now these are the bigger threat."

Hank stood frozen in confusion and shock, "what the fuck did that bastard bug do? And what the fuck are you?"

"It can harness crimson magic like no other I've seen before." Arcturus looked out to see hundreds of insetille, siscrati and scorthic surrounding them. "We cannot surrender now, using everything we've got is our only option."

If the insetille can use the crimson without it consuming them, what else can they do with it?

"Well, I guess I could think of worse ways to die." Hank readied his axes.

Gathera stood panting with rage and sadness, "you will fuckin' pay for everything you've done!"

20
NO TURNING BACK

Chitinous echoes drummed throughout the streets as the swarm fought against the surrounding warriors. Scorthic tore apart the less experienced mages with ease as they pushed through the city. Drones and carabus breached the bastion as Greystone and his guards held their ground. Hails of arrows and cannonballs pelted the assaulting scarek before being silenced by volleys of crimson bolts.

"How does it feel, skell, to know you are the ones who doomed this city?" The prophet taunted them. Maveri unleashed torrents of azure magic into the swarm. "The fabled skell losing their home as we lost ours." Gathera snarled and burst her axe through the head of a carabus. "Skell, it is a joy to watch you, thinking you have a chance to survive." Arcturus braced Aegis before burning golden light through an assaulting scorthic. "Zatel was only a sacrifice, skell. Her life was given so that we could achieve victory." The soil and sandstone crackled below Hank as he beat down multiple drones. "She will be remembered whilst we tear you apart, skell."

Seraphina and Bleu stood parallel, cutting through the fray with glorious precision. "Scraktor fel atire crorse!" The prophet yelled and the horde erupted in screams, storming toward the group.

Maveri swiftly clicked his fingers, igniting them in azure flames to cast a blazing fireball. Soaring through the horde, the magical blast immolated the creatures before dispersing against the prophet's crimson field. Wreyth raised his hands as the ground below the oncoming horde cracked with ethereal green light. The insetille screeched as their souls burned with each step along the tainted ground. Wreyth smiled before furling his fist and thrusting his palm at the creatures to release multiple bolts of soul magic. Falling to the ground, the creatures turned to crimson dust as their souls glided into the calastain. The group locked deeper into glorious combat as their allies fell around them.

Arcturus deflected blows as he protected Maveri. Swinging Karek'Thur, he carved through the creatures with ease as the ground below their feet ruptured. Hank commanded loose shards of rock, sending them hurtling through the insetille. Feeling the heads of each creature concave, the dwethren pummelled through them with his stone axes. Corpses piled up as the group tore through the beasts. Limbs and shattered chitin were pushed aside while more drones clambered atop their fallen brethren. Gathera lodged her axe within the abdomen of a carabus before a razor-edged barb pierced through her left bicep, skewering into the ground behind her. Clenching her jaw, she gripped her axe tighter and tore through the bug and tossed it aside.

Bleu shredded through the assaulting scorthic, dismembering them, and flinging their ligaments back into the horde. Gracefully twirling, Seraphina swung her swords while cleaving through the drones. Her azure blades left sparkling trails of magic behind each sweep. Beneath the pile of corpses, a scorthic clamped its claw around her ankle. Before she could react, the beast twisted and snapped her bone. She screamed out in agony as she fell to her knees. Forcing her blade through the bug, she tore it apart and forced open its claw. Blood spurted from the wound as ice-cold agony ran up her spine. Bleu leapt in front of her and beat back the assaulting creatures. Swiping back and forth, his claws ripped through the beasts with ease as he defended his master.

Aegis clashed through the swarm; its golden image ruptured their bodies as it ricocheted amongst them. Suddenly, the image ground to a halt. Arcturus watched the prophet grasp the magical buckler, holding it, resonating within its grip until the shield's golden light turned crimson. Focusing its sight upon the legionnaire, the prophet sent the image hurtling back toward him. Arcturus raised Aegis to block the image. The magic clashed against his buckler. Its impact rang out in deafening tintinnabulation sending bolts of searing pain through his mind. He grasped his helm and tossed it aside as his eardrums convulsed. The piercing ring echoed through his skull before the pain burned out his consciousness.

Arcturus? My Love? Stand up!

Maveri continued to pelt the drones with magical, azure missiles. Shards of chitin chipped away before finally, the beasts fell. Within the corner of his sight, he saw Arcturus collapse. Karek'Thur hummed as it crashed onto the sandstone before its light extinguished.

"I'll protect the legionnaire; you deal with those prophets!" Wreyth moved over to Arcturus. He slung bolts of ethereal magic at the closest beasts before rupturing their souls with a flick of his wrist.

The prophets raised their arms and linked a beam of crimson magic surrounding the group. "Skell, it is time to end this!" The creatures locked eyes with Maveri while aiming their claws towards him. He watched crimson beams of magic surge from every direction. Waving his hands, the wizard summoned an azure barrier to cover the group. Holding strong, he clenched his entire body as the beam began converting his azure barrier to crimson. Maveri tensed his core while doing his best to maintain the barrier. The pressure eased as the beam broke, and the body of a prophet slammed to the ground.

"You need to leave, now!" Greystone lifted his mace before decimating the fallen prophet. The other prophets turned and began casting their beams of crimson at the king. Greystone raised his hand as white lightning burned through the skies. The bolts struck the surrounding prophets burning them to dust. "Maveri, you have to leave! Tell the beings of

Murimia what happened here!" The ground rumbled and cracked beneath Greystones's feet before the gaping maw of the gorthrel consumed him as it burst into the skies. It turned its hulking body and dove towards Maveri. An ice magic dome blossomed around the group as the archmage pulsed into existence beside Hank.

"Quickly, adventurers! With me!" He slammed his stave upon the ground and swiftly, they became engulfed in a blizzard. Hank watched as the gorthel's silhouette faded away.

The mage lifted his staff, allowing the storm to disperse. Maveri looked over the group to see both Arcturus and Seraphina lying unconscious.

Gathera clutched her arm as blood poured from her open wound and glanced over her surroundings. "Where are we?" Her sight flicked over the dark empty room. She forced herself up, "Anile?" her feet dragged upon the sandstone as she moved to the reptiare's lifeless corpse.

"I'm sorry, I was too late to save him. Too late to save so many of our warriors," the archmage's voice resounded in their minds.

Gathera fell to her knees and pulled Anile onto her lap. "Anny, no..." She pulled back his niqab to reveal his pale aqua scales, "what has he done to you? No, no, no... he didn't mean to do this. It wasn't his fault; he wasn't in control. I can't lose you, Anny. Please..." Tears formed in her eyes. "Trey loved you so much. This fuckin' crimson! Anny, please just breathe..." Her voice wavered. "You were one of the only people I could trust, Anny, you were my healer. I'm so sorry I wasn't here for you, I could've stopped him, I should've stopped him." A hand squeezed her shoulder.

"He's a great loss, Gathera. Anile was the best of us. He was kind and loving and he never insulted me...which is a first for anyone really. You couldn't have saved him. Once the tower fell, there wasn't anything that anyone could do." Gathera held Hank's hand.

Tears rolled down her cheeks. "He was my family, Hank. He's not just a loss. I should have saved him. The tower wouldn't have fallen if it wasn't for that fuckin' wizard." She scraped her hand across her face. "Come to think of it, was that your plan all a fuckin' long?" Carefully lying Anile's corpse against the sandstone, the or'kerec stood to face Maveri. "It's your fault this city fell!" Raising her palm, her enchanted hand axe flew to her.

"Hey! Woah, woah, woah! It wasn't his fault!" Hank placed his hands on her abdomen as he tried to hold the or'kerec back.

"Fuck off, Hank!" She pushed the dwethren aside. "You fuckin' bastard!" Gathera hurled her axe with almighty force. After helping Wreyth check over Arcturus, Maveri stood, his eyes focussed on the glimmering jade axe swirling toward his head. He watched its blade shimmer in the setting sun then closed his eyes to await the impact. He paused for a moment then opened his eyes to see the weapon frozen in white ice, barely millimetres away from his forehead.

"Stop this petty squabbling! We have all lost people in this battle!" The axe dropped to the ground as the archmage lowered his stave. "Yes, it is a great shame the druid has passed but you could not have saved him. This crimson magic shows power beyond our wildest imagination. It's a miracle I was able to reach you all in time. Look, adventurers, we must band together to stop this madness. The city is lost, our king and the seven have fallen and our homes were laid to ruin. We must leave here and recover; we need to warn others of the dangers of this crimson. My kind can help us; let me take you to them. We have restorers for your wounds, and we have beds for you to rest. Once I convince them to help, we can all work together."

Gathera snarled, "your people? I thought this city was your people?"

The archmage turned to face her. "I am not the being you might think I am, or'kerec. I opted to live within this city's walls to help adventurers such as yourselves, but I am not one of you." His voice echoed in their minds.

"I'm sorry bud, but why can I hear you in my head and not with my ears?" Hank clenched his fists.

Wreyth smirked, "I was thinking the exact same thing."

"He's speaking through telepathy," Maveri uttered the words cautiously.

"Thank you, Maveri." The archmage looked over the group. "Come with me, I have a portal down these stairs. It will take us to my home."

Gathera reclaimed her axe and latched it to her hip. "I'm not ready to lose anyone else. How can I be sure that you're our best option?" The screams and snarls of scorthic and insetille echoed around them.

"The way I see it, right now you don't have many options. With me and my kind, you might finally stand a chance." The archmage's eyes smiled.

"But I can't just leave Anile here like this," Gathera looked to the corpse of her friend.

Relieved, the archmage stood tall. "We shall take him with us. My people can bless his soul and gift him a proper burial."

Bleu nudged Seraphina and licked her face. "We need to bring these two also," Maveri gestured to the pair of unconscious fighters.

"I'll bring the lass with the help of the cat, someone else can carry the big guy." Hank strolled over to Bleu, "whatcha say, tigaris? Wanna help me carry her?" Bleu tilted his head before bowing and allowing Hank to drape Seraphina over his back. Gathera lifted Anile onto her shoulder and sneered at the shards of pain sent through her arm. "You good, or'kerec?" Hank tilted his head.

"I'm fine," she replied sharply with tears rolling down her face. Maveri attempted to drag Arcturus, scraping his armour along the floor.

"Here, let me help." Wreyth knelt and lifted the legionnaire's legs, "archmage, can you carry his weapons and helm?" The archmage nodded. "I get why you're helping them, but why are you letting *me* come?"

The archmage paused for a moment. "Nor'ai will need all the help it can get. There will be no judgement for your kind from mine." They moved down the dark, spiralling staircase to the lower level of the building. Dim torches lit their path as the fragile stairs crumbled beneath their feet. Its sandstone walls seemed damaged and unkept with loose bricks protruding from the structure.

"I have had this place hidden for a while now." The archmage guided them down the staircase. "It is my portal for any time I want to return home."

"There's something unsettling about the way you move, archmage," Gathera uttered the words through her clenched jaw.

"Aye, you can say that again," Hank smiled.

The archmage glanced back, "I levitate; walking is a waste of energy."

White light shimmered from the end of the stairway as they turned down the final spiral. The slim circular room had two benches fixed around the wall connected by a singular wooden table. In the centre of the room glistened an icy-white portal and below it lay a light dusting of snow.

The archmage turned to Hank, "geomancer, do you know your fortifications?"

Hank stroked his hand over Bleu's forehead. "Of course I know my fortifications."

The archmage nodded. "You may want to fortify yourself and your friends with some personal warmth. There isn't much heat where we're going and not one of you is dressed for the cold." The dwethren nodded and held his fist before his face, raised two of his fingers and closed his eyes. Gathera and Maveri felt their bodies rise to a comfortable temperature as warmth poured through their souls. Bleu purred as he rubbed his face against Hank.

Wreyth looked around at their comforted faces. "Wait, was something meant to happen?"

"Interesting," the archmage paused. "Right then, adventurers, follow me." He moved to the portal, "oh, calastain, you may want to use caution when walking through this portal. Drekaiek might travel differently through our portals, you may well end up in a different place."

Wreyth scowled, "what does that mean? Are you saying I could end up somewhere random?"

Chuckling, the archmage strolled through the portal. "Just a warning to you, is all. I will come and find you if that happens." The group looked at one another and then followed behind. Their forms dispersed into the white light as they stepped through before the portal swept them off their feet.

21
COLD HANDS, WARM HEART

Arcturus lifted his head. His eardrums still rang with the piercing tones of the clash. Familiar figures reformed within the ice-white light beside him. He slammed onto the smooth floor as Maveri's grip wavered. Dragging his hands from beneath him, he noticed the way they glided with ease. He glanced down at the opaque crystal before him, almost able to see the depths below.

Finally, you're awake.

"Woah there, big guy, let me give ya a hand." Hank helped the legionnaire up, "there, now keep ya-self steady, lad." Hank's muffled voice hummed through the crystalline atmosphere. Arcturus rubbed the side of his head trying to clear his mind. The group stepped around him as they filled out the pristine spherical room.

"It's good to see you on your feet, legionnaire," the voice spoke into his subconscious. "I feel introductions are in order before we go any further." Placing his hands together, the archmage's body hummed, "my name is

Yatuul Haquel. I am the archmage of this city."

Maveri placed his hand on Arcturus' shoulder. "You're safe now." With great difficulty, the legionnaire deciphered the wizard's words. The group watched as the archmage's guise lifted. His sharp, icy features slowly revealed themselves as shards protruded from his elegant humanoid form, like curved rising stalagmites. His pointed geometric fingers gripped his long icicle stave and his almost featureless face gazed down upon them. Beautifully formed patterns shimmered up to his large turquoise glowing eyes; it was as if he wore a bauta mask formed solely of ice. Gracefully curved frozen horns extended from his forehead and an elegantly draped verglas cape flowed over his translucent body. A light white mist surrounded him, trailing each motion he made.

"I can imagine you have all figured out why we talk through telepathy now?" Yatuul's eyes smiled.

This is so very odd; I can hear his voice in my soul.

Hank stroked his hand over his long, dark beard, "Is it because you don't have a mouth or nose?"

The archmage's shoulders lifted in amusement at the dwethren's comment. "That is correct, dwethren. Although, you don't talk through your nose."

Hank gestured back to Maveri, "some of us do."

Yatuul raised his elegant finger, "now, now, dwethren." He looked to the group, "I doubt any of you have seen this land. I would imagine you haven't ventured to Deythron before now?" Yatuul's eyes shimmered.

"So, all of this time you've been...this?" Maveri's frown grew quizzical.

"I have indeed, wizard." Yatuul turned to Maveri, "I did not feel the kind of Vavarinu would be quite ready to accept my truest self."

Maveri paused with his mouth agape. "I can't believe I didn't know."

"No one did." The archmage's eyes smiled.

"Am I correct in thinking you said we are in Deythron?" Placing his hand against his forehead, Maveri muttered.

"Yes, you are currently inside the teleportation tower within the city of Paerlowe," the archmage lifted his arm as if to present the room.

"There are no cities in Deythron; the land is uninhabitable." Maveri's face became awash in confusion. "The permafrost here is so vast and the temperatures are beyond frigid. Even you said that nothing inhabited these lands."

Yatuul's eyes shimmered, "correct, I did say that to keep my kind safe. I wasn't lying; it would be uninhabitable for beings such as yourselves. But we are velgart, we are beings born of ice." Maveri's eyes darted back and forth, trying to understand Yatuul. "I see you are confused, Maveri. Let me show you our city, this land, and my kind. Maybe then you will understand." Yatuul turned to Gathera, "and a proper burial for your friend is in order." The or'kerec cracked a slight smile as the archmage spoke.

"A burial? Amongst our lands? Yatuul, why would you think to bring these seven foreign beings here?" A second voice resounded in their minds before an icy figure emerged in the graceful, arched doorway.

"Seven?" Gathera looked around and counted the group, "wait, where's that weird guy gone?"

Maveri looked back to where the portal stood. "Where's Wreyth?"

I knew it! I knew I didn't sense Wreyth nearby!

Yatuul stepped toward the figure. Its features were much like his yet sharper and more aggressive. Its long verglas kilt emerged from its shimmering light blue, rime-frost belt, swaying in the wind. "Khain, it's good to see you." He glanced back to the group, "oh my, I did worry this might happen. Since your friend is both drekaiek and undead he travels through portals differently than the living. Worry not, I shall find him and bring him back to you."

Khain stepped closer to the archmage, his turquoise eyes scowling in disgust. A frost serpent swirled around him and rested its head upon his shoulder. "Do not change the subject, archmage." His voice sounded much harsher than Yatuul's soft welcoming tones.

"I have brought them here to help them. We have discovered the damage those meteors have done and can do to this realm."

"We have been researching that here too." Khain looked over the group.

"These outsiders won't be of any use to us."

"Yes, physically they offer nothing, but their knowledge may prove useful. They need us and we may well need them. Let me speak to the Empresses, I shall explain everything. It shall be their choice if we let them remain here."

Khain grasped his twisted ice glaive as the turquoise gem upon his forehead glimmered. The slim frost serpent hissed at the group between Khain's resonating horns. "Fine. The Empresses have requested you in their presence anyway. You may bring these outsiders with you. Although, one false move from any of them and I shall have their heads."

Yatuul's shoulders eased, "thank you, honour guard. I promise this will all make sense soon enough." The archmage gestured for them to follow. "Please let me know if you hear of the whereabouts of a calastain." Khain nodded and the group walked out into the darkening snowstorm.

Arcturus felt the swirling storm pelt his skin as each flake melted into soft warm water, "Maveri, does this climate feel cold to you?"

The wizard handed Arcturus his helm and weapons. "No, the dwethren has bolstered us so that we create our own warmth. Without it, we would be dead within a matter of minutes."

Arcturus holstered his weapons and looked upon his almost frozen helm. "Well, that doesn't sound good. How long does his spell last?"

Maveri shrugged, "it's not one of my spells so I couldn't say."

"Until I decide to stop it. So, I wouldn't piss me off if I were you." Hank glanced back at the pair of them as he guided Bleu across the bridge. The blizzard eased a little to expose the glimmering archways along the sides of the vast glacial walkway.

Keep an eye on Khain, I don't trust him.

Arcturus nodded as the group strolled along the bridge.

"By the go—" Gathera abruptly stopped, gazing upon the immense ice structures ahead of them. They halted behind her as the looming frozen towers transcended before them.

"Welcome to Paerlowe." Yatuul's soft voice graced their minds as they looked over the magnificent city. Its glacial structure rested upon an expansive ice sphere that extended deep into the frozen lake below. Four towers stood adjacent to the city; two were linked with walkways to the surrounding mountains, and the others stood deep within the icy expanse. Each had its own elegant walkway connecting to the city centre.

"Those towers linked to the mountains are our gatehouses, the one we have just left is our portal tower. The last is The Tower of Reflections, which is where we can commune with our memories and amplify our ethereal communications." Maveri locked his eyes upon the tower in question.

"Do you think this is where that beam resonated from?" Maveri shunted the legionnaire.

Arcturus gazed over the majestic buildings. "I couldn't say. I'm sure we will find out soon enough."

Approaching the doorway, two giant frost elementals blocked the path with their hulking shields. Their forms were forged from great shards of ice connected by the same ice-white mist as Yatuul. "Greetings, Yatuul. Greetings, Khain. You seem to have foreign beings with you."

Khain looked over the group and then back to the elementals. "Believe me, this wasn't my choice. We need to enter the city. Yatuul would like an audience with our Empresses. He has some information about the meteors."

The blank expressions of the living shards of frost stared back at Khain. "No need to explain yourself, honour guard. You may enter." As the elementals moved aside, the monumental arched doors unsealed and slowly opened. Before them sat a huge hexagonal crystalline room. From each corner sat smaller doorways leading to walkways around the city. Circling the centre of the room were bustling market stalls carved from ice. Traders negotiated with fellow velgart while selling their unknown mystical wears. The group noticed the crowds of velgart citizens stop and keenly observe them as they passed.

"We have never had any of your kind here, apologies for our curiosity," Yatuul's voice seemed uneasy. Khain moved them through the crowds, his frost serpent glaring back at the group. They passed shops selling glowing gems and misty white substances. Warriors trained against one another with glacial weaponry and mages formed new structures with frost magic. In the centre of the city stood an enormous, opaque, spiralling ramp with astonishing decorative railings. Droves of velgart and frost elementals bustled around them. The group admired the crystalline architecture and graceful beings, each sight more elegant than the last.

"How is it I have never heard of this place, or of the velgart for that matter?" Maveri moved to the front of the group to question Yatuul.

"We are a private race. To travel to your land takes magic and spells to keep ourselves alive. We cannot live in your climate without it much like you cannot live in ours. We have seen no need to alert the realm to our existence and it is rare other beings ever venture to Deythron. When they do, they do not survive long. The land here is mountainous and treacherous. Only a few can traverse it. Our last recorded encounter with outsiders was many moons ago." Yatuul's eyes flickered.

Khain halted them. "Up this elevation is our royal quarters. To enter you must leave all weaponry with these guards," he gestured to a large chest.

"I have to ask, Kriss, or whatever your name is, how do we climb a slippery, ice ramp? We can't float like your lot." Hank pursed his lips and gestured to the group.

Khain scowled. "It's Khain. Fine, let me make a simple adjustment." With a click of his finger, stairs lifted from the ice forming a beautiful staircase. "Better?"

"Aye, it'll do," Hank smirked.

"Outsiders, please place all weaponry within this chest. Casting spells or using magic of any kind is prohibited. Do not speak unless requested or urged to by our Empresses. Please drink these vials, it will reduce any pain you are feeling from any open wounds. They shall only cleanse you momentarily." The guards opened a large frozen chest as the group disarmed themselves. Hesitantly, they placed their equipment within the case. The group looked to Maveri as he stood clutching his satchels close.

I'll speak to you again soon, my love.

"I don't use weaponry, only magic. These bags just contain some of my personal items." The wizard's eyes darted around the group. As the chest closed, a soft white mist rose from its lock, sealing it shut.

"Drink these." Ice-formed vials were handed to each of them. Arcturus looked upon the sparkling blue substance inside before taking a sip. He felt the freezing cold liquid trail through him as his body tried desperately to heat it. Within seconds, the pain from his ears subsided to reveal the crisp atmospheric sounds of the velgart moving within their city. "Let us take your wounded, we shall transport them to our holding chambers." Bleu snarled as the guard attempted to remove Seraphina.

"It's probably best to take the cat too, he's not a fan of leaving her side." Hank stroked Bleu's forehead. "Go on buddy, we will see ya soon." The guards lifted Anile off of Gathera and guided Bleu.

"If I find you've touched a scale on that lizard, I will personally shatter both of you." The or'kerec bared her teeth. They blankly stared at Gathera before moving away.

"Careful, or'kerec, a temper like that won't end well for you here. I understand you are grieving but you need to keep a level head. Don't let your heart do the reacting for you." Yatuul's eyes looked caringly at Gathera. The group dusted off as they prepared themselves. Arcturus wiped the blood from his head and rested his helm upon the frost chest before him.

Khain guided them up the stairs, "the Empresses grow impatient."

Yatuul's eyes smiled, "adventurers, are you ready?"

"Do I look okay?" Maveri brushed his quaffed hair and looked at Arcturus.

"Oi, wizard! This ain't a date, laddie!" Hank chuckled.

"You look oddly well-kept for someone who's just been in a fuckin' battle," Gathera snarled a little as she spoke. "Maybe you should have tried a little harder." She exposed her sharp canines.

"Look, now is not the time, or'kerec. Yes, Maveri, you look fine. Though, we are here to ask questions and exchange knowledge, not to woo them."

Arcturus shifted his pauldrons.

"In my experience, wooing them is all part of winning them over," Maveri winked.

"Outsider, if you try anything in there other than laying down facts, I will not hesitate to end your life there and then." Khain glared at Maveri. The stairs shifted to the correct height of each member's footing as they climbed higher and higher. Arcturus looked over the passing balconies as they moved. Velgartian residents stared before shaking their heads and moving away.

"We really aren't fuckin' welcome here, are we?" Gathera grunted.

Arcturus raised his eyebrow. "It doesn't seem like we are, no." Finally, the group reached the top of the vast spiral staircase.

Khain stopped in front of two almighty crystalline doors. "Our Empresses await you inside."

22
MEETING ROYALTY

Khain placed his hands against the ice. Beautiful turquoise patterns blossomed to life through the architecture as a welcoming hum unsealed the doors. Ahead of them sat a second great staircase within a long hallway edged with gracefully smooth glacial archways. Beautiful crystalline chandeliers softly swayed above them as if dancing at their arrival. With each step they took, pulses of turquoise beat beneath their feet. The sound of their footsteps echoed amongst the monumental walls. Each stair before them lay broader and thicker than the one they previously climbed.

"Ah, great, more stairs. Hopefully, these move like the last ones did." Hank lifted his foot, but the stairs remained still. "Gah! People never make these places for short folk such as me, do they?" He dragged himself up the first step. "Just 'cause all you ice people are tall. Do you not have any little ones in your ranks?"

Yatuul turned to watch the dwethren struggle up the polished steps. "Apologies, geomancer. Our shortest is still at least as tall as this one," he gestured to Arcturus. "I'm sorry, I know none of your names besides

Maveri."

Arcturus smiled at Hank, "I can carry you if you like?" He chuckled. "Oh, Yatuul, my name is—"

A voice erupted within their minds, "Arcturus Pythare, son of Tahmaliea Pythare." His sight flitted back toward the top of the staircase. "We know you; we know all of you. Please, come and join us." Turquoise light gleamed through the blue, ice, arched windows, reflecting off the distinguished structures. They climbed up the final step as Hank trailed behind. The room was astonishing. Layers of majestic frozen benches lined the Great Hall in place for some form of audience. Ahead sat two strikingly curved, rime frost, ornate thrones. Their decorations formed the backs of the seat with fine white layers of verglas softly draped over the bases. A pair of tall feminine beings stood gazing out of a trio of frosted windows. The figure on the left was exquisite. Her fiercely sharp verglas dress flowed precisely down from her hips. Light blues and whites swiftly adjoined by defined golds and purples streamed in needle-like lines toward her shoulders. Ornate shards of ice protruded from her collar, spreading outward across her shoulders like frozen lotus petals. At the end of her slender angular arm, she held a bending and twisting stave tipped with a floating ice shard.

"It seems you've made it. I'm glad our stairway didn't prove too much of a task for you," the figure turned. Her etched gold, purple and white featureless face focussed on the group. Stark bright white eyes pierced from her ornate profile. Curved purple frost horns surrounded a levitating turquoise crystal. "My treasure, our guests are here." The Empress glided effortlessly toward the throne, leaving a glistening trail of turquoise sparkles behind her. "Welcome, outsiders. Please let me introduce myself. I am Empress Zearelna." Her voice was commanding and raspy yet welcoming. The second figure turned to face the group; her lower body shrouded in a soft white mist as her sky blue and rose-pink torso formed from above it. Silvered details pencilled in amongst the smooth lines of her glossy body. Her form was much softer than Zearelna's. A light white verglas cape draped over her shoulders, revealing only her gentle slender hands. Her ice-white featureless face was etched with gloriously swirled lines that beat with turquoise. From her forehead blossomed antler-like frozen horns centred with a rose gold gem. She didn't seem to have eyes like the other velgart but as she examined the group, the swirled etching ignited in turquoise light.

The Empress drifted to Zearelna's side. "It is good to finally meet you, outsiders. We've learned much about you all. I am Empress Lamiere." Her peaceful and reserved voice seemed almost calming as the group felt her speak.

"My majesties, I understand that it is not our policy to allow outsiders within our city. As you know, I left here to research how others live. To gain knowledge on whether there might be any chance of our kind being accepted into their world. During this time, I took up residence as the archmage within an arid city named Vavarinu. The residents there suffered through poverty and hunger while adventurers gathered from around the realm in search of glory and riches." Yatuul paced.

Khain's eyes flickered as he gripped his glaive, "is there a point to your story, archmage?"

Yatuul nodded. "Of course. I witnessed races being shunned and corrupted as politics overtook their lives. Not so long ago, those meteors cursed our skies and plunged into the lands. Within each is a form of magic unknown to this realm. Magic with almost necromantic qualities. These brave adventurers helped defend the city from this crimson, but I am afraid to say we were unsuccessful."

Arcturus frowned. "We did everything we could."

Zearelna turned her vision to the legionnaire, "I'm sure you did, adventurer."

"Forgive me, your majesties, but it is our theory that the beam resonated within these lands." Maveri ran his fingers over the rough stubble forming on his cheeks.

The velgart all focussed on the wizard before Lamiere finally spoke, "you are correct. Deep within the mountains is where the source of the beam resides. We did send a patrol out to discover more insight, but they regrettably have not returned."

Yatuul turned to the Empresses. "The power of this magic is unfathomable. Within the wrong hands, it could be catastrophic to our realm."

Zearelna looked to Arcturus whilst Yatuul spoke, "that was not your first encounter with this 'crimson', was it, legionnaire?"

"No, Empress, it was not." A look of anguish washed over Arcturus as he bowed his head.

"I do believe that it was Uzarian that took one of the first assaults. I can imagine you lost a lot." Zearelna compassionately tilted her head.

Arcturus frowned. "How do you already know this information?"

The Empress placed her hand upon her throne. "I have my sources." She glided to the arched windows. "You are one of the last remaining legionnaires. Your kind could not handle this magic even with your all-powerful virago. It seems that divided, we don't stand a chance of fighting back this threat."

Gathera stepped forward, "then let's not stand fuckin' divided." Khain raised his glaive, halting Gathera.

"Stand down, Khain. Gathera Kinjale, daughter of High Chieftain Balorgas Kinjale. This is what we would like to achieve, but alas not all races want to fight a battle they believe is not theirs. We must fight this crimson at its source." Lamiere held her palm toward Khain as she spoke.

"Then let's do that," the or'kerec snarled at Khain.

"I admire your passion, Gathera. Without finding the beam's location we will never know what summoned this magic here," the Empress paused for a second, "maybe with your help we can find its source, then together, we can end this nightmare." Her body hummed with hope. "You all need to rest and heal before we can progress any further as shortly your potions shall wear off. We grant you our blessing to remain here as our guests. Chambers shall be prepared for you, and we shall show you to our restorers. I know we will figure this out together. Tomorrow Yatuul shall guide some of you to the Tower of Reflections; maybe your souls shall help us find some answers." Maveri tried to disguise his excitement as the Empress spoke.

"We don't know these beings, my majesties. I do not trust them to remain here unguarded." Khain turned his back on the group.

"Honour-guard, this is not your choice. If it will place your mind at ease, we will be having them escorted by guards whenever they leave their chambers. We shall keep their weaponry until we require them to use it." Zearelna turned. "Now leave us."

The honour guard's frost horns shuddered, "I understand."

Lamiere glided to join Zearelna by the windows. "Take our guests to the restorers, we need them ready for whatever may come." Khain nodded and gestured for the group to follow.

"You go on ahead, adventurers. I have some tasks to attend to before tomorrow. I've been away for a while so I must make some preparations." Yatuul turned away as if dismissing them.

Arcturus smiled, "thank you for your help, Yatuul. I hope that together, we can fight back this crimson." Yatuul nodded before promptly leaving the hall.

"Come." Khain guided them down toward the door.

"Outsiders, please do feel welcome here but do not mistake our hospitality for acceptance or complacency. You are here to help the realm with a cause greater than yourselves. You would be wise not to test us." The group looked back up the stairway to see the Empresses watching them leave.

"Yeah, and don't mistake you carrying me for a new development in our friendship." Hank hopped from Arcturus' arms as they reached the bottom step. Khain rested his palm upon the grand doors as they unsealed and slid open once more to reveal a small group of guards.

"Show these outsiders to the restorers. Then once they are ready, escort them to their chambers. You are to watch them at all times. They may gather for socialisation but nothing more. Oh, and we are keeping their weapons." The guards surrounded them, acknowledging Khain's orders.

As the group walked down the spiralling staircase, the velgart once again watched in bemusement.

"Now, I know how you feel each time you enter a new city, Gathera." Hank chuckled. Gathera thumped him on the shoulder and grinned. Whilst they walked, Arcturus and Gathera felt the pain of their wounds slowly seeping back. They strolled down into the city centre, passing by the stands of traders.

"You are not welcome here, mud-dwellers." The velgart glared at them as their voices resounded in their minds. Arcturus looked aside, feeling the overwhelming displeasure loom down upon him.

"We are here, outsiders. Enter through these doors and follow the restorers' instructions. We will be back to escort you momentarily." Glistening turquoise doors stood before them. Arcturus and Gathera pushed them open as Hank and Maveri attempted to follow. "Not you two, we see no pain within you. We shall take you to your chambers." The guards halted them, pulling them back.

Hank raised his brow to Maveri. "What about my emotional pain? I'm not over the fact I've lost my tavern." The guards stared blankly at the dwethren. They gripped his shoulder, forcing him and Maveri away.

Arcturus glanced at Gathera. "Just us then, I guess." She grunted and pushed past him into the room.

"You do not deserve our restorers." Arcturus felt the velgart's disapproving glare upon his back as he slowly walked into the room.

233

23
A BRIEF RESPITE

Arcturus stepped inside the expertly designed, angular room. Swirls of gorgeous turquoise and mint green magic entwined like clouds around the atmosphere.

"What have you done to him?" Gathera bared her teeth.

"Welcome, outsiders. There's no need to worry about this reptiare; it seems this crimson magic has claimed his soul." The restorers stepped aside to reveal Anile floating in the centre of the room. His arms and legs were restrained by streams of focussed magic as his once timid face sharpened with aggression. "We have two options here: we attempt to cleanse its soul which will surely kill the being, or we leave it living to study this magic. Gathera, we would like to offer you this choice." One of the five Restorers guided Gathera closer to Anile.

"You're going to make me choose?" Her jaw twitched as she fought back tears. "Can you not do something to save him?"

"There is a minimal chance that if we can cleanse its soul, the being may live. But during our examinations, it seems the body has taken substantial damage and is only being kept alive by this magic." The Restorer's eyes saddened. A tear rolled down Gathera's cheek. "If we can cleanse its soul but the being dies, we shall be able to imbue it within a frost gem. This can be worn as an amulet to keep its soul close to your heart."

The or'kerec picked up a shimmering emerald gem off the table beside her. "That sounds like a beautiful idea. If there is no way of saving him, then yes, I would like that option." She nodded at the restorer as his turquoise eyes glimmered back.

"A grand choice, Gathera Kinjale. Now please stand within the centre of the room with your chosen gem upon the reptiare's chest. Arcturus Pythare, please, may you stand beside her." They walked onto the small platform and glanced at each other. Anile snapped and writhed as the pair moved closer. The crimson seared his eyes as he glared at Gathera. "Now, if you could refrain from any unnecessary movement and try to relax. This will take but a moment." The restorer glided back to his corner as the others moved to theirs.

An ice-white mist began filling the room while the restorers raised their arms. Arcturus felt himself being lifted off his feet as his pain eased. Strikes of turquoise energy blinked across the room into Anile. Each strike through the reptiare seemed to rip shards of crimson from his soul. Gathera locked her sight on the gem as it hummed and vibrated in her palm. Anile's body became shrouded in a mint-green haze and started trailing into the gem. The reptiare writhed and pulled at his restraints as his crimson eyes dimmed.

"Goodbye, my friend." Gathera held the gem firmly against Anile's chest as pulses of green light beat within. More and more turquoise sparks beat through the reptiare until finally, the room fell silent. Both Gathera and Arcturus dropped softly to the ground as their bodies thrummed with sensitivity.

"Gathera, please release your frost gem." The restorer gestured forth.

She opened her hand and the gem remained levitating before her. Its green light hummed peacefully as a crystalline chain formed around it. Slowly, it floated to her and latched around her neck before resting carefully on her chest.

"I cannot thank you enough for this." Gathera's eyes were awash with tears.

"No need to thank us." The restorer's eyes gleamed. "Please use caution when returning to your chambers. We have never restored beings that aren't velgart before. There may be some side effects. Nothing major we hope, but some emotional fluctuation or hormonal imbalance is likely. This should only last until morning." Arcturus shared a concerned look with Gathera. "The guards await you outside." The pair walked out of the room.

"I'm sorry about Anile, he deserved so much better." Arcturus gripped the or'kerec's shoulder.

Gathera wrapped her hand around the gem. "He helped me in so many ways, not just as a healer but as a part of my family. I just never thought I would lose him, ya know? He was the kindest soul I've ever known. So many lives were saved by him and his magic. It's shit that he lost it all due to somethin' like this. He and Trey were so good together, I just fuckin' hope that draegorth is alright. To know it was him that killed Anile hit me in a way I didn't know it could." She looked at the legionnaire and her face softened. "You're a good man, Arcturus, even if you are a heavy-footed oaf."

"We shall take you to your chambers, outsiders." The guards led them back into the city centre.

"No, bloody no! You cannot tell me that your healing potions here are stronger than a greater healing potion. I will not have it!" Maveri flung his arms in frustration. Arcturus glanced over to see the wizard waving his cane at a merchant.

Hank grabbed Maveri's wrists. "Don't worry lads, I'll hold him back!"

"Unhand me you buffoon!" Maveri slapped his cane against the dwethren's forehead. Unlatching a coin purse from his hip, he fumbled, and hundreds of gold coins poured onto the floor. "Oh, bloody hell!" Swiftly, he knelt and scooped them back into the purse.

The dwethren's jaw fell agape. "You're one fuckin' rich old bastard!" He knelt and started siphoning away some of the coins.

Maveri pulled the coins from his fingers. "Stop it!"

"You owe me for that fuckin' drink you pompous fuck!" Hank slapped away Maveri's hands.

"What the fuck is goin' on?" Gathera scowled.

"This flipping merchant is trying to have me believe that the healing potions here are better than any I have ever known!" Maveri swiftly stood and brushed himself off.

Arcturus chuckled, "okay, caster, calm down. Is it not possible that since these velgart have been keeping to themselves, maybe they have stronger magical potential than we know?"

"It might be a possibility..." the wizard grunted.

Arcturus turned to the disgruntled merchant, "I do apologise for his behaviour." The merchant shook its head and began straightening up its goods.

"Outsiders, it is time to go to your chambers." The guards surrounded them.

Arcturus nodded. "I think you're right. Come on guys." He urged

Maveri away.

"You haven't seen the end of me, merchant," the wizard yelled out as Arcturus dragged him by his wrist. They moved through the twisting and turning outer corridors of the city. Through the opaque ice, they could see the shrouded formations of towering mountains on the horizon.

The walk to their chambers was long and confusing and almost impossible to map out without prior knowledge of the city. Finally, after what seemed like an eternity, the group were presented with several angular doors. "Here are your chambers, outsiders. We have grouped you together to make it easier to watch you." The guard placed its hand against the door. It hummed to life and slid open before the guards pushed the group inside.

"Well, that was rude!" Hank looked back to the sealing door, "just 'cause we ain't from he doesn't mean they get to treat us like animals!"

Gathera chuckled, "if anyone should be treated like an animal, it's you, mate." A heavy thud thundered from the corner of the room. "By my fuckin' axe, what the fuck was that?"

"None of your business!" Maveri knelt next to his bag to retrieve an ornate teapot and several similar cups. "Who's for tea?" He looked about the room while pulling out a carved wooden box, "anyone?"

Arcturus stood beside a baffled Hank and Gathera, "it seems I must be the one to ask, what is tea?"

"What is tea? Oh, you're in for a treat!" Maveri grinned. "Here, each take a cup and let me boil the water!" He handed out small finely crafted cups to each of them.

Gathera unnaturally palmed the ornate crockery as her hand engulfed the cup. "Umm, have you not got anything bigger? Maybe a tankard?"

"Don't be silly! Here, you hold it like this." Maveri lightly lifted the cup by its handle with the tips of his fingers, "lift this finger as you take a sip." He raised his little finger as he pretended to drink.

Hank sneered, "why the fuck would I do that?!"

"I don't actually know why it's done." Maveri glanced aside and began using a subtle spell to carefully boil the water. "Any preference on flavour?"

Gathera raised the cup as if to throw it at the Wizard. Arcturus placed his hand against hers to stop her, "surprise us." He disapprovingly glanced at the or'kerec as he lowered her hand. Maveri hummed while searching through the wooden box, then stopped and slowly pulled out a diamond-shaped bag. He smiled and blissfully dunked the bag into the teapot. Majestic sparkling swirls of greens, blues, pinks, and purples climbed into the air to reveal a blissful aroma. Arcturus stepped back a little as the scent reached his nose. The exquisite combinations perfectly blended together in seamless enjoyment as they reached the legionnaire's taste buds. Fruits and sweets of all varieties were entwined with a distinct tang that twirled together to create an exciting yet playfully light flavour.

Maveri moved over, carefully pouring the liquid into each of their cups, "sip cautiously, it's hot." The three looked at one another.

Gathera shrugged and gulped the tea, "ah, fuck!"

"I told you it's hot," Maveri chuckled. The group simultaneously slurped at the mystical liquid. Arcturus paused while absorbing the flavours. They twisted and turned, almost dancing upon his tongue until suddenly, his mind was met with pristine clarity. He gazed out over the mountainous glacial landscape through the vast verglas window. The night sky ignited with an astonishing turquoise glaze as it streamed along the horizon. His sight focussed on several peagorth rolling and swooping above the crystalline peaks, weaving their way amongst their young. Their great ice-like feathers bristled in the breeze while their curved, angular beaks peeled open with each caw.

"This realm is truly breathtaking. Why in light's name would anything or anyone want to change it?" The legionnaire pressed his hand against the cold verglas. "Never have I seen such large creatures fly with such elegance and beauty."

Maveri stood beside him, nursing his tea. "An old friend of mine once said: 'The realm is full of hatred. Races, gods, and rulers all fight for the same thing yet none of them realise it. Selfishness is the route of all Nor'ai's problems and until the day when we forgo our petty squabbles, we will never truly appreciate this world in which we co-inhabit.' That man was Wreyth. I sure do hope he's okay."

"Wreyth does make a good point. To be ugly in a world full of ugliness does not make you stand out, it only makes you blend in." Arcturus glanced over. "I too worry about him. Yatuul seems to be on the case though."

Hank smiled, "I mean, he was fuckin' odd! And that magic he was usin' was like nothin' I've ever seen! Fuckin' drekaiek give me the creeps."

"How so?" Arcturus cocked his head.

Hank sipped his tea while gazing at the liquid. "Can't trust the fuckers. They make a deal with a demon to have these great powers and will not think twice about crossin' ya."

"I don't believe Wreyth is like that." Arcturus sipped the last of his tea. "From what I could tell, it was a deal made out of desperation to save his people. More like a friendship or companionship... and his demon seems friendly albeit a little blunt."

Hank spat out his tea, "his fuckin' what? You met his demon?"

Maveri chuckled. "Oh yes. Aleiá is quite lovely. Although I wouldn't piss her o—" Before Maveri could finish, Arcturus fainted, cracking the ice flooring as he landed.

Hank glanced down. "That reminds me, you still owe me for that dri—"

"Oh, I forgot to say that this tea might—" The group followed suit as they all slammed to the ground. "Oh my..." Maveri glanced around at the sleeping party members. "At least they will be in for a good night's rest!" He turned to find his bed, "now which one is mi—" His body grew limp and he slammed to the ground atop Hank. The light dimmed on the group as the setting sun crept behind the mountains, leaving only the silhouette of a great winged beast watching from the horizon.

24
ETHEREAL COMMUNICATIONS

Arcturus rubbed away the sleepy haze as he opened his eyes. It had been several hours since the group had passed out into their deep slumber. Extending his limbs into an almighty stretch, his muscular back eased as he felt the sudden shift of his bones clicking back into place. "Hmm, I haven't slept like that in weeks!" Arcturus lowered his hands to push himself up, "wait, what?" He looked down to see a triangular frame crafted of ice; within its centre was a sparkling turquoise mist holding him aloft. "How did I get here?" He rolled over to see Gathera snarling and growling away in her sleep, like a wolvren pup having a bad dream. The floor sparkled as the beautiful beams of the morning sun crept over the horizon.

"Oi! Ya sleepy shites! Get up!" Hank's voice echoed around the room.

"Uh, fuck. What does that little bastard want now?" Gathera wiped her hand over her face.

"It's morning and I'm guessing Hank has heard something about food."

Arcturus stood.

"Come on guys! Yatuul says he has breakfast for us!" Hank slapped Maveri across the face.

"Ouch, you shit!" The wizard rolled off the turquoise mist before slamming against the ice flooring. "Fucking hell! I thought I was already on the floor!"

Gathera smirked and clambered out of bed, "Ha! Looks like you're getting to know the lil' fella quite well, Arcturus."

Arcturus watched the sun gloriously beam between the mountainous peaks through the clear ice window. "There truly is such beauty in our world."

Gathera joined him and looked over his shoulder, "yeah, I guess it's alright." They all lazily prepared themselves and walked to the doorway. Effortlessly, the frost door slid open to reveal two guards.

"Come on, quick! Before they eat it all!" The dwethren pushed past the group.

Grabbing his shoulder, the guards moved him back, "we shall guide you to archmage Yatuul." Hank huffed as his shoulders dropped.

They moved through the angled walkways around the city centre. Velgart drifted amongst the city with ease and their turquoise eyes gleamed. They pressed their foreheads together in a sort of morning greeting before going about their day. Maveri gazed upon them in wonder until he slammed into Arcturus' back. "Archmage Yatuul is inside." A door ahead of the group slid open, and the guards urged them inside. Before them lay a large spherical room with tubular frozen structures carved into the walls.

"Wait, what's this place?" Hank gazed around the room.

Yatuul glanced back to the door, "ah, you're here! Good morning, adventurers!"

Hank scowled, "I thought you said you had food for us!"

Yatuul turned to the distraught dwethren, "oh, no, I said I had sustenance for you, not food. I apologise for the confusion."

Gathera frowned. "Wait, there's no food? I'm fuckin' starvin'!"

Yatuul moved to the centre of the room and extended his arms towards the tubular structures. "We velgart don't eat food as you beings do. We survive off of the elements and magic coursing through our realm. These capsules will quench your hunger as if you had eaten a feast! Just step inside and let the sustenance flow through your very soul." Hank chuckled and darted his eyes before speeding past the group into a capsule.

"I guess he's really starving." Seraphina rolled her eyes as she looked at Bleu.

Arcturus glanced at Seraphina and Bleu entering the room behind the group. "Seraphina, you're, okay? I didn't see you at the restorers." Arcturus looked over her as relief washed over him. Yatuul glided across the room and placed a hand on Seraphina's shoulder. "She needn't visit our restorers. The beauty of being Shadowborne is that you are unable to be healed by magic. Instead, you have to allow the darkness to replenish your wounds."

Seraphina's eyes widened. "Wait, you know what we are?"

Yatuul turned to Seraphina. "Of course! Don't worry, we do not judge you here. You and Bleu have some of the kindest souls we have ever seen."

Arcturus tilted his head. "Shadowborne? I don't think I've heard of that."

Gathera grunted, "it's somethin' to do with a thing born during an eclipse."

They turned to Maveri as his eyes scanned the room, "oh, uh, yes. A Shadowborne is a creature born of night. If both conceived and born during the midst of an eclipse, then you do not follow life like a normal being. Instead, you feel more comfortable in darkness." He turned to Seraphina, "that would explain your very powerful magic. Although I did think that all known Shadowborne had been culled."

Seraphina released a coy smile. "I mean, they did try their best to kill me."

"Ah, that thing is absolutely amazin'! Don't ya think guys?" Hank rubbed his stomach whilst exiting his capsule.

"We wouldn't know. We haven't been in yet." Gathera glared at him with a smirk.

"Oh. Well, what are ya waitin' for? Get your ass in there!" Hank wiped the drool from his beard. Arcturus chuckled as the group all walked into their capsules. The fractal doors sealed shut behind them while its ice-white construction started pulsing with vibrant turquoise light. Swirls of white mist circled each of them, encasing them in clouds of magic. Mouth-watering flavours erupted upon their tongues, surging energy through them. Stewed meats blessed with fresh vegetables and zingy spices blossomed over their taste buds. It was almost as if they were swallowing the food while their stomachs grew full. The capsule flared again in turquoise light as it ignited the mist. Sparks of magic darted around before passing through their bodies until finally, the capsules became dormant. The fractal doors reopened.

"These capsules are fascinating!" Maveri inspected them as he walked out.

"Yeah, these are amazing, Yatuul!" Seraphina and Bleu grinned at each other while the tigaris licked his lips.

"Have you got a travel-sized version of these?" Gathera grinned.

"I am glad they worked and didn't end up killing you all. That would have been mighty embarrassing." Yatuul clasped his hands together in pride.

"What do you mean?" Arcturus frowned.

"Well, as with our restorers, we haven't used these with beings other than ourselves. You never really know what this magic might do when it comes to other lifeforms." Yatuul grasped his stave from his back. "Now, we must try and find some answers." The group slyly glanced at each other before moving back to Yatuul. "I do believe that you, Arcturus, and you, Maveri, both encountered this crimson magic before the others. What about the rest of you? Did you encounter it before Vavarinu?"

"Well, umm, I did see some strange stuff happening in the caves below..." Seraphina descended into a mumble as Bleu shunted against her hip.

"Hmm, interesting. What about yourselves?" Yatuul turned to Gathera and Hank.

"I gotta be honest with you, no. I didn't even see the meteor things," Gathera shrugged.

"Well, I mean I heard things in my tavern, but I just thought it was crazy talk. So, I just gave 'em more drink 'til they shut up about it," Hank scratched his head.

Yatuul paused for a moment then turned to Arcturus and Maveri. "It seems you two are the best choice to take to our Tower of Reflections. Arcturus and Maveri shall come with me so that I can see if there is more information within their souls. The rest of you can either tour the city with our guards or return to your chambers. This will work best if only the ones who are communing enter the tower." Gathera and Hank grunted.

"Yeah, I guess that makes sense." Seraphina smiled.

"Fantastic!" Yatuul clasped his hands together. "We shall return soon!" The velgart led them out and around the outer edge of the city.

"You seem well rested, Maveri," Arcturus chuckled.

"Thank you, I do feel more attuned with my magic again. Although I still don't know how I ended up in that bed." Maveri stroked his moustache. "At least planting face down on the floor doesn't seem to have done you much damage."

"I did what?" the legionnaire placed his hand on his face.

Maveri glanced aside, "well, I may have forgotten to warn you about the side effects of the tea." He chuckled. "I wouldn't worry too much, Gathera fell much harder than you."

"I'm sorry I didn't get to see that," Arcturus grinned. "I must admit, I haven't slept that well since before all of this happened." The legionnaire adjusted his armour. "I just wish I could figure out why someone would want to unleash such disturbing magic upon this realm."

"You think it might just be one person looking to wreak havoc on

Nor'ai?" Maveri's brow furrowed.

"Well, either that or there is a much bigger, more terrifying agenda," Arcturus glanced aside.

"Fascinating..." The wizard stroked his hair in thought. "I wish I had a library to conduct some research." He looked to Yatuul, "Archmage, do you happen to have any form of a library here?"

Pausing, Yatuul turned back. "A library? What is this being you ask of?" The archmage's eyes shimmered in confusion.

"No, no, it is a structure. It houses books full of knowledge and information." Maveri lifted his book from his hip. "They normally look similar to this."

"I did wonder what that was. I thought it may have been a strange extremity. I have seen many beings flick through those in Vavarinu, but no, we do not have any of those. We envelop our knowledge from each other. If we need to learn, then we talk to others and experience it for ourselves." Yatuul paced away.

"You mean to tell me the whole time you've known me and worked alongside the other mages in Vavarinu, you thought these were strange growths?" Maveri recoiled.

"Yes. I didn't dare ask as that would have been rude if I was correct." Yatuul's eyes smiled.

"Well, I never!" Maveri placed his book upon his hip. "You truly do learn something new every day." The group stopped. Before them lay a pair of enormous, elegantly carved ice doors shimmering with turquoise magic. Yatuul placed his hand in their centre. They softly opened to reveal a long glacial walkway shimmering in the sunlight.

"I'm very interested to see what information we might be able to drain from you two." Yatuul faced ahead as he spoke.

"Drain? That's a very strange way of wording that," Maveri glanced over to Arcturus.

"I don't like the sound of that at all," Arcturus stroked his hand over his hair.

"My apologies, I mean it more in the playful sense." Yatuul guided them across the walkway. "You see the only way to find what might be hidden deep in your soul, is to course our magic through you to see what might come out."

Arcturus frowned and looked at the clear skies. Miles of snow-kissed mountainous peaks softly breached the clouds above. "This truly is a spectacular place." Arcturus glanced back at Maveri, whose eyes stayed fixated upon the structure ahead. The vast ice tower was graced with swirls of turquoise magic circling up to its monumental spire.

"Welcome to the Tower of Reflections," Yatuul waved his hand toward the tower as if to reveal it.

"Good morning, archmage. Do you wish entry into the tower?" A hulking frost elemental stood with its weapon blocking the pathway.

"I do. I shall be bringing these adventurers inside too." Yatuul's eyes smiled.

The frost elemental looked over Maveri and Arcturus, then back to Yatuul, "outsiders are not allowed entry to our sacred tower."

Yatuul's shoulders slumped. "We have been granted special permissions from the Empresses themselves."

The elemental gripped its weapon tighter, "I have not received this request, archmage. Please return to the city centre."

Yatuul pulled his stave from his back. "I am requesting access now. Step aside." Shards of ice formed behind Yatuul.

"Stand down, archmage. Yes, they have been granted permissions, Grattus."

The elemental lowered its weapon. "Then access shall be given, honour guard."

Khain pushed between Maveri and Arcturus as he walked to Yatuul, "I told you to wait for me."

"I didn't realise I needed babysitting." Yatuul placed his stave onto his back. The doors opened as the elemental stood aside.

"You don't. They do." Khain pointed at Maveri and Arcturus before moving into the tower. Yatuul looked back and gestured for the pair to follow.

Arcturus lent to Maveri and raised his brow, "we really aren't wanted here, Maveri. Could you do me a favour if you get the chance in here and scan to find an aetherwell?"

Maveri frowned. "I suppose I could search for an aetherwe…" They froze in awe as they entered the great open room. Its decorative ice flooring reflected off four surrounding angular mirrors placed around the centre of the room. The pentagonal shape of the space only seemed to enhance its majesty as pulses of turquoise revealed what seemed to be past events of history.

"This room is exceptional, Yatuul." Maveri watched the turquoise ripple from the centre of the floor.

"This is our greatest structure within Paerlowe. Any soul that passes through here before entering the ether will share its life with us. Let us not waste time. Maveri, please stand in the centre of the room." Yatuul gestured for Maveri to walk forwards. Khain fixated upon the wizard as he analysed his movements. Thrums of magical energy began rapidly flowing beneath Maveri. He walked forwards as his distinct azure magic formed an aura around him. A glacial hum rumbled around the room before swiftly falling silent.

"Maveri Borealis of Tarlgoan." The voice boomed into life as it filled the room.

"Who in the name of Nor'ai are you?" Glancing about, Maveri addressed the room.

"Half aelveth, half human in descent and trained in the arts of azure wizardry. Let us see what your soul carries." The voice crackled. A turquoise light burned from the floor into Maveri as his eyes opened wide. Magic flowed from the wizard's core into the room. Slowly, it formed into the hazy image of a ruined town. The crumbling buildings were made from a familiar, crisp, white marble and lay upon a great open plain. Three adventurers made their way across a torn landscape, sidestepping weaponry and armour from fallen warriors. One of the beings knelt and lifted any remaining corpses to check for forms of life before they continued into the town.

"I don't know how many times I need to tell you, Maveri, the weapon's gone."

The whisp-like voice carried around the room as if trailing on a breeze.

"It can't be gone! I still feel its magic resonating here."

In a swift pulse, the image pulled away from the adventurers to reveal a great wyvern circling the rubble. Its head tilted as it scanned each fallen creature as if searching for something. A second, much more distorted creature glided down to meet the wyvern. Its size was almost twice that of an adult wyvern as its almighty wings flapped. Arcturus stepped forward. "What is that? There was no other beast there." The hazy image shimmered to almost reveal a being riding the large creature.

"Well, it seems we aren't the only ones looking for that blade. Hjaele, if those pesky adventurers find Karek'Thur, be sure to kill them before retrieving the blade." The tone of the voice seemed masked by the haze of unclear magic. "Once you have it, bring it to the crypts. I will prepare the aetherwell." The wyvern looked up at the hazy figure riding the great beast and nodded in acknowledgement.

Khain stepped forward, "Archmage, can you focus the image? Who is that rider?"

"I'm trying to." Yatuul raised his hands as the images twisted and contorted. "It seems something has corrupted the memory. Whatever it might be is fighting back against me!" A golden light beamed through the glacial structure and into Arcturus.

My love, I fear now it is time to trust your gut. We need to leave this place and venture for the Ancient Crypts. There we might find more answers, there it seems we may find an aetherwell.

A fractured look of confusion and worry glazed over Yatuul's eyes.

Arcturus fell to his knee, "as you wish, my love."

"Who are you talking to?" Yatuul tilted his head.

"My, my soulbond." Arcturus stood. "We've been shown where we need to go."

The archmage slammed his stave upon the ground, "this image has been tampered with, we have no certainty of its authenticity."

Khain looked over. "The image stated that they wanted to bring a blade to the crypts. There is only one structure with that name within our lands, a structure from which a great spell could be cast without interference."

"We do not know for sure that it meant the Ancient Crypts, honour guard." Yatuul turned to Maveri, "let it show us more."

"No!" Khain slammed his weapon on the ice. Maveri dropped to the ground as Arcturus rushed over to aid him. "We must let the Empresses decide what is to be done next."

Yatuul blocked Khain. "Let us check the legionnaire's soul first."

The honour-guards verglas serpent hissed as Khain stood his ground. "Move out of my way, archmage."

"Do you honestly believe the information given is enough for the Empresses?" Yatuul's eyes shimmered. "If we come to them with half-baked theories, we shall be laughed out of the room."

Khain raised his glaive, "is there something you're specifically trying to find, archmage? I saw your eyes glimmer at the name of that blade."

"We did not find the sword. Unfortunately, it seems Karek'Thur might have been lost or taken before we arrived there." Maveri tentatively stepped forward, "the demon I was accompanied by managed to save this legionnaire's life. But unfortunately, the blade was nowhere to be found."

Yatuul glanced at Maveri, "is that true?" He looked back to Khain. "That sword could hold the answer to stopping this crimson magic."

"Well then, it's a shame it's gone." Khain pushed Yatuul aside. "We will have to find some other way to defeat this new enemy."

Yatuul clenched his fist. "Fine. Let us speak to the Empresses." The doors thrust open and the archmage stormed out to see a great crimson hue trailing over the surrounding mountains. Khain turned to Maveri and Arcturus, "It is here."

Arcturus scowled, "I see that."

Khain grasped his weapon tighter. "We need to warn my people, now!" Arcturus and Maveri exchanged glances before following the honour guard back into the city. Khain gazed over the mountains. "If this crimson magic is here now, we are all in grave danger."

25
PLAN OF ACTION

Khain, Maveri and Arcturus rushed back into the city, pushing through the crowds. Velgart turned as they moved aside for the honour guard.

"When we are in there, both Yatuul and I shall be speaking. You do not speak unless spoken to." Khain's voice seemed slightly softer than usual.

Arcturus glanced aside. "I understand."

"This is a very delicate situation that could change the fate of my people." Khain stopped. "I still don't fully know you or trust you."

Maveri smiled, "the archmage knows our kind."

Khain glared at the wizard, "don't test me." He closed his eyes and then looked aside. "I will do anything to defend my kind. Now, come on." Khain gestured for other guards to join him as they pushed on through the city. Maveri flashed a look of concern to Arcturus.

"Hey, guys! What's all this rushing around for? What happened in there?" Seraphina waved at them from between two guards before being silenced.

"As I have said to these two, do not speak unless spoken to, outsiders." Khain moved up the spiral staircase.

"Ah no! These fuckin' stairs again," Hank's shoulders slumped.

Gathera chuckled at Hank's displeasure, "come on, short arse." They swiftly climbed the staircase up to the throne room.

"Welcome back outsiders. Seraphina, Bleu, we haven't officially met. I am Zearelna and this here is Lamiere." Seraphina smirked as Bleu glanced up at her.

"I'm sorry my Empresses but we do not have time for any more greetings. From the image we saw, it seems there might be activity at the ancient crypts within these lands." Yatuul paced. "Although the images were extremely hazy so I don't know how much of them we can trust."

"We understand that there was an unknown voice within this soul spark. Is that correct?" Lamiere turned her sight to Khain.

The honour guard stepped forward as the Empress addressed him. "You are correct, your majesty. Yatuul seems to believe the image may have been tainted; that could be the reason why we couldn't identify the rider."

Zearelna turned to gaze out of the window to watch the crimson magic trailing along the breeze. "If that is true, then could the wizard not be touched by the crimson?"

Lamiere joined her and placed a hand on her shoulder. "We have tested their blood, there is no unknown magic amongst them."

Zearelna looked at Lamiere. "Then this rider may have known in advance that they might be watched through a soul spark." She moved back to the group, "Arcturus, Maveri, you spoke about fighting a wyvern within Uzarian, correct?" Arcturus and Maveri nodded. "Was there any sighting or evidence of a second wyvern?"

"There was not," Maveri spoke up. "It is rare for one of them to even leave the Isle of Dynestrael, let alone two."

"I think we need to travel to the crypts," Lamiere spoke without turning.

Zearelna glanced back. "You trust the image?"

Lamiere glided over to Zearelna's side, "it is our only hint of where this magic may have originated from. I fear if we don't act now then this crimson will be sieging our home before we know it."

"I don't mean to interrupt." Yatuul tentatively glided back to the group. "But is it wise to send our forces deep into the mountains on what could just be a hunch? Especially as the magic already seems to be here."

Lamiere gazed at the archmage, "you don't trust it?"

"I do not." Yatuul closed his eyes. "Maybe we can find more information by using the legionnaire. For instance, his soulbond did manage to send him a message through the ether."

Zearelna turned to Arcturus, "is this true?"

"It is," Arcturus nodded. "She spoke of trusting my gut and leaving sooner rather than later."

"Why not tell them of the blade you seek, Yatuul," Khain moved to Arcturus' side.

Yatuul's eyes softly closed, "of course."

Zearelna's light grew quizzical, "which blade do you speak of?"

"Karek'Thur, but it seems to either have been lost or destroyed," the archmage glanced aside. "We unfortunately have no idea what this blade might look like."

Lamiere softly raised her hand, "this is a waste of time. We should prepare our forces and move on the crypts."

Zearelna turned, "you wish to react with force already? What if we are attacked here? The crimson surrounds us as we speak."

"We know not what may await us in the crypts." Lamiere placed her hand on Zearelna's forearm. "Sending in a small patrol may result in their certain death."

Zearelna titled her head, "yes, but if a vast army does await us, there is no guarantee that a larger force can defeat it either and it leaves our home vulnerable."

"Of course, that is true, but a larger force may have a better chance of retreating," Lamiere turned to gaze out of the window once again.

Zearelna shook her head. "In that sense, a smaller force may do better at staying hidden and avoiding danger."

Lamiere closed her eyes. "Then let me go with them."

"Treasure?" Zearelna glided to Lamiere.

"With me, a smaller force joined by our adventurers may stand a chance. It would also mean a sizable force remains here with you to protect our home." Lamiere softly turned to Zearelna.

Khain gripped his glaive tightly as his frost serpent swooped around his body. "Then I shall join you, my Empress."

Zearelna raised her hand, "but we are stronger together."

"I shall join them too." Yatuul pulled his stave from his back. "If anything were to go wrong, I shall portal us back home."

"Fine." Zearelna reluctantly nodded. "My treasure, at the first sign of danger that you can't handle, you return here to me. I will ready our defences and prepare for an assault."

Lamiere's face pulsed with turquoise light. "I shall do just that." She gripped Zearelna's neck. "Even when I am not physically here, I am always by your side." The Empresses pressed their foreheads together and held for a moment. Lamiere turned to Khain. "Ready a small force of a thousand warriors, we leave soon."

"I've gotta be honest with ya, why doesn't Yatuul just portal us into the crypts, like he did when he brought us here?" The Empresses moved apart before glaring at the dwethren.

"It's not as easy as that, Hank. I can't just portal us to a random unknown location. Even if I could, who knows what sort of forces we would be appearing in the centre of? I need a location to act as a recall point. Hence our portal tower is used for that precise purpose." Yatuul placed a hand on the dwethren's shoulder.

"But, if we appeared by them, they wouldn't see us comin' and then—".

Gathera slapped Hank across the back of his head, interrupting him, "for fuck's sake, just shut up." The or'kerec clenched her fist, "otherwise next time it won't just be a slap." She snarled as Hank rubbed his head.

"Go and prepare yourselves, outsiders. Retrieve your weaponry from the chest and be ready when we call for you." Zearelna briskly gestured for them all to leave.

"Adventurers, follow me." Yatuul led them out of the hall and down the tall spiral staircase. Ushering the guards away from the sealed glacial chest, he placed his hand upon its lock. An ice-white mist erupted from the seal as the lid gracefully swung open to reveal each of their weapons. "Please retrieve your weaponry and prepare yourselves. I shall call you when we are ready." Arcturus leaned down and grasped Karek'Thur.

I've missed you, my love.

"Arcturus, you alright?" Gathera's voice pulled him back to reality.

"Yeah, yeah, I'm fine. Just feels good to hold it again," he rolled the blade and smiled.

Gathera grinned, "great. Now fuck off out the way, I want my bow back." Arcturus chuckled and stepped aside.

"Maveri, please may I speak with you, alone?" Maveri glanced up to Yatuul. "Of course. Is there an issue?"

Yatuul's eyes smiled. "Not at all! Just one magic wielder seeking to blend his thoughts and tactics with another. I feel you could help us prepare for this battle and our defence."

Maveri smirked. "It's nice to be appreciated." Yatuul moved over to him and placed a hand on his shoulder as they walked away.

"Outsiders, you have free roam of our city, please use it as you wish," Khain nodded to the group.

"Thank you." Arcturus nodded in return and watched him leave, "what's the plan then?"

Hank smiled. "I know where I'm going!" He quickly turned and ran toward the sustenance room.

"That fuckin' greedy bastard..." Gathera grinned. "What you thinkin' of doin'?" She turned to Arcturus.

The legionnaire smiled, "I need to level my head."

"Well, that's boring." The or'kerec turned to Seraphina and Bleu, "what about you two?"

Seraphina looked surprised, "us? Oh, uh, we were actually going to go look around the markets if you want to join?"

Gathera looked blankly at them. "Yeah, no. That quite frankly sounds shit." She bit her lip. "Shame, looks like I'll have to go solo..."

"Did you want some company?" Arcturus smirked.

The or'kerec suggestively raised her brow, "well, I am interested to see what you can do with that weapon." She winked and pushed him aside, "maybe another time." Gathera strutted off to their chambers.

Maybe we should have joined her, it could have been fun.

Arcturus raised his brow.

Yes, yes, I have a little bit of a girl crush.

"I'm guessing she's off to do some practising or something," Seraphina and Bleu turned and walked into the market.

"Maybe next time, my love," Arcturus glanced aside then adjusted himself. "Great, now I'm worked up."

Maybe you could do with some fun too then.

He shook his head and strolled out onto the walkway toward the portal tower. Stopping halfway, he leaned on the elegant railings and looked up to Paerlowe's towering glacial structure. Great feathered rocs circled its pointed spiral with their young and called out to one another in echoing chirps. He stood for a while to contemplate the events leading to this moment. Anxious emotions mixed with fueled excitement rolled through his body as thoughts poured into his mind. He was almost certain that if they could find the source of the beam they might actually be able to stop the crimson in its tracks and maybe even bring Maeve back.

"I could lose all of this. The only home I've ever known could be gone, just like that." Khain glided over and leant beside him.

Arcturus nodded, "you could, but surely that is more reason to fight."

The honour guard closed his eyes. "Do you know why I don't trust outsiders?" He looked over. "It's because the one time we did, they took advantage of us."

"How many outsiders have you met?" Arcturus turned to him.

Khain looked out over the landscape, "enough to know you're all the same." He dismissed his ice glaive. "But, maybe I judge you too harshly, maybe you even see me as your equal, but you have to understand that I may lose everything. You outsiders come to our home with your crazy theories and for whatever reason, we believe you. Living this life at peace with a warring realm around you makes you realise how much will truly be gone if it disappears." The honour guard stood. "I really hope I can trust you, Arcturus. I hope we can defeat this threat so then I can return home to my peaceful life."

"Peace is all I want for this realm and your kind." Arcturus smiled. "I understand your worry, Khain. I lost everything back in Uzarian to this crimson. My fear is if we don't stop it, it could end all life in Nor'ai as we know it."

"Hmm, then we can't let it go unchecked," Khain grunted then walked away. The legionnaire nodded and turned back to the landscape to gaze into the pristine white snow.

He reminds me of Sigmund; hot-headed and forceful, yet with a kind heart.

"He really seems like a grumpy sod," Seraphina smiled as Bleu jumped onto the railing.

"I think it's a show he puts on," Arcturus smiled. They gazed over the crimson hue on the horizon as sparks of turquoise light began dancing out into the skies. Arcturus frowned then turned to Seraphina. "Did you buy anything?"

"Turns out you need money to buy stuff here," she stroked Bleu, "and we're broke."

The legionnaire chuckled, "you and me both." He turned back to the horizon. "I have to ask, how long have you known that you're Shadow-borne?"

Seraphina tensed up. "For as long as I can remember. It's been a life of exile and keeping out of harm's way. I guess it's a good thing I was born to favour the darkness because ever since I had to leave Murimia, I've barely seen daylight until I met you guys."

"That sounds like a very difficult life." Arcturus leaned back against the railing and moved his hand to stroke Bleu, but the Tigaris backed away. "I can't believe I have never met any of your kind before."

Seraphina nodded to Bleu, and he rested his chin on Arcturus' palm. "It's because they fear us. The velgart are only really partly correct about us; beings don't like the idea of us. Disappearing and reappearing on command doesn't sit right with them and they especially hate that we heal in darkness. But the strangest thing I have ever heard was something Trey once told me. He said, 'they will always fear something that is so undeniably close to the Rift.' To this day, I have no idea what he meant."

Arcturus frowned, "the Rift? What's that?"

"No idea." Seraphina leaned beside the legionnaire. "Gods I really hope Trey is okay."

"Ah fuck me, I feel so much better!" Gathera swayed across the walkway. "I wouldn't go back up there. I made a right fuckin' mess." She glanced aside. "I should have asked for a towel or summit to clean up with."

"Do the velgart even use towels?" The legionnaire asked quizzically.

Gathera smirked. "Ah yeah, fair point," she paused, "wait, do these things even cum?"

"Feel free to ask them," with a smirk, Arcturus slowly stood up. "Although they aren't sexual beings so I would presume not."

"Yeah, they probably don't." The or'kerec chuckled and leaned against the railing, "what are you guy's talking about?"

Arcturus tilted his head, "we were talking about—"

"What happens if we all die tomorrow..." Seraphina subtly glanced over while interrupting him.

The legionnaire caught himself, "yeah, we were saying that this realm will probably never be the same again."

"Yeah, that's probably very true." Gathera drew her axe and ran her finger along its blade, "but, I sure as shit am not goin' down without a fight."

Arcturus smiled, "that makes two of us."

Bleu snarled, causing Seraphina to laugh. "You're right, Bleu, we will kill 'em all and be back in time for dinner!"

"Someone say dinner?!" Hank strolled out holding his stomach. "Yeah, I could eat again." The group turned and laughed.

Arcturus tilted his head as a crimson bolt of lightning sparked across the mountaintops before an almighty glacial explosion rang out. The legionnaire placed his hand on Karek'Thur.

What is that, my love? Are we too late?

"I fear that is the end of our relaxation time." Arcturus glared into the skies to see a bright beam of crimson jolt up and pierce the clouds. "That," he stuttered, "that is exactly what I saw the first time!"

Gathera stood tall, "that looks really fuckin' bad." They stared in shock as the skies began to crack like glass, leaving trailing crimson lines.

"We need to act now before it's too late!" Arcturus glanced around. "Yatuul? Yatuul? Are you seeing this?"

"I see it." Yatuul's voice resonated in their minds. "We've had reports of our outer towers falling to the crimson and multiple fallen velgart. Come back to the city, we will be leaving immediately." The group nodded at one another and rushed back towards the city.

We must protect this realm, my love. It is our duty.

26
GLACIAL MOVEMENTS

Maveri latched a turquoise gem to his cane, "will Wreyth be joining us?"

"Of course, Maveri," Yatuul nodded.

"You've spoken about Wreyth?" Arcturus raised his eyebrow.

"Yes, it seems he had ended up rather far away. He should still be joining us in the battle." Maveri stroked his goatee.

Arcturus tilted his head, "I see. Is he safe and unharmed?"

"Of course! One of my scouts picked him up. He was a little frustrated but thankfully undead don't really feel the cold." Yatuul's eyes glimmered a smile then turned to concern. "Although now is not the time to speak of this. Our enemy has attacked our outer encampments and we must retaliate." He ushered them toward an immense doorway. "They cannot be allowed to enter this city so the sooner we find the source, the sooner we can stop this crimson." Two gigantic frost elementals pushed the doors open, unleashing piercing winds through the city.

"I know this may be a great risk and I understand that these circumstances aren't ideal, but these are our lands and Nor'ai is our home. This unknown magic has entered this realm and we must figure out how. We cannot wait around for war, instead, we must take the fight to them and cut away this infection at its root! I shall be beside you and together we will find the answers we seek. For we are velgart!" Lamiere stood before a thousand of velgartian warriors and mages, each thrumming with glorious turquoise light as the Empress rallied them.

"Let us join the front line," Yatuul pushed through the gathered warriors. They moved along the great ice-made bridge as the winds howled above them.

I understand why we need to go, but does it not seem odd that the velgart are willing to separate their force with the enemy so close?

Arcturus frowned as the question washed over him. "A little odd, yes..."

"Welcome, outsiders," Lamiere nodded.

"Mount up, velgart! It is time we move." Khain clutched his hand into a fist. Ice-white mist erupted from below, engulfing him. The group heard a snarl before the mist cleared to reveal a glacial leocrin pulsing with turquoise light through its opaque structure. He pulled its verglas reins, turning it to face Arcturus.

The legionnaire smiled, "very impressive, Khain."

A chorus of growls resonated from behind the group urging them onward. The group turned to see the army of velgart all mounted upon similar creatures.

"Not really, it's something we are all able to do." Khain's eyes smirked.

Arcturus looked back to Khain, "Well, unfortunately, it's not something we can do."

"Here, outsiders." Lamiere raised her stave, and a similar mist surrounded the group, summoning leocrin beneath them. The creature's solid structure almost rattled with each breath it took. Sharp angular horns protruded from its crisp, cat-like structure. Arcturus felt the beast lift him from the ground as verglas reins formed in his hands. The leocrin glanced at the others, then at Arcturus and snarled.

"Now you can experience my way of travel!" Seraphina grinned, climbing atop Bleu.

"Bleu, take this blessing of speed. You'll be able to keep up with us that way." Yatuul placed his hand on Bleu's back, igniting his paws in turquoise.

"Velgart! Once we leave these mountains, keep in formation and stay watchful, we do not know what we may encounter." Lamiere waved her hand before furling her fingers, summoning a majestic purple snow Leocrin with a golden crown-like mane. "Our city may come under siege during our expedition, if so, our Empress will beckon us and Yatuul shall return us home!" She lifted her stave and pointed toward the mountains. "Forward, velgart!" Arcturus felt the leocrin bound forth, following

Lamiere and Khain. He latched on until the rhythm of his body synced with the creatures.

"I've gotta get me one of these, "Gathera rode her beast with snarls of joy.

"Yeah, I'm not so keen." They glanced back to see Maveri tightly clutching his leocrin's reins.

"Oh, come on Maveri, it's easy!" Seraphina pulled Bleu, urging him to rear his head. The tigaris leapt forward into the deep snow and carved a path while purring with excitement. Arcturus gazed upon the vast mountains towering high around them. Pulses of turquoise beat through the exposed ice as the glaciers sang in the crisp air. The howling winds lifted layers of snow and swept it across the crystalline landscape.

"Fantastic, isn't it? Without the Permafrost, none of this would exist." Yatuul pulled back as he spoke.

"I have to ask, Yatuul, what is 'Permafrost'?" Arcturus stroked his rough, stubbled chin.

"Ah, of course. The Permafrost happened many new moons ago. Potentially even long before your time, I would imagine." Yatuul's eyes smiled.

"There are theories as to how it was created, whether natural or otherwise. But, as this magical, unyielding cold graced the lands of Deythron, so did we."

"So velgart are a part of this Permafrost?" Arcturus raised his brow.

"Myth has it that we are the lost souls of fallen warriors within these lands formed into living ice. Given a second chance at life but with no memory of our former existence," Yatuul paused for a moment, "I don't believe that. Instead, I believe, like any creature, we exist because the realm wants us to. Because we have a purpose to fulfil."

Arcturus watched the emotion change within Yatuul's eyes. "I must say, that is hauntingly beautiful."

Yatuul looked over at him. "We keep our lives private to not bring unwanted attention to our lands or this magic. If something knew of our presence, who knows what they might try. Some beings can be so cruel."

Arcturus nodded in acknowledgement. "Of course, many would relish being able to create structures such as your kind do." The landscape opened up into vast mountainous valleys as they left the grounds of Paerlowe. Wide frozen rivers weaved through towering cliffs with protruding glacial structures breaking up the flat surface ahead. Pulses of turquoise magic thrummed in the darkness below the ice.

"Brace yourselves!" Lamiere leaned closer to her leocrin. The howling icy winds grew louder as falling snow whipped around the group.

"Hank, make sure you don't drop that spell. Without that warmth, you'll all be frozen within seconds," Yatuul's voice pierced through their clouded minds. Suddenly, an arctic blizzard textured by turquoise flickers of magic engulfed them. Within seconds, the group lost sight of everyone around them. The sound was deafening as the titanic winds battered against their armour.

"Don't panic, adventurers, let our leocrin guide you. Bleu, use your shadow-sight to follow us." Yatuul's warming tones eased Arcturus' worry. The leocrin beneath bowed their heads and forged on through the storm. Squinting into the distance, Arcturus spotted flickers of crimson light sparking amongst the turquoise.

"Arcturus, do you see this?" Lamiere's voice spoke crisply in the legionnaire's mind. "If you wish to speak with me, just think and I'll listen."

Arcturus' brow furrowed, "I see it. How close are we to these crypts?"

"We are still a while away," Lamiere's voice seemed concerned.

I can't shake the feeling that Paerlowe is in danger.

"It can't be good that we saw crimson so close to Paerlowe. Do you not worry about your home?" Arcturus raised his hand to focus his sight.

Lamiere paused for a second, "of course I do, but some voice in me just seemed to urge me to make this choice. Like it was the right one, you know? Something primal and foreign is coming and we need to stop it." The frozen river beneath them rumbled and cracked as the once glorious pulses of turquoise turned to crimson. "No! My treasure!" Lemiere's voice became tainted with concern.

Arcturus recoiled at the changing magic. "We must leave this frozen river; this magic can't be allowed to taint your kind!"

"Velgart, move off the river!" The Empress commanded the army up toward the hazy silhouettes of the mountains surrounding them. Arcturus kept his head down, grasping the verglas reins. The cracks within the ice grew larger as explosions of crimson magic burned into the air.

My love, watch out!

Arcturus' ears perked up and he pulled his leocrin's reins to avert the blast. Cracks in the ice tore the river in twine as crimson magic rumbled through the landscape back toward Paerlowe. Arcturus looked over his shoulder to see velgart warriors slung from their mounts.

"Avoid the cracks!" Arcturus yelled out into the blizzard.

"Yatuul, you need to return us home!" Lamiere's voice became engulfed in panic, "Yatuul? Archmage? Answer me!" The remainder of the army reached the snowy base of the mountains as the blizzard began to subside.

Maveri glanced around his snow-covered surroundings, "did everyone make it?"

"I think we all did, but I think some of the velgart didn't." Arcturus counted his fellow adventurers.

Lamiere rode amongst the group, "has anyone seen the archmage?"

"I fear we may have lost him," Khain pulled his leocrin onto the snow. The river behind the warriors calmed as pulses of crimson light beat back along the route they trod.

"Then we must return home. That magic is heading straight for Paerlowe," Lamiere gazed around her remaining force. "Can anyone else here create a portal home?" The remaining velgartian mages attempted to craft portals but something seemed to be blocking their magic.

Khain bowed his head, "I fear this crimson will not allow us to return home." He looked back over the shattered ice floating down the crimson river. "At the speed that magic is travelling, we won't be able to beat it. The river is too dangerous now and the mountainous path takes hours longer."

"We can't abandon our home, honour guard." The Empress stormed over to Khain.

"I don't think he's suggesting that." Maveri moved closer. "Correct me if I'm wrong, Khain, but I believe he is suggesting that we continue our journey and end this corruption. Maybe then, we can save your home." The wizard lifted his hands as light sparks of azure flickered between them. "Even my portal magic cannot be used right now."

The honour guard nodded, "if we can defeat this enemy at its source, surely we will save our kind." Lamiere gazed along the river in silence.

Arcturus frowned, "where's Gathera?"

Hank looked around, "Gathera, you oaf! Where are ya, lass?"

Lamiere scowled, "I can't sense her leocrin anywhere."

"Gathera? Call out if you can hear us!" Arcturus yelled out across the settling snow.

Bleu sniffed the grounds around them before grunting at Seraphina. "Bleu says her scent leads over here."

I don't like this at all, my love.

"We can't have lost another." Arcturus shook his head in disbelief.

"Fuck off! Gathera ain't gone! She's a tough bitch!" Hank scanned over the snow.

"Hank, she must be here somewhere." Seraphina watched the dwethren's face drop. "Come on Bleu, let's go find her!" Seraphina bowed her head and stroked Bleu.

"Yes, little tiggy, let's go get her!" Hank yelled out.

Arcturus smirked a little, "he's like an excited child."

"We must forge on if we are to save my kind and yours," Lamiere urged the remaining warriors up the mountains. They followed her through the deep snowy landscape, pushing their leocrin harder and harder as the peaks around them shuddered with the sounds of marching armies. Lamiere raised her stave. "This fight will decide the course of Nor'ai's future. We must prevail!"

27
THE FROZEN CRYPTS

The wind whipped lashings of snow from behind as they reached the brow of the hill. Crisp white clouds shrouded the skies, allowing only narrow rays of sunlight to pierce through.

"It will take a few days ride to reach—" As Lamiere spoke, she spotted a great towering structure made of ice. "What in Nor'ai is that?"

"It looks to me like a velgartian structure," Arcturus moved to her side.

"But how? We have never built this deep into the mountains," Lamiere stared in shock.

Arcturus looked up at the spiralling angular tower, examining the great crimson beam sparkling through it. "Are you sure? That looks extremely similar to the towers back in Paerlowe."

"I can promise you, we have never sanctioned construction here," Lamiere looked to Arcturus.

"That's definitely where the crypts once stood, but how did we get here so quickly?" Maveri pointed to the base of the tower, "see look, you can just make out the old stonework through the ice. I can even feel the subtle pulse of the aetherwell from here."

"This can't be right, the velgart has nothing to do with this crimson. Let me speak with Khain, maybe he knows something," Lamiere moved back to address the honour guard.

"That is definitely velgartian." Maveri looked to Arcturus, "I thought the Empresses were meant to be all-knowing?"

Arcturus removed his helmet, "something seems off. You can't tell me that she had no idea that her kind built such a momentous structure here."

My thoughts exactly. This place is ominous, but we can't let that stop us now.

"Is that Paerlowe?" Seraphina and Bleu trudged through the deep snow before stopping at the brow. "Wait, have we done a full circle?" Bleu growled.

"No, that's the crypts." Arcturus flit his sight as a silhouette passing by the crimson caught his eye. "There, look! It's the beast we fought back in Uzarian!"

Maveri frowned, "where?" Arcturus turned the wizard's head to face the tip of the spire. "Oh my, you're correct!"

Seraphina stepped back, "you mean that bird-looking thing?" Seraphina nervously smiled.

"That's no bird, Seraphina, that's a wyvern." Arcturus kept his sight locked on the vast silhouette.

"What're we discussing? Oh, fuck me! That's a big tower!" Hank's jaw fell agape. "I bet that thing has so many fuckin' stairs."

"Oh, don't worry, we can just fly up on the bastard wyvern!" Maveri placed his head into his hands.

Lamiere returned to the front with Khain. "We have no knowledge of that tower ever being constructed. Either someone built that in secret, or we have other beings out there that can build as we do."

"Other velgart?" Hank tilted his head.

Khain looked to the dwethren, "possibly." He glanced back to see the thawed river flowing with crimson magic. "I believe that river must have brought us here quicker than we realised."

"Then what do we do?" Arcturus turned to the Empress.

Lamiere looked over the tower, "I think our only option is to-" The great beam of crimson thrummed in power through the tower, forcing more great cracks to rip through the skies. "Legionnaire, is that the same beam you saw all those moons ago?"

"Exactly like it but this time it seems much more powerful." Arcturus donned his helm.

Khain nodded, "then we know what we have to do."

"What are we doin'? What's goin' on?" Hank looked about the group to see them all readying themselves, "oh for fuck's sake. Guess we have to stop this and find that fuckin' or'kerec." Before he had time to react, the leocrin stormed forth.

Plumes of snow burst out from behind the creatures as they bounded almost vertically down the mountains toward the tower. Sudden cracks of crimson burned through the ground beneath them and pulsed through the landscape.

"By the gods!" Arcturus watched as multiple corrupted warriors clawed out of the snow before them. Their glowing crimson eyes pierced through the sunlight as they snarled at the group.

"Let me clear a path!" Maveri whipped his spellbook from his hip and raised his palms. Erratic azure magic sparked to life around him until he released the torrent into the oncoming horde. Plumes of snow and crimson dust blossomed into the atmosphere as the beam ripped through the corrupted warriors.

Arcturus focussed and drew his weapons. A quickly brightening glow of crimson enveloped the casters ahead as they readied their spells. They released flaming orbs back at the group. Arcturus lifted Aegis as its golden barrier formed around his allies. Clenching his grip, the corrupted magic exploded against the golden light forged from his shield. Hank looked aside as he watched the velgart beside them disappear into the crimson flames.

"Ready your weapons!" Arcturus dismissed the barrier as his leocrin pounced into the horde, knocking some enemies to the floor with thunderous speed. Ice weapons clashing against plate armour pierced the air as the remaining velgart joined the fight. Arcturus watched his leocrin clamp its jaws against a corrupted draegorth's head before shattering its skull. Raising his shield, he defended himself from the surrounding enemies and weaved Karek'Thur through their attacks to rip them apart.

Another erratic beam of azure lightning pulsed through several enemies as Maveri held his ground beside his fallen leocrin. Effortlessly, he thrust glowing missiles into the beasts while priming other spells. Forging a great azure fireball between his hands, the wizard slung it into the horde. Seared flesh horrifically graced the air as the corrupted beings turned to dust. Arcturus' leocrin forced him deeper into the fight until a sweeping battle-axe carved through the leg of his beast, throwing the legionnaire to the snow. He gambolled to his feet and raised his shield to deflect the second blow. Leaping to his defence, the leocrin took the full force of the axe as it buried deep into its skull before shattering into shards of mystical ice.

Arcturus clamped his hand around Aegis, sending a surging pulse of golden magic through his attacker. He forced the corrupt human aside before carving through its leg with Karek'Thur. The warrior stumbled as it fell to the snow and turned to dust. Arcturus took a breath before pressing on. He glanced over to see a group of crimson legionnaires.

"Sigmund?" His sight locked on the aelveth's familiar face.

The creature tilted its head and glared back. "Good to see you again, brother, now submit to the power of the crimson!" Sigmund leaped forth.

Arcturus deflected each swing of the corrupt warrior's sword. "Brother, you don't have to do this, you must resist!"

Sigmund locked his sword against Aegis, forcing Arcturus to his knee. "Oh, but I do. Let me show you the true purpose of life!"

That is not the Sigmund we knew anymore, Arcturus. You must end his misery.

The legionnaire closed his eyes. "I know, my love." Focusing, he forced a pulse of golden magic from Aegis, blinding Sigmund. He pushed away the warrior's blade and thrust forward, carving through the aelveth's chest. "I'm sorry, brother." He pulled back his blade and watched his old friend burn to crimson dust. Clenching his jaw, Arcturus continued into the fray. A zigzag of azure light bolted amongst the crimson warriors as their torsos ripped open. They stopped, dropping their weapons before turning to dust.

"Don't worry! We got you, my dude!" Seraphina leaped down from Bleu, drawing her glowing swords. Gracefully, she breached through the onslaught as she sliced through her foes. Blissfully powered by her skill, her gorgeous weapons swept through the crimson horde. A devastating mace stormed down upon her from an almighty or'kerec. The impact dispersed a greyish shadow as Seraphina's form dissipated. Reappearing, she grasped Bleu's mane and flung herself onto his back. Smiling at Arcturus, she pulled a kunai from her belt and slung it into the or'kerec's head. "Oopsy." She winked, and then she and Bleu disappeared into the fight. Arcturus clashed against several foes as he shook his head in disbelief. He ignited Aegis as their attacks battered against its golden barrier. Suddenly, their bodies became encased in ice before shattering in front of him.

"You're welcome, outsider," Khain stood behind the shattered foes. The legionnaire listened for a moment then rushed to the honour guard's side. Expertly, he launched the image of Aegis toward a crimson spear, deflecting it away from Khain.

"You're most welcome too, honour guard," Arcturus grinned.

Khain looked to Arcturus in frustration, "we need to get inside." He turned, plunging his glaive through an oncoming warrior before casting a frost-storm into the face of two others, freezing them in place.

Arcturus nodded. "We need to clear a path to the door." Reigniting his blade, the legionnaire blissfully sliced through his surrounding enemies.

"I'll do what I can," Khain's eyes smirked, and his frost serpent whipped through the cores of several crimson foes. An almighty explosion of rocks sent three enemies flying over the fight before they turned to dust. Hank smashed the crimson warriors until they knelt before caving in their skulls. Sharp shards of rock followed him, pelting into nearby foes. The dwethren jumped, slamming his weapons down causing the ground to quake and stumble his foes.

We all fight by your side, my love. Harness my power; together we can end this.

Arcturus instinctively raised Karek'Thur to the skies in the manner of the virago. Flashbacks of his past battle enveloped his sight. He watched the graceful image of Maeve and her fellow virago appear beside him. They raised their weapons in turn, parting the clouds above. Golden light blistered into a bright golden beam down into the fight. It decimated a large section of the crimson horde with ease.

In an almighty screech, the wyvern circling the tower's spire swooped down. Arcturus' eyes widened as he saw the beast storming toward him. He raised Aegis as bellows of crimson fire immolated the ground around him.

"I was wondering when you might show up," Arcturus planted his feet firmly as he held strong.

"We meet again, wyvern!" Maveri yelled out from behind the legionnaire. "Keep that shield up!" He raised his palms at the hulking beast and released two beams of glorious azure magic toward it. An ear-shattering cry filled the air as the beams glanced across the creature's side. The wyvern clamped its jaw shut as it attempted to avoid the magic. Maveri followed the beast, burning through one of its wings. Locking into an uncontrollable spiral, the wyvern smashed through the side of the tower.

"Well fought, wizard," Arcturus nodded at Maveri.

"Enough!" A wave of ice shimmed across the landscape, freezing the surrounding crimson warriors in place. "Arcturus, you and the others need to get inside." Lamiere stood towering over them as mystical ice burned forth from the tip of her stave.

"I agree." Arcturus dismissed his barrier and stood tall, "allies, on me! We need to get inside that tower!" Seraphina and Bleu sparked into existence beside him as Hank sprinted over.

"Ya right there, we gotta get inside that place," Hank panted as he gripped his earthen mauls firmly in his hands.

"I shall clear a path, but my magic won't hold them for long." Lamiere looked around the frozen warriors as their crimson magic slowly cracked through the ice, "quickly, follow me!" She pushed forward, freezing all the foes that stood in her way.

Khain joined their side as he sliced through the frozen crimson warriors. "Empress, I shall stay with you and hold them off while the adventurers deal with what's inside."

Seraphina smiled, "aww he called us adventurers!"

"No, honour guard, you shall join them inside," Lamiere glanced down, "they will need all the help they can get." Khain reluctantly nodded as they pushed closer to the doors of the tower. The group glanced back as the crimson warriors burst from the ice and the fallen velgart rose once again.

Maveri hurled magical, azure missiles as he sprinted alongside Arcturus. "We have no idea how many of them are inside that tower."

"Let's hope this was most of the army that managed to make it up to Deythron." Arcturus launched the image of Aegis, shattering several enemies. Finally, they reached the frozen stone steps of the crypts. Moving to the great square door, they searched for some sort of handle.

Hanks peered through the ice. "The handle is stuck behind this frozen shite!" He lifted his weapons and slammed them against the structure. Pulses of crimson rippled with the impact before sending the dwethren flying into the snow.

"This place is sealed by magic," Maveri placed his palm on the door.

Arcturus glanced at the wizard, "do you think you can open it?"

"I think so, but I'll need time." Closing his eyes, Maveri levitated his spellbook.

Khain looked back over the defrosting crimson horde, "you need to hurry!"

"Let me try." Lamiere placed her stave against the door. "With your help wizard, I think we can make quick work of this."

Arcturus walked to the top of the stone stairs, "then we will hold the line." He raised Aegis and readied Karek'Thur. Khain, Seraphina, Bleu and Hank all moved to his side. Several remaining velgart shifted to the bottom steps as they turned to hold back the oncoming crimson warriors. The horde stormed forward, slinging bolts of magic toward the group.

Arcturus summoned his golden barrier as magic immolated the velgart before him. "I don't know how long we can hold this!" Crimson flames beat against the golden light as the horde reached the stairs.

"I've got this!" Hank charged forward and slammed his weapons to the ground. The almighty impact cracked the stone stairs. They held for a moment before shattering, falling into the darkness below. "Wait, how high up were these crypts built?" The dwethren gazed down to see the remnants of the almighty staircase that led to where the group stood. Crimson casters pelted their magic against Aegis' barrier as the warriors beside them charged around another route.

"How long left?" Seraphina turned to Maveri.

The wizard clenched his fists, "hopefully...not...too...long..." His words barely escaped his tensed jaw. A pulse of solar magic rippled amongst the group as the golden barrier fell.

Arcturus stumbled back into Bleu. "Sorry, I couldn't hold it any longer.

"Wizard, it's up to you now." Lamiere pulled her stave away from the door, "Khain, look after them." She glided over the fallen stairs and raised her hands, levitating her stave, "this is for you, my treasure." Clenching her hands, the turquoise light inside her burned bright. Her glorious, elegant structure cracked as ice-white mist poured from within her core. In a sudden burst of frost, her body shattered, freezing the crimson horde in its tracks.

"Lamiere, no!" Khain attempted to run to her aid, but Hank pulled him back.

"She's gone." The dwethren bowed his head.

Maveri opened his eyes. "I've done it!" The tower echoed as the door slid ajar.

"Everyone in, now!" Arcturus urged the group inside. "Maveri, can you reseal the door?"

"Let me do it." Khain slammed his glaive on the frozen stone floor, forcing shards of ice to seal the door shut. He turned to the group clutching his glaive. "This is our final stand warriors. Do not fuck this up."

28
<u>EMBELLISHED</u>
MEMOIRS

The group gazed over the stunning angular glacial walls. Crisp whites and crimson sparkled along the twilight hallway as they walked across the old stone flooring of the crypts.

"Hey, guys, look here!" Hank gestured over as he pressed his face against the opaque wall.

Arcturus stood over the dwethren and wiped his gauntlet over the ice. "What do you see, dwethren?" He narrowed his vision. The silhouette of a large humanoid wolvren-like figure stood frozen in place. "Is that a fenrick?"

"Oh, shite lad! You got a fenrick in yours?" Hank pulled his face from the ice, "I got some proud fancy lookin' fella."

Maveri frowned. "No, not possible. The fenrick have not existed for over a thousand new moons!" Strolling over to the legionnaire, he pushed him aside. "Let me see." The wizard pressed his face against the ice. "By Nor'ai's light!"

"When you are finished, adventurers, I think I've found a way up." Khain stood beside a sealed triangular door.

Arcturus adjusted his helm and drew his weapons, "honour-guard, are you sure your kind knew nothing of this place? This tower resembles your structures within Paerlowe almost exactly."

"Yeah, I gotta say, my dude, it looks just like your stuff here." Seraphina stroked her hand over the frozen structure as Bleu sniffed the ice. "No, Bleu, don't!" The tigaris slapped his tongue against the ice before his eyes sprung open wide. Seraphina placed her head in her hands, "why do I bring you places?"

Maveri turned to see the tigaris slowly starting to panic, "oh, for the sake of the gods, here." Lifting his hands, a small azure flame flickered in his palm as the ice warmed. Bleu purred at the warming sensation and pulled his tongue away. "There you go, you daft sod. Now don't do it again."

"Well, I honestly didn't think you would make it this far. Bravo!" The oddly familiar voice resonated in their minds. "What do you think so far? It's glorious, isn't it?" The crimson beam thrummed through the body of the tower.

Arcturus readied his weapons. "I know that voice."

Of course. It had to be the loyalist nut that betrays us!

"Indeed you do, I would be offended if you had forgotten me already."

Khain's eyes scowled as he looked about the corridor, "archmage."

"Yes, yes, welcome, honour guard. Although can you still be named that? I mean, you did allow your Empress to sacrifice herself. Surely that should have been *your* job?"

Maveri strolled forward. "Yatuul? I thought you perished on that river."

"You thought wrong, wizard. Instead, I used its magic to bring you here faster. The crimson and I, well, we are one. To be perfectly honest, I had hoped to convert more of you on that river, especially that pesky or'kerec. But she disappeared so that solved part of the problem for me."

Hank slammed his fist against the ice. "She better not be dead you icy fuck!"

"Oh, such a fiery temper for such a little being." The voice chuckled. "One can only hope that she perished." Yatuul paused. "I see you've met some of the lost souls that are frozen here in time, aren't they fantastic specimens?"

Maveri stroked his goatee. "You have quite the collection."

"A collection I add to every day. Although I admit these rarities have taken a little longer to submit to the crimson. You see, the velgart weren't always what they are today, they were once a disgusting race of demonic-looking beings plagued by the fantasies of evil. The calastain were not fit for this realm. So, I changed them, I made them, perfect..."

Khain clutched his glaive tightly as his frost serpent swirled around him, "what do you mean by that, archmage?"

"You'll find out soon enough, honour guard." The ice wall beside Hank began to crack. "Or maybe you won't. It seems one of my specimens is ready to show you the true way of the crimson. Good luck."

Arcturus raised Aegis. "We need to get through that door."

Khain placed his hand against the triangular door. A spark of crimson energy repulsed him as it burned across his palm. "It looks like we aren't getting through it very easily." Hank stepped away from the cracking ice. Splinters of verglas shattered against the stone floor as an almighty howl echoed through the structure of the tower.

"Well, I suppose I get to meet a fenrick in the flesh," Maveri pulled his spellbook from his hip. "Don't let that thing bite you."

In an explosion of ice, the beast burst from its tomb. It towered over the group as its claws unfurled and its crimson eyes flared to life. Ruffles of dark brown fur covered its muscular body as it reverberated with rage. Two long canines extended past its lower jaw and an exposed bone-like horn lay across its snout before protruding out from its forehead. The beast snorted as it glared at the group, scanning over each of them while running its tongue over its razor-sharp teeth. Pulling its claws to its chest, it clenched its body and its form spasmed. The creature fell to its knees.

Seraphina summoned her two azure swords as she and Bleu stepped back to the rest of the group. "What the shit is happening?" A shard of crimson ice burst from the fenrick's chest, splitting into multiple fragments before then plunging into the rest of the beast's form. It shuddered as its once dark-furred body ruptured and turned opaque. The creature pulled itself to its feet as a white and crimson mist swirled around its silhouette. Two crystalline clawed hands breached through the mist as the fenrick ripped into sight. Great stalagmites sprouted from its shoulders and its now angular ice-born form shimmered in the twilight.

"What the fuck has happened to that thing!?" Hank lifted his fists, urging the stone beneath his feet to form into two elemental maces.

Maveri's brow furrowed. "It looks almost velgartian."

Arcturus clutched Karek'Thur, "whatever it is, it needs to die."

"Is this what I am? Is this how I was made?" Khain looked down at his hands.

Maveri glanced over, "we will have time to discover that after we have dealt with this beast." Unleashing a ravenous howl, the fenrick leapt at the group. Arcturus lifted Aegis as its golden barrier blossomed. The beast's claws slashed against the shield, leaving trails of crimson through the golden magic. Stepping back, the fenrick slammed its shoulder into the barrier, shattering it.

Arcturus steadied himself, "two can play at that game." He pushed forward, gripping Aegis as its golden core shone brightly. With each strike, the beast effortlessly stepped aside before lunging back at him. A rib-shattering slam smashed against his cuirass as the beast's almighty claw breached his defence. The force threw him into the glacial wall cracking the ice around him while he slid to the floor, gasping for breath. Bleu flashed to life in front of the legionnaire. He snarled at the fenrick as his stripes glowed in azure light.

"Gotcha!" Seraphina screamed out as she landed on the velgartian beast's back. She plunged her blades deep into its core and grinned. Shards of ice rattled before launching from the fenrick's shoulders. They sliced through Seraphina's arms and forced her from its back. The beast turned and grabbed her by the neck, lifting her from the ground. Crimson light thrummed through its body as it glared into her eyes. It slowly began to clench its fist. A glacial glaive ripped through the fenrick's wrist, forcing it to drop Seraphina back to the ground.

Khain stepped beside her, "go into the shadows; you've done your part." Seraphina nodded and dispersed into the darkness.

The fenrick snarled and grabbed the honour guard's weapon. "Why do you fight me, brother? We are one and the same, you and I." Its gruff rumbling voice pulsated in the group's minds. "Let us show you the path to true perfection."

"No. Let me show you something instead." The honour guard tore his weapon from the beast. Pulling back, he angled his glaive at the fenrick, "consider this a welcome present." He threw the weapon as it spiralled through the air, crashing against the beast's chest with a sundering force.

The fenrick's feet scraped along the stone while it tried to hold its ground. Hank sprinted from behind the creature. Slamming his maces against its ankle, he shattered its glacial structure. Maveri followed as he pelted azure missiles into its core before reaching Khain's side.

"Let me help ya with that," Hank lifted his hammers. Two large stone bricks ripped from the floor behind him and into the air. He thrust his weapons forward, commanding the stone into the fenrick's chest. The beast flew back with such an almighty impact that it smashed through the triangular door and into the centre of a large hexagonal pillared room.

Arcturus clutched his abdomen. "Well fought." Bleu searched the room for Seraphina before whimpering and dispersing into the shadows.

"It looks to me like we found a way to open that door," Maveri smirked.

Khain lifted his hand as his glaive returned, "it does seem that way." The group moved to the door to see a great spiral staircase leading up to a second platform.

"Where's the fenrick?" Arcturus looked around the room.

Hank chuckled, "looks like we might have shattered the poor thing."

"I don't think so, dwethren," Khain gestured to a trail of splintered ice leading up the stairs.

"Then I guess that's where we go next." Arcturus cracked his neck and took a deep breath. "Seraphina, Bleu, if you can hear me, we are moving to the second floor." The group moved deeper into the room as they walked to the stairs.

"So many beings all trapped here, and for what? To be turned into velgart?" Khain gazed over the frozen tombs along the walls. "Is this really how my kind was created?"

Hank shrugged, "no clue mate, but it sounds like that Yatuul fella might have the answers."

"It would make sense." Maveri ran his hand through his quiff. "For aeons, no one has entered this land due to its harsh conditions. What if it wasn't a natural occurrence?"

Khain looked to Maveri, "what are you trying to say, wizard?"

"Deythron wasn't always the harsh icescape we know it to be now." Maveri glanced at the honour guard.

What if during all this time, Deythron had been used as a veil for some horrific experiment?

Arcturus' brow furrowed. "Are you saying that Yatuul turned Deythron into what it is today?"

"Maybe not Yatuul, but someone or something might have. I don't know, I'm just thinking out loud." Maveri turned back to the stairs, "come on, we have to finish off that fenrick." They climbed the stairs in silence as their footsteps echoed around the glacial structure.

I think he's onto something.

"It seems, my dear Torric, that we have some guests." A slender feminine velgart draped in verglas robes stood in the centre of the room. Her form was smooth and polished with a more skeletal outline. She stepped forward and pulled a great staff carved from bone from her back.

"Ah, it seems you're right, Fanelda." Beside her stood a slender, flamboyant velgart with a sharp almost serrated structure. "Isn't this sweet? Our reunion brought to light for such pathetic idiots."

"Well, Torric, I believe it was this beast here that freed us." Fanelda urged her bone staff toward the wounded fenrick.

Torric's crimson eyes glimmered, "aww no, the poor thing is hurt. We can't let them kill it, can we now?"

"No, no! Of course not. Maybe I should give us some more friends, just to make sure we keep them away from this poor beast." Fanelda's eyes sadistically smiled.

"What a stupendous idea!" Torric's core glimmered as he adjusted his cufflike verglas on his wrists. Fanelda raised her staff as her form ignited, pouring her crimson essence into the stone. Energy swirled amongst the cracks before forming into frost-born skeletal elementals.

Arcturus glared as the clattering army raised before the group, their eyes bursting to life in crimson flames. "Why is it never simple?"

"Because a simple life is a boring life, lad. Now let's kill these fuckers and stop this crimson shite," Hank grinned, readying his maces. Pulses of crimson ignited the room as the high anticipation of combat thickened the air.

29

A VELGARTIAN END

Maveri levitated his spellbook as glorious, azure magical glyphs swirled around him. He pelted missiles of pure energy into the shamble of enemies, carving off chunks of ice with each hit.

"I got ya, lad!" Hank stormed forward and countered two of the skeleton's attacks. Smashing his maces into their abdomens, he shattered them. "Oh, this is the stress relief I needed today!" Gambolling forward, he stood between several enemies and chuckled. "Where the fuck is Gathera? She would love this!" Golden light ricocheted around him as he watched the image of Aegis decimate the foes with ease. He looked to Arcturus, "now you're just showin' off, laddy."

Maveri pulled his palms apart as crackles of azure lightning formed between them. "Kill the necromancer, then all these things di-" In a thud of almighty force, the fenrick charged into the wizard. Trapping him in its vice-like grip, it slammed him against the glacial wall.

"Legionnaire, help your friend. Let me deal with these two!" Khain sprinted at Fanelda while twirling his glaive. An ice torrent surrounded the honour guard as he unleashed a serrated blizzard at the velgart.

Fanelda raised her staff as a crimson barrier engulfed her. "My, my, you're a feisty one!" She slammed her staff against the floor, sending a pulse of crimson at Khain.

The honour guard dodged aside before shunting Fanelda against the ice. "You are a disgrace to my kind!" He thrust his glaive against her throat.

"Tut, tut," Torric ripped Khain's glaive from his grasp. "I believe it is you who is the disgrace." Before the honour guard could react, the velgart plunged the weapon into his back.

Fanelda's eyes smiled as she watched the pain burn through Khain's soul. "Oh dear, it seems your little manoeuvre didn't work." She glanced over to Torric. "Maybe you should show him the true path." Sliding away from the honour guard, she chuckled.

Arcturus, help him!

"Khain!" Arcturus screamed out as he fought through the onslaught of skeletal enemies. He clutched Aegis and unleashed a burst of solar light, melting his immediate foes and clearing a path to the fenrick. The beast turned and swiped at the legionnaire. Arcturus slid onto his knees and carved Karek'Thur through its glacial legs, "you are really pissing me off." As the creature lost its balance, Arcturus stood behind it with his weapons primed. "Maveri, you need to get up." Glancing at the wizard, he saw a large tear in his glorious cloak.

Blood spurted from Maveri's shoulder as he clutched his wound. "This can't be good." His jaw clenched as he spoke.

"You're hurt?" Arcturus' face became awash with concern. "Shit, do you have any potions?" As he spoke, the fenrick dragged itself along the ice towards him.

Maveri nodded. "In my satchel, but it's over there," he gestured to the worn leather bag lying where the wizard once stood.

"Of course they are." Arcturus scowled at the bag, then back to the fenrick and the assaulting skeletons. "I can't get to it without leaving you vulnerable."

No, don't leave him, we need him.

"Just go! I can defend mys-gah!" As Maveri pulled his hand away, he felt the pain tear through his arm and into his chest. Arcturus shook his head and slung Aegis at the skeletons. A deep bellowing groan echoed out from the floor above as footsteps rumbled on the ice ceiling.

"Oh, I don't like that at all!" Hank looked up to see a large, silhouetted figure moving around above them, "what the fucks up there?!" Slamming his maces into the skeletons surrounding him, he didn't break sight of the ceiling.

Fanelda's eyes smirked. "Seems we have another guest, Torric, hurry up and sort out that pesky warrior."

Torric nodded and wrapped his hands around Khain's skull. "Let me show you perfection." He pulled the honour guard's head back and glared into his eyes. Crimson began purging from Torric's soul into Khain's. Writhing in agony, the honour guard attempted to break free. A gorgeous spark of azure magic tore through Torric as Bleu ripped the velgart into pieces.

"Leave him alone you shits!" Seraphina burst to life from the shadows as she carved through the surrounding skeletons with her azure blades. Falling to his knees, Khain slammed his head against the glacial wall. Seraphina turned and knelt beside him, "no, no, come on dude, you got this. You're gunna be okay."

The turquoise glimmer in Khain's eyes grew weaker. "Thank you, Seraphina. I know you will be a beacon of hope in this world."

"I'm sorry, I should've been here sooner," she placed her hand against the honour guard's face.

Khain's eyes focussed on Seraphina. "No, you've done all you could. Never forget your worth."

Bleu growled as he scratched at the ice next to Khain. "What is it, Bleu?" Seraphina looked up to see a faintly familiar face in the tomb, "wait, that's that guy from Vavarinu." She slowly placed Khain against the floor and summoned her blades, "well, let's hope he's still alive and on our side. Bleu, cover me!" Driving her azure swords into the ice, she tore apart the tomb.

Faint glimmers of ethereal light began sparkling before her while she carved deeper. The tower rumbled as cracks formed along the glacial walls.

"Finally." The figure raised its head and smiled. Clutching its fists, it became surrounded by ethereal magic before exploding out of the ice. "I appreciate the assistance." Wreyth placed his hand on Seraphina's shoulder.

"Dude, we really need your help," Seraphina smiled.

"If that archmage didn't lock me up in there, I would have been helping you from the start." Wreyth looked down at Khain, "who's that? And do I need to kill it or help it?"

Seraphina crouched down. "Help him if you can!"

Wreyth nodded. "Aleiá, fancy helping this thing out?"

"It would be my pleasure." A haze of ethereal light blossomed beside Wreyth as the demon appeared. "His soul is weak; I will need time to heal him." She glanced up at Seraphina. "Please keep those things away from me." She gestured at the incoming skeletons.

Frozen in shock at the demon's form, Seraphina raised her brow, "uh, yeah, sure."

"Let's play," Wreyth pulled his hands to his sides as bolts of ethereal magic formed in his palms. Slinging them effortlessly forward, he punched the magic through the skeletons. Seraphina twirled her swords and joined Bleu in the fray as they fought their way to Fanelda. Seeing the skeletal horde before him being ripped apart, Hank looked back to the ceiling and then to the leather satchel on the ground.

The dwethren picked up the bag and shook it. "Hey, anyone lost this?"

"It's Maveri's! We need it over here!" Arcturus called out as he held Aegis' barrier against the claws of the assaulting fenrick, "even with no legs you're a pain in the ass!" He clutched his buckler tightly and released an explosion of solar magic. The beast howled as the blinding light cursed its vision. It swiped and writhed to find the legionnaire until Karek'Thur's burning blade burst through its chest. Arcturus twisted the sword while watching the crimson disperse and the fenrick turn to dust.

"Here ya go lad!" Hank tossed over the satchel.

"Not so fast," Fanelda glided over and caught the strap around her staff.

The dwethren shook his head. "For fuck's sake." He jumped forward. With a smirk, the velgart slammed her staff on the ground. A crimson shard of ice burst from the floor, slicing Hank in two. His dismembered body slammed against the frozen structure with a dull thud and his maces slid to a halt by Fanelda's feet. "It's been a joy fighting with you, but you took one of mine, so I'll take one of yours." She strapped the bag around her shoulder and swiftly climbed the spiral staircase.

No! Hank!

"Hank!" Arcturus screamed out as he launched Aegis at the remaining skeletons. Storming through their ranks, he tore them apart as Wreyth,

Seraphina and Bleu all fought beside him. The legionnaire slid to his knees as the final foe fell, gripping the dwethren's head in his hands.

Hank coughed and spluttered blood. "I really didn't see that comin'." He tried to swallow. "Don't worry lad, you got this. If ya ever see Gathera again, tell her how brave I was, won'tcha? I feel like this is a sacrifice that you'll tell in the great tales of this war…" His jaw fell agape as the final breath seeped from his lungs.

Arcturus placed his forehead against the dwethren's. "I will, Haeckel. You will be remembered."

"Wreyth, I think it's too late…" Aleiá pulled away from Khain as his core began burning with crimson light.

Seraphina dropped her swords. "No!" She sprinted over to the honour guard. "What did that bastard do to you?!"

"Looks to me like whatever wounded him has cursed his soul with crimson." Wreyth placed a hand on her shoulder, "there's nothing we can do for him now." He looked to Aleiá. "Could you check on the wizard for me? I'll deal with this."

The demon snarled. "Fine." She walked off, "I'm always saving this bastard wizard."

Wreyth turned back to Seraphina, "did you want to do it, or should I?"

"Surely there's another way." Tears rolled down Seraphina's cheek.

Wreyth exhaled. "If anyone can save a soul, it's Aleiá. We just don't seem to be able to do anything about curing this crimson plague." He paused, "it seems the only way to cure it, is to kill it."

Seraphina wiped her eyes and sat in silence for a while. "I'll do it." Wreyth nodded and walked away to Maveri and Aleiá. The distinct sound of shattering ice resonated behind him as he knelt to the wizard, "how are you doing? Not feeling all crimsony, are ya?"

Maveri smirked. "No, I'll be fine," he looked up to Aleiá. "What would we do without you?"

"You would die." The demon growled and stood. "He needs a potion or a proper healer, but he should be stable for now."

Thank the gods!

Arcturus lay the dwethren's torso down and wiped the tears from his eyes. "It looks like we have a satchel to find." He turned to the group as Seraphina and Bleu joined them. "There's something else up those stairs and we don't know what other things that velgart might have summoned. We need to tread carefully and fight with our heads, not our hearts." The group moved to the base of the stairs and slowly began to climb to the next floor. Arcturus stopped as his sightline raised over the ice flooring to see an empty room much like the ones below. "Hmm, I don't see anything." They walked into the room and scanned the area to see one of the walls smashed apart.

"There are no stairs in this room, how do we climb higher?" Wreyth looked to the ceiling, "this definitely isn't the top."

Maveri slowly walked to the shattered wall. "It would seem the staircase is on the outer of the building from here on." He felt the piercing cold beat against his skin and moved back to the centre of the room. "But going out there might prove challenging without the dwethren's spell."

I might be able to help, my love. Keep them close as you climb those stairs, and I will keep them warm.

Arcturus nodded. "Stay close to me, I should be able to warm us for a short while out there."

"As long as it's long enough to get us to the next floor," Wreyth paused, "then sure, let's stand by the legionnaire."

Aleiá rolled her eyes, "we don't need the heat, Wreyth. I'm a demon and you're a soul."

"Ha, good point," Wreyth chuckled, "then fuck it, do what you want." He moved to the smashed wall and looked out into the treacherous snowstorm. "You guys are really gonna need some heat though, it's not nice out here." The group huddled behind Arcturus as he lifted Aegis against the snow. Karek'Thur hummed gently in his hand as a faint dome of golden light surrounded them in comforting warmth.

Go now, I can't hold it for long.

30
<u>FOR VENGEANCE!</u>

A sudden rupture shook the floor. Arcturus glanced up to see splinters of ice cascading down. "Move!" The legionnaire pushed the group out onto the ledge. Blinding sunlight screamed through their unadjusted eyes before the vast, mountainous landscape blossomed before them. Thick snow beat against the glacial tower, leaving a soft layer on the stairs.

"Careful, we don't know how solid this ice is." Maveri carefully led the group up the steps. Arcturus gazed over the vista; the great mountains breached the clouds with their erratic points as glacial rocs flew around them with playful glee.

Even in times like these, you still enjoy the view.

"I'm sorry Seraphina, I'm sorry I couldn't save your friend." Aleiá looked over her shoulder.

Seraphina ran her hand across Bleu's mane, "don't worry, I know you tried. I just wish I could have done more for him."

"His kind did this to him, not you. You can't feel bad for that." Aleiá released a coy smile. "It's sweet you care so much though; you remind me of this one. That is when he's not being a dick." She gestured to Wreyth.

Seraphina chuckled, "thank you. Hey, he doesn't seem too bad."

"Go through the shit my people and I went through, and you'd be a dick too." Wreyth glanced over to Aleiá.

The demon rolled her eyes. "I know the shit you went through; you wouldn't still be alive without me." A strong gust of wind lifted the snow and pelted the group. Maveri uncovered his eyes and wiped away the snow. His sight focussed on a large silhouette masked by the bright sun. Tilting its head, the creature released a bellowing roar.

"I know that roar!" The wizard pulled his spellbook from his hip and flicked open the pages. An almighty torrent of crimson flames flourished from the wyvern's cavernous maw. Maveri locked his wrists together as an azure barrier formed between him and the flames. Holding strong, he glanced down to the stairs as the ice swiftly began to melt.

"Wizard!" Wreyth pulled his arms aside as ethereal magic formed in his palms. He pushed his left-hand forwards as ghost-like vines swirled at the beast. As the ethereal magic entwined around the wyvern's throat, Wreyth pulled. Its jaw closed and the flames halted before it writhed back and forth, trying to break free.

Maveri stumbled away from the melting steps. "Quickly, the ice won't hold much longer!" The group moved up to meet the wizard. "Wreyth, come on!" The calastain glanced over as he tried to keep his grip on the beast.

"Ugh, fine." Turning as the ethereal vines dispersed, he ran up the stairs. His boots crunched with each step until they met the frictionless slush. Slipping, he slammed against the frozen stairs and clawed for grip. Cracks splinted in the weakened structure as the stairs behind him crumbled into the abyss.

Arcturus knelt and grabbed the calastain's hand. "Hold on!" A piercing screech called out from beside them as the wyvern recovered. "Maveri, deal with the beast!"

Pull him up, my love. We need all these allies alive for what might await us.

Fighting through the searing pain in his shoulder, the wizard lifted his hands as azure glyphs circled him. "Already on it." Sparkling missiles soared at the wyvern as they beat against its scales.

Aleiá knelt beside Arcturus and gripped Wreyth's wrist. "Seraphina, help the caster." Seraphina nodded and pulled several azure kunai from her hip. In a graceful flurry, she hailed them at the beast. Distracted by the onslaught of magic, the wyvern failed to avoid the blades. One span through the commotion and lodged into the beast's eye. Screaming in pain, the almighty creature thrashed in the skies before slamming into the structure above the group.

Maveri glanced up. "Watch out!" He pulled Seraphina aside as Bleu leapt over them. Great shards of ice broke from the structure of the tower and smashed through the staircase between the group.

My love, we don't have much time left. I feel my magic faltering.

Arcturus clenched his jaw as he pulled Wreyth up with all his might. With the combined strength of the demon and legionnaire, the calastain clawed back onto the remnants of the stairs. Attempting to steady its flight, the wyvern faced the group.

"Shit, we need to get over that gap." Arcturus moved to the edge of the stairs to size up the several-foot jump.

Wreyth scowled for a second then looked to Aleiá. "I have an idea. Come back to me." The demon nodded as her physical form turned ethereal and she melded into Wreyth. "I'll get over there first, then you jump to me."

Arcturus frowned. "I can't make that jump!"

"Just trust me," Wreyth smiled. Furling his hands, he stepped to the ledge as his form turned ethereal. In a dash of glorious soul magic, Wreyth appeared on the opposite side in a cloud of eerie green smoke. Arcturus stood in disbelief. "Now, legionnaire, jump to me!" Wreyth gestured for him to follow.

We have no other choice.

Arcturus shook his head and stepped back. As the beast beside him released a bellowing roar of flames, the legionnaire sprinted and leapt at the group. The searing heat exploded against the structure and decimated the stairs behind him. Arcturus watched the ledge drop before his eyes, still a couple of feet away. Dragging the flames to follow the legionnaire, the wyvern adjusted its flight path. Exhaling in disbelief, Arcturus' heart dropped until a strange sensation engulfed his core. He gazed at the ethereal vines wrapping around him before being pulled up to Wreyth. The ice crunched as his breastplate slammed against it and the group hauled him to his feet.

"I got you," Wreyth dismissed the vines.

Arcturus' eyes welled with relief, "thank you, Wreyth."

"Don't think you can relax yet, legionnaire." Maveri stood clutching his shoulder. "This will take all I have left," he held his palms against each other and formed a great ball of azure flames. "I need you all to get behind me."

Arcturus crouched before him and raised Aegis, "slay the beast." Maveri smirked before releasing the blazing magic. The hulking orb of erratic fire exploded against the wyvern's chest, engulfing it in bright azure light. Screams echoed out over the icescape as the body of the creature burned to a cinder.

Aleiá stepped beside the wizard. "I'll take the kill if you don't mind." She lifted her scythe before hurling it at the wyvern. Its blade sliced through the beast's burning skull, silencing it. Aleiá recalled her weapon and lifted her hand, ripping the soul from the beast as it plummeted out of sight. The structure of the tower reverberated as a pulse of crimson rose to the large hexagonal structure at its tip.

"We need to get up there." Arcturus turned to the group, "Seraphina, do you see a way back into the tower?"

"It looks like there's some sort of door here." She placed her hand against it and the ice slid aside. "Oh, it's open!" The group sprinted up to join her.

Maveri ambled beside Arcturus as he aided him up the stairs. "We need to get you that potion."

"Your dumb man-bag has nothing inside it, why do you want it back so badly?" The necromancer smiled. "Not to worry, you won't need it now anyway." She slammed her staff against the ice. Her body cracked and fragmented with crimson light as her form changed. A shocking blast of crimson light sundered from Fanelda as her new body burst to life. Eight angular spinelike legs clamped against the ice, holding her bulbous glacial abdomen in place. Six glaring eyes locked upon Arcturus as he slowly stepped back.

"A fucking arachgnite, how did she turn into that?" the legionnaire scowled in disbelief. A booming guttural cry exploded from Fanelda, reverberating upon the cracked floor. Her form spasmed as she launched several crimson bolts at the party. Splitting to opposite sides of the room, Arcturus dragged Maveri aside with Wreyth. At the points of impact, the bolts ruptured into four-foot-tall arachlings. Their appearance was much like that of the arachgnite, yet slimmer and sharper. Wreyth's eyes widened as the creatures lunged toward him. Dodging their ghastly fangs, he awaited an opening to strike. He thrust his hand forward to release a spread of erratic ethereal magic. The arachlings beside him shattered.

"My babies!" Screeching out, Fanelda began scaling the wall, "you will die for that!" The arachgnite's body reverberated as the satchel swung from its core. Arcturus beat another arachling aside before spinning his blade in his palm and driving it through, shattering the creature.

"We need that satchel," the legionnaire looked over to a paling Maveri, "and we need it now."

Wreyth nodded. "Protect the wizard. I'll grab it with the others." Punching through the arachlings, he forced himself to the opposite side of the room. Arcturus readied his shield as swarms of arachlings scaled the walls and floors around him. Hurling Aegis, its image tore through the crystalline insects. He spun and carved apart the arachlings as they pounced at him. Fighting one, then another, then another, he felt the fatigue surging through his muscles.

Bleu and Seraphina appeared beside him. "We thought you could use some help." They aided in carving through the creatures before Bleu's body slammed against the wall. "Bleu?" Seraphina looked aside to see the Tigaris pinned to the wall by verglas webbing. She moved over, readying her blades to free her companion before being pinned to the floor by a similar webbing.

"You will all die here! There is no stopping perfection!" Fanelda screeched out from the ceiling.

Aleiá rolled her eyes, "we need to kill her, she's really pissing me off." She grasped two arachlings and smashed them together. "Got any ideas, Wreyth?"

"That web looks like it holds anti-magical qualities. If we get stuck in that, we won't get out." Wreyth looked around the room. "I can't reach her from here, but there has to be a way." He spied the image of Aegis returning to the legionnaire's shield. "Ah-ha! That can reach her. Once she's down with us, then she's fair game."

"Great id—" as Aleiá spoke, verglas webbing pinned her to the wall, "fuck."

Wreyth chuckled, "surely it doesn't work against soul magic, right?"

Aleiá attempted to dismiss her physical form as the web ignited in crimson light. "Shit! That fucking hurts!"

"Oh wait, yeah, no she's a necromancer, so yeah it works against sou—" Wreyth's body slammed to the ice, "of course." Arcturus glanced around at his webbed allies and shook his head. Looking at Fanelda, he hurled Aegis. The golden image of the shield sang as it ripped through the oncoming verglas webbing. Fanelda recoiled in shock, barely avoiding the buckler. The shield tore apart the webbing holding up the arachgnite, dropping her to the floor. With a resounding crack, the flooring splintered in several places as her feet pierced the ice.

"Legionnaire, you don't win this fight. Your allies are incapacitated, and your magic is weak. You won't stop perfection, Yatuul has promised so much." Fanelda circled Arcturus.

The legionnaire clicked his shoulders and adjusted his weapons. "You know, I try my best to see the beauty in everything I can, but this crimson is nothing more than a plague. Nor'ai has lived through it all; the Great War, famine, conflict, unyielding deserts and racial extinctions, but against all odds, this realm survives. What makes you think this plague is anything more than just another blip in history?"

Fanelda chuckled, "because this is no plague. This magic is a beautiful blend of chaos and harmony, life and death, good and bad. Everything you could ever want to be is given to you with not a moment lost. Combine all of that with the boundless existence of the velgart and what do you get? Perfection."

"You all talk of this 'perfection'; every single one of you cursed by this plague mentions it. This is not perfection; this is blind ignorance. For magic that possesses your soul and contorts you to do its bidding. You become nothing but pawns in a game. Do you truly think that magic from outside this realm is just going to allow you to harness it without an ulterior motive?" Arcturus scowled as he gazed into Fanelda's multiple crimson eyes.

"Don't talk wet! You know nothing of the crimson!" She slammed her spined feet into the ice.

Don't talk wet? She's the worst. Kill this damn arachgnite and be done with this.

The legionnaire shook his head. "I know that it's taken everything from me, everything I've ever loved or cared for. I know that if my mother was here, she would be sickened by how this realm has been plagued by false promises and lies. And I know that no magic is ever given without taking part of you for itself, especially magic like this." Arcturus clenched his jaw as tears formed in his eyes. "For years we study the magic of this realm, whether we are born with it, learn to handle it or have it bestowed upon us. Nor'ai gives us so much while asking us to use it honourably. Magic is not a just gift; it is not something you just harness without ever giving it a second thought. Magic is life, a life that Nor'ai breathes into us so that we can use it in harmony with her, not against her."

Fanelda scraped her spines along the ground. "Oh you sweet little idiot, do you not see that we are trying to improve this realm? The velgart will be a peaceful race born of power, nothing will ever be able to harm these lands again!" She pulled back as her body furled under itself and launched a hail of verglas webbing at the legionnaire, pinning him to the wall. "In some ways, it's a shame that you won't live to see this new world." Her spindly leg scraped across his cheek, slicing his skin, "but then again, you would never appreciate a perfect world. What you might appreciate is me devouring all of your friends as I force you to watch." Fanelda pulled away and clawed her way over to Maveri, "what about this one? The little wizard pet," she turned to Seraphina, "or that sorry excuse for a shadowborne? Oh, so many choices…" Pulling back, she exposed her glacial fangs and then lowered herself to Maveri.

31
LIGHT A PATH

Arcturus clutched Aegis and Karek'Thur as he glared at Fanelda. "Maeve, if you can hear me, I need your help." He shifted his body trying to pry himself from the web. Karek'Thur hummed in his palm. "Is that you?"

Fanelda glanced up, "to whom are you talking? You're ruining this for me!"

I'm trying my best!

Arcturus frowned, "I'm ready when you are!" He closed his eyes. Several jade arrows punched into the glacial magic holding his arms.

"Did someone call for some help?" Gathera grinned as she readied more arrows.

"Gathera!" Seraphina called out with glee as she watched the or'kerec free her allies.

"Told ya I'll be a fuckin' hero one day!" The or'kerec turned to see Fanelda. "What the fuck is that?"

Arcturus pulled his arms from the wall, ripping through the verglas webbing. Carefully stepping back to the floor, he nodded to Gathera and smiled, "thank you." His weapons shone with the majesty of the sun as he stepped toward the arachgnite with the or'kerec by his side. He glanced to Gathera, "that is some velgartian, arachgnite, necromancer amalgamation that we need to kill."

I knew she would be back.

"I see! Ah, ah, ah, back away from the wizard!" Gathera loosed a storm of jade arrows into the oncoming arachgnites.

Arcturus grinned. "Oh, and we'll be taking that satchel now." He slung the image of Aegis, smashing Fanelda aside. Lunging forward, he swung Karek'Thur with all his might. The blade seemed to tear through the crisp atmosphere before eviscerating Fanelda's legs as she tried to defend herself.

"You can't win this. There is no point in trying!" Her glacial body quivered in pain as she scurried back. The ground crunched as she stepped on the remnants of her legs and arachlings decorating the floor. In desperation, she launched bolts of webbing at the legionnaire. Karek'Thur carved through them with ease as the golden image of Maeve flickered around the warrior.

Arcturus smiled, "legionnaires don't try, we succeed." His voice harmonised with Maeve's glorious tone. He carved Karek'Thur through her head and ripped the satchel from her core. Fanelda's body shuddered before falling to the ground, convulsing in golden light. The webbing encasing the party melted as Fanelda's corpse turned to crimson dust.

"Well fought, Arcturus." Wreyth nodded and turned to Maveri to see his bloodshot eyes and pale complexion. "Shit, you really aren't looking great bud, I have to say." The group surrounded Maveri as he lay motionless.

"Wizard, we have your bag." Seraphina patted him gently on the forehead, but Maveri didn't respond. Without hesitation, she slapped him across the face. "Dude?"

That's one way to do it...

Maveri's eyes sprung open. "What in the dammed halls of Xelkorth was that for?" He glanced about the group as they waved the satchel at him. "Oh, right, I see now. Well, it took you long enough." He gestured to Gathera. "Where the bloody hell have you been?" He caught the bag as Arcturus carefully tossed it over. After rummaging around for a few seconds, the wizard removed a glass vial containing a shimmering maroon liquid. Without hesitation, he popped the cork and chugged the solution. Maveri sat up as the colour rushed back to his skin, "mmm you can't beat the taste of pure, unfiltered magic." He looked over his beaten allies. "Arcturus, I don't know how much more of this we can take."

The legionnaire crouched beside him. "I know, but I fear if we don't stop this now, it could be the end of Nor'ai."

"We have to keep going, we are so close." Seraphina grabbed the legionnaire's shoulder.

Aleiá looked over to Wreyth. "We've still got some fight left in us, right?"

"You can't stop the party now that I've finally arrived." Gathera grinned, looking around for Hank. "Wait, where's the stubborn little fucker and the ice guy?"

Arcturus placed his hand on her shoulder, "they didn't make it."

Gathera paused for a second, "oh."

"But Hank wanted me to let you know how brave he was. Although I think he might have meant that sarcastically now I say it out loud." Arcturus looked caringly into the or'kerec's eyes.

"Fuck." Gathera clenched her jaw and bowed her head. "I fuckin' knew he wasn't strong enough to come. I should never have let him join us."

"He wanted to fight for the realm," Maveri stood, "as we all do." He gestured to the wavering party. "Although, I didn't have this much trouble when all I did was search Nor'ai for riches. Oh, speaking of riches!" he muttered to himself as he rummaged around in his satchel once again. "Ah, ha! Here, each of you take one of these." Opening his hand, he revealed several shimmering crystals.

Seraphina picked one up and held it to the light. "What are they?" She watched glistening stars twinkle in the centre of the crystal.

"I call them 'oh shit' gems, but the proper term is warp crystals. If you crush that in your hand, it will portal you to a safe location within this realm in a heartbeat." Maveri ran his hand through his quiff. "I have been keeping them for a time when things might go royally south, and I have a feeling now might be that time."

Seraphina licked the gem. "Woah, that's so cool!" she looked over the group as they all stared at her, "what?!" Bleu brushed against her. "Oh yeah, what about Bleu?"

Maveri raised his finger and paused. "Just make sure you're touching him when you crush it."

Arcturus chuckled. "Maybe once this is done, wizard, you'll be able to return to your life of riches and rarities."

Maveri rolled his eyes. "Your optimism is annoying. I think I have enough left in me for a few more spells, but I'll drink a mana potion just to be sure."

"Smart thinking, caster. We haven't consumed too many souls but I'm sure we will have enough in us." Wreyth clicked his neck. "Aleiá, if shit hits the wall in there, return to me. If you die, I die."

Aleiá grunted, "I know how it works, dipshit, I was the one who brought you back, remember?"

Wreyth chuckled. "I remember."

Gathera turned to Maveri, "how do you know these gems won't kill us? Have you used them before?"

Pausing mid-swallow, Maveri pulled the potion from his lips and wiped his goatee, "define 'used them before...'"

"It's a fairly simple question she asked; have you had first-hand experience with using one of these gems?" Aleiá walked over to the wizard.

Maveri cocked a smile. "Well, not personally, no. But I have studied them."

"Studied?" The demon tilted her head. "Surely the study would be to use it?"

Maveri glanced aside to Wreyth, "umm, well yes, but there are many magical tests one can do without using the item."

Wreyth recoiled, "don't look at me like that, answer her questions. I'm not here to protect you."

Looking at Maveri, Arcturus frowned. "And you trust these tests?"

"Well, yes! Of course I do!" Maveri stood tall.

"And you're happy to risk all of our lives on tests?" Seraphina wiped her gem.

Maveri scowled, "yes. I do not know where you will end up, but I know you will be safe."

"You do realise the beating you'll get if this fuckin' gem doesn't work properly, right?" Gathera pulled her axe from her hip.

"I fear I do now." Maveri looked aside cautiously.

"Well, let's hope we don't have to use them," Wreyth shrugged and placed his gem in his pocket. The group moved to the large spiral staircase at the edge of the room and slowly began their ascent. Arcturus led the way as he held Aegis primed. Walking around twists and turns, the group watched as the structure of the tower hummed increasingly violently with crimson. Eventually, they stopped at a great glacial door blocking the way ahead.

"Once through here, I can imagine there's no turning back." Arcturus turned to the group, "are you all ready?"

Seraphina grinned as Bleu raised his back. "Ready."

Wreyth pulled his hands to his sides as ethereal magic bloomed to life around him. "Ready."

"I'm fuckin' ready." Gathera firmly gripped her bow.

Aleiá dragged her scythe along the glacial wall. "Ready." They all paused for a moment as they waited for Maveri. Glancing back, they watched the wizard as he twirled his moustache in his reflection.

"Maveri?" Arcturus frowned.

"Hmm?" The wizard looked aside.

"Are you ready?"

Maveri dismissed the question, "yes, yes, open the door."

Arcturus chuckled and turned to the door, "my love, are you ready?"

Always.

"I thank you all so much for what you have done, I couldn't imagine fighting beside anyone else." The legionnaire pressed his hand against the ice. It ignited in crimson light before slowly sliding aside.

32
IN CRIMSON WE TRUST

Their eyes scanned across the great pentagonal room. Its features closely resembled that of the towers back in Paerlowe but with a sharper angular twist. The ceiling extended high above the group into a great pointed tip and the walls surrounding them crackled with pulses of opaque crimson light.

"Welcome, welcome adventurers." Yatuul glided across from the dimly lit edge of the room and clasped his hands. "I hope your journey wasn't too perilous."

Wreyth stepped forward as the ethereal magic swirled around him. "Enough, velgart, we are finishing this little crimson nightmare you've created."

"Oh, really? That is a great shame. You see, I have barely even started. To finish now would be foolish." Yatuul's eyes smirked. "Oh, good. You found your green friend."

Gathera snarled, "yeah it is good. Means I can rip you apart."

Yatuul rolled his eyes. "I'm sure you will."

"Can you not see what you're doing to this realm? This crimson will consume all of Nor'ai if you don't stop." Arcturus walked toward the archmage.

Yatuul shook his head. "Do you not see that that's my intention?"

"Archmage, what are you saying?" Maveri clenched his fists.

"I guess I'll have to spell it out for you." Yatuul glided over to an altar in the centre of the room. Its appearance was dark and sharp as if carved from ancient stone. Runes were etched along its side with ripples of crimson pulsing within its core. "You see, the races of this realm are awful, poorly designed and weak. You squabble, you fight, you kill all while doing nothing with your lives or furthering Nor'ai's progress. In my design, I will make you peaceful and powerful, an intelligent race with no memory of your former lives."

Seraphina shifted around the group. "You want to make us all velgart?"

"Precisely. No more deals with disgusting demons, no more war, no more hatred, just life. Wouldn't that be better for this realm? Do you not see it? All of your kind have torn your own little holes in this world and for what? To feel like you own something. I have already wiped one race clean from this world and I can tell you that we are better off for it." His eyes scowled at Wreyth, "or at least I thought I had."

"I knew it was you!" Aleiá stormed to Wreyth's side "You are the one who led the mages into the forests of Leltanor and killed thousands of defenceless calastain!"

Yatuul pulled back a little while pressing his hand against his chest. "I knew I felt a demon's presence here. So, it was you who saved this abomination then? That's good to know. The calastain were not helpless or defenceless, they were demon worshipers! A race solely born around the purpose of leading your kind to our realm."

"No, you're wrong. My people were mostly druids, in tune with nature and Nor'ai herself. We preserved this realm, helped her become the goddess she is today." Wreyth clenched his fist, "you took everything from me."

Yatuul clasped his hands together. "I turned your kind into something more. No longer a plague on this realm, instead, something valuable and perfect. The calastain were a blight, much like every other race."

"Let me get this right, your plan for peace and perfection begins with mass genocide and war?" Maveri stroked his goatee in thought.

"You are so narrow-minded. You see only what your life has conditioned you to see, not the truth, not the solution." Yatuul gestured to the tip of the spire. "Yes, I may have had to use a little help to get me here, but with this crimson, I have the means to create a better world with ease."

Gathera snarled. "If anyone here is narrow-minded, it's you mate. You bring this shit here and kill my family for this. That's twisted."

Arcturus clutched Karek'Thur. "Do you even know what this crimson can truly do? Or where it's from? This power does not want to be controlled, let alone used for some idiot's idea of peace."

"Everything can be controlled, legionnaire, your kind should know that best. You just have to have the means to do so." Yatuul glanced back to the group. "I fear we could dance around the true answer to this realm's problems all day. Instead, why don't I just show you the meaning of true perfection? Why don't you just give in now and join me?"

"I will never become one of your experiments." Arcturus raised Aegis as he snarled.

Maveri lifted his hand as sparkles of azure magic followed. "Your kind helped us fight against the crimson so your plan for peace and control seems like it has already failed."

"You're correct. That was not against my will, though. Yes, some of them were able to retain more of their former selves than I had hoped. Khain for one was a nightmare, but the rest were worthy sacrifices to drag you all here. You see, you are the only ones that have braved these harsh lands in an attempt to find the source of the crimson and stop it. The others will fight back against the immediate threat, but without people like you urging them to actively seek it out, they will leave me be until I'm ready." Yatuul tilted his head. "It's so easy to manipulate beings when you are the one who created them."

"You killed your own people just to drag us here?" Seraphina's brow furrowed. "You talk about all of this peace and perfection yet you're more than willing to sacrifice hundreds of your own kind to bring some adventurers to a big tower."

Yatuul's eyes smiled, "those were calastain, they were still worthless to me even as velgart."

This is disgusting. He is the plague that swamps these lands, and he doesn't even see it.

"I've heard enough!" Wreyth clenched his jaw. "You tore my kind and my life from me so now I'll do the same to you." He slung several ethereal bolts at the archmage.

"Worthless." Yatuul effortlessly flicked his staff as crimson light burned away the magic. "You are nothing, all of you are nothing, but with me, you could finally have a purpose."

Maveri pulled Wreyth back. "His magic is much stronger than ours."

"Then we fight him together; we have to end this," Wreyth snarled.

"Keep him focussed on your magic," Arcturus readied himself.

"The beautiful thing about speaking through telepathy is I'm already in your heads." Yatuul lifted his staff as multiple crimson ice shards formed before him. "I also know that you've used most of what you have on what came before me." The shards hurtled toward the group. Arcturus beamed Aegis' barrier around them as the magic pelted against it. Azure missiles, bolts of ethereal magic and glorious, jade arrows burst through the golden barrier. Yatuul stepped back as he countered each projectile. Arcturus pushed forward as his allies followed closely behind him, slinging their magic at the archmage. Swiftly forging a wall of ice, Yatuul repositioned himself. Raising his staff, he pointed it at the group. The gem upon its tip began to spin as a glacial steam burst from the weapon. In blinding white and crimson light, a beam of corrupted ice seared the golden barrier, freezing it instantly. Yatuul raised his hand and with a clench of his fist, he shattered the magic.

Aegis shuddered as if in pain. Holding it firmly, Arcturus attempted to form another barrier, but the shield lay dormant. Yatuul's eyes smiled as he readied his staff to form another beam of ice. In a flash of azure light, Seraphina appeared before the archmage, shunting him aside. The beam of corrupted ice resonated against the wall of the tower before dispersing. Yatuul locked his sight upon Seraphina, lifting his hand to her throat. Ice crept from the floor, encasing her feet and arms as he locked her in place. Seraphina attempted to meld but the crimson tore at her soul and locked her in place.

"Stay there, shadowborne." The archmage turned as Bleu pounced out from the shadows. Lifting his staff, he locked it against the beast's chest before a blast of ice magic sent the tigaris hurtling across the room. Ethereal vines formed around Yatuul's core as Wreyth slung his arm forth and wrenched him close. Without a second thought, he blasted him with erratic sparks of soul magic. Shards of ice shattered from the edge of the archmage's form and scattered across the floor. Yatuul thrust his hand forward, surging glacial magic through Wreyth's chest. Raising his staff, he effortlessly blocked Karek'Thur as Arcturus swung from beside him. Slamming the butt of his staff against the legionnaire, he pushed him away with a pulse of crimson. Erratic sparks of azure lightning burned against the archmage's shoulder as Maveri pushed his palms towards him. Yatuul's structure cracked as he tried to rebuff the magic. Turning his staff under the beam, he launched several shards of glacial magic at the wizard. Maveri broke focus as he formed an azure barrier to negate the attack.

Yatuul stood tall as the cracks in his shoulder pulsed with crimson. "Do you not see, wizard? The ways of the azure are nothing compared to crimson."

Maveri dismissed his barrier, "you're blind, Yatuul, that magic will consume you!"

"Good." The archmage lifted his staff as a beam of crimson stormed toward Maveri. His eyes smiled as he watched the manic desecration unfold. As the beam made contact, it split into smaller beams creating a cone around the wizard. Arcturus smirked after rolling to his aid to block the beam. Yatuul shook his head as Arcturus turned Aegis to direct the beam back at him, "nice try, legionnaire." He pulled his staff back and lifted it to the ceiling, forming a rain of glacial shards above them.

Gathera readied her bow and launched a volley of jade arrows to decimate the falling shards. "I'm so fuckin' fed up with your kind already." She sprinted across the room through the shower of ice. In a swift, elegant movement, she leapt against the wall and readied an almighty jade arrow. Loosing the projectile, she watched as Yatuul attempted to deflect the blow.

The archmage's body jolted as a burning green scythe ripped through his core. The searing pain screamed through his soul as Aleiá forced him down to his feet. His eyes narrowed in pain. "No!" The jade projectile ripped apart half of his face, scattering verglas across the room.

"Fitting that your end should come from a demon and an or'kerec," Aleiá smirked and grabbed the back of his head as her clawed fingers wrapped around his remaining skull.

"Your kind are weak, pathetic abominations that should never have existed within this realm!" Yatuul Raised his staff as a storm of glacial power poured through him.

Aleiá's eyes narrowed. "Strong words for a weak shard of frozen water!" She ripped her weapon from the archmage and turned him to face her. Shards dropped from Yatuul's cracked body, shattering on the ground.

Yatuul's eyes locked onto hers. "You can't stop it, it's too late."

Aleiá grinned. "It's never too late." Plunging her scythe into his core, she dragged it through his core allowing the crystalline shards to pour out. Her eyes darted from the shattering ice to Wreyth's lifeless body. "Fuck, no!" Aleiá sprinted over and placed her hand on his chest. Ethereal magic poured from her core into his as his eyes ignited back to life. "Get up you idiot!" Wreyth looked up as Aleiá's concerned eyes met his. "I will not have you dying on me!"

Wreyth scrambled to his feet as he gasped for air. "Fuck, thank you."

Aleiá glanced over to Seraphina. "Not her too!" She watched as Arcturus and Gathera slid to Seraphina's aid and began shattering the ice encasing her.

Glacial shards rattled along the ground as crimson magic began weaving Yatuul's body back together. "I told you, it's too late!"

Wreyth snarled, "wizard! We need to end this!" He rushed over to Maveri's side, "on my cast." He lifted his hand, forcing the ground surrounding Yatuul to burn with ethereal light. The wizard smirked and pulled his arms aside; the azure letters floating around him stopped and formed a circle. In one almighty push, a glorious beam of pure azure magic ignited the room. Wreyth pulled his hand down, causing a decimating explosion of soul magic to entwine within the azure light. The almighty desecration engulfed Yatuul and dispersed the crimson surrounding him into a hailstorm of mystical ice.

33
A CLIMACTIC END

Wreyth and Maveri exhaled as their magic slowly disappeared and the room fell silent. Arcturus pulled Seraphina free and Aleiá fell to her knees.

"Is there anything I can do for you?" Arcturus glanced at the exhausted demon.

Aleiá smirked, "once I take that velgart's soul, I'll be fine." Arcturus nodded.

"Bleu!" Seraphina dropped to the ground and dragged herself to Bleu's side. The tigaris lay against the glacial wall, heaving and panting in a pool of his own blood. Opening one eye, Bleu purred as Seraphina stroked him.

Arcturus frowned. "Is that it? Is it finally over?"

"Has anyone got a potion? I can't lose him!" Seraphina sat back against Bleu.

"It's okay, we have the aetherwell's magic in our possession," Maveri strolled over. "Wait, where is the aetherwell?"

"Don't worry, this will make sure he's okay for now." Gathera flashed a smile as she latched Anile's amulet around Bleu's neck. Subtle mint green magic shimmered over the tigaris as his pain eased.

Seraphina glanced up with a tearful smile, "thank you, I almost panicked and crushed this thingy." She looked to Bleu while holding the warp crystal in her palm, "you'll be okay buddy, I promise?" Bleu grunted in return.

"Give me a moment, I'll use my magic to locate the well," Maveri lifted his hands and scanned the room with his azure magic.

Seraphina wiped her face and helped Bleu to his feet. "I really can't thank you guys enough." She stepped forward and slipped on a shard of loose ice. Fumbling the crystal in her hand, she slammed to the ground.

"Careful!" Arcturus recoiled. In a blink of azure light, the warp crystal shattered against the floor in a glorious explosion, vanishing Seraphina, Gathera, and Bleu from existence.

Maveri turned to see the remnants of the portal dispersing, "what happened?"

"She smashed her warp crystal." Wreyth watched on in disbelief.

"Wait, and it took all three of them? Fascinating..." Maveri scratched his goatee. "So, if you smash it with such force, it creates a bigger portal. Good to know."

I can't believe those gems work.

The room shuddered as an erratic beam of crimson soared through the tower's structure, shattering its frozen aesthetic. As the ice crumbled the building on which they stood trembled and groaned.

"What in the hells is happening?" Arcturus shifted about the room to find some support. "I thought it was done!"

Wreyth steadied himself as best he could. "I think it might be time for us to use those gems too."

"No! I can't leave without finding that well!" Arcturus yelled over the sundering noise.

"Soon we won't be left here to use the damn well!" Maveri retorted as he searched the room. The floor slowly split open in its centre to reveal a pyramidic, well-like structure. They gazed over the glorious aetherwell as it rose up to meet them. Ancient markings decorated its perfectly crafted, pyramidic, brimstone structure. Ethereal wisps swirled around its centre as a beautiful green orb rose above it.

Arcturus gasped, "is that it?"

"Yes." Maveri stood in awe. "I have never seen one in person before." As the well settled in place, so did the surrounding structure.

"Think of the soul energy residing in that." Aleiá licked her lips.

Arcturus stepped forward, "you can use it after I bring her back. I can't have you sapping the life out of it."

What if it doesn't work, my love?

"It has to work." The legionnaire examined the well. "How do I use it?"

Maveri moved to his side. "If the rumours are true, you place the gem inside it and if it has enough remaining power it will bring her back to life."

Arcturus lifted Karek'Thur. "Well, here goes nothing then." He raised the blade. Ethereal wisps swirled from within the well and surrounded the weapon before pulling it from his hand. They watched Karek'Thur rise peacefully above the well for a moment. Arcturus smiled, "Come back to me, Maeve." The whisps slowly began seeping into the soul stone within the sword's guard turning it gently in the air.

I feel it, it's working!

"Wait, what's that in the well?" Wreyth glanced into the centre of the aetherwell. "That can't be right." A small spark of crimson light flickered in the deep viscous substance.

Maveri stepped back as crimson whisps slowly crept up to the blade. "No, I imagine that's not supposed to happen." He looked back to the group in concern, "Arcturus, remove the sword."

"What?" The legionnaire glanced over the Maveri.

"Take the damn sword away from the well!" Maveri yelled out as worry engulfed his voice.

Arcturus frowned, "no, I will not remove the sword. I can feel her, she's coming back to me."

"The well is corrupted, you fool, remove the sword!" Aleiá stepped forward.

Arcturus raised Aegis. "You will have to kill me before I remove that blade!"

Maveri gazed at the legionnaire in utter confusion. "What! Don't be an idiot! We will find another way. We are here to fight the crimson, not bond with it!"

"What if there is no other way? What if all the other wells are lost?" Arcturus positioned himself between the group and the well. "If this is my only chance, then I will take it!"

Wreyth clenched his fists, "don't be a fucking twat!"

"Don't test me, calastain, I am not afraid to put you back in that grave!" Arcturus clamped his hand around Aegis, forcing its solar light to shine bright.

"Oh, you can fucking try it!" Wreyth readied his ethereal magic.

Maveri stormed between them, "stop it you two!" He turned to Arcturus, "I understand your pain, I lost everything too. We all did. I would give anything to get it all back, but this is not the right way, we will find another!"

Arcturus paused for a moment and stared into Maveri's eyes. Taking a deep breath, he turned to the blade to see the crimson light swelling in the well. "Shit, you're right. What in Nor'ai's name am I doing?!" He climbed the side of the well and grabbed the hilt of the sword. Pulling with all of his might he was barely able to shift Karek'Thur. "It's stuck!"

"What? How?" Maveri questioned.

"I don't know how! Just help me!" Arcturus urged them to aid him as the whisps of ethereal crimson light crept up to cover the majority of the sword. "Help me reclaim this sword!" The group rushed to him as they tried to pry the sword from the well. With each second that passed, the crimson engulfed more and more of the weapon. Desperation poured from Arcturus' soul as he wrenched at the blade.

I think you need to leave, my love...

"No! I can't leave you!" Arcturus pulled one last time. He watched as the crimson light kissed the final tip of the weapon. "No!" An almighty explosion of crimson light tossed the group across the far side of the room. The wave resonated out across the lands of Deythron, shattering the ice like thin glass and melting before it could retouch the ground. Crimson rivers poured from the mountains down through the valleys and the once turquoise-tipped mountaintops now shone with sickening crimson light.

Wreyth dragged himself to his feet and gazed down the gigantic structure which the group stood atop. "I don't think this was a velgartian made tower." He gazed over the almighty brimstone tower decorated with great horrific emblems of crimson horrors. "I think they just disguised it as one."

"What the in the hells has this magic done?" Aleiá moved to his side as she gazed over the ruined landscape. "The ice has just... gone."

Arcturus stood in disbelief, "what in light's name have I done? I am supposed to protect Nor'ai, not ruin her!"

"I think it's too late to pull the blade." Maveri pointed to Karek'Thur floating high above the shattered aetherwell. Veins of crimson light whipped against the surrounding structure as the soulstone slid from the weapon's guard. The stone trembled and twisted before shattering to form a great crimson beam down to the centre of the well and down through the building. The room shifted as great towers raised around them while the architecture of the room changed before their very eyes. Above them the ceiling split open, allowing the floor to lift to the tower's peak in a spiralling motion. In an attempt to hold steady, the group grabbed onto anything they could find. Brimstone churned and groaned into new positions as crimson veins sealed the new structure in place. The cracked skies above them sparked furious bolts of lightning and thunder that lashed at the ground. Each point of impact forged a new nightmarish structure, dragging it high into the skyline.

"Guys, look!" Wreyth gestured to two great claw-like archways ripping through the ground at the far end of the mountains. They curved to almost meet at their tips and a great staircase shifted into place beneath them. Crimson magic rushed up their spines, coursing like blood through the cracks in the brimstone structure. "What the fuck is happening?"

Arcturus lifted Aegis as the strong, oddly warm winds weaved amongst the group. "I don't know but I know our fight isn't over!" He gazed over the once glorious landscape that now lay tainted and ruined. Looking over the great citadel where they now stood, he knew there was no way down, no escape. A bolt of crimson light burned down to Karek'Thur slicing the weapon in two and shuddering the citadel beneath them. Arcturus held steady and squinted his eyes to see a silhouette below the blade standing where the aetherwell once stood. As the beam subsided, his eyes focussed to see a familiar form. "Maeve?"

"Arcturus?" Maeve stood donned in dark, black plate armour with veins of crimson light beating through it. "You did it, you brought me back!" She lifted her hands to inspect them. "I can't believe it." Clawed gauntlets glared back at her before a dark, plate, corinthian helm slowly forged in her palms with a dreadful plume of crimson magic trailing from its peak. "This is... different..."

"You look... different." Arcturus edged closer to her.

Raising her head, she locked eyes with the legionnaire. Her golden eyes flittered and sparked to life. "I, I don't feel like myself, Arcturus."

Arcturus clenched his jaw. "It's okay, my love, we will fix this. Everything will be okay."

"I can hear a voice; she's telling me to wear the helmet." Maeve turned the helmet in her hands.

"Don't listen to her. Listen to me, you are back, and we can fight together again." Arcturus' face became awash with concern and regret.

Her eyes flickered with a flash of crimson. "I...can't, please help me!"

Trying to resist the corruption, she slammed to her knees. "It hurts, Arcturus please!"

Arcturus rushed to her aid. "Hold on!" He grabbed her shoulder and turned to Maveri, "wizard, do you have a potion of healing?"

"I don't, I'm afraid." Maveri stared on in shock.

"Or a spell or anything, please, we need to help her!" Arcturus cried in agony.

Maveri turned his head. "I don't think we can."

Maeve slid the helmet onto her head. "I, please, my lo—"

Arcturus frowned, "Maeve? Don't..."

"I feel it. I see why now. It all finally makes sense." Maeve slowly raised her head and glared at Arcturus. Her golden eyes slowly shifted until they finally burned with crimson light. "This was always going to be our path, there was no sense in trying to fight it."

Arcturus stepped back, "no, please, no! Together we will defeat this enemy, you must resist!"

Maeve smirked, "resist? You are weak. Your love for this realm, your love for your sun gods and your love for me makes you weak!" Clenching her fist she forged a great, black, plate kite shield edged with crimson light.

"You're wrong!" Arcturus snarled. Wreyth, Aleiá and Maveri moved to Arcturus.

"I don't think that's your Maeve anymore." Maveri placed his hand on

Arcturus' shoulder and pulled him back.

"Get your hands off me!" Arcturus shunted him back.

Wreyth looked to Aleiá. "We need to leave this place."

"You will do no such thing!" Lifting her hand, Maeve beckoned the corrupted blade from above her. Karek'Thur landed in her palm and ignited in crimson light as its split blade housed a beam of pure crimson magic. "You will watch the fall of your realm!" She pointed the blade's tip at the group. Crimson tendrils whipped from the floor and wrapped around them, lifting them from the stone. "Then you will die."

"Maeve, no! Release them! This is between you and I." Arcturus writhed as he attempted to break free.

Maeve smirked, "no, *my love*, they are as much involved as you are. Oh I almost forgot, there's someone who wants to see you." She turned and slammed her blade into the brimstone. Crimson tendrils lashed out from the cracked stone, erratically whipping around the room. "This realm needs salvation, and we shall bring it!" The tendrils slowly calmed before wrapping around one another to form a deep crimson portal. "This is our destiny!" Paralyzed, the group watched on as the portal swirled to life.

A powerful female silhouette formed within its centre. "It's good to see you again, my son."

34
WHENCE IT CAME

The figure smirked. "So, it seems the rumours are true. You did survive." Arcturus' ears perked as he heard the strong, sharp voice. "I may have underestimated you." The legionnaire squinted in an attempt to gain a better view. Crimson light shimmered over her familiar designed silver ribboned armour with plumes of glowing crimson blossoming from her angular helm and pauldrons. She lifted her large kite shield; its crimson accents flickered to expose the ancient symbol of the virago within its centre. "Or maybe I overestimated that velgart to be able to take down the legionnaires even with the power of the crimson." She kicked the shards of Yatuul across the stone. "What a pathetic excuse of a mage." The large glyph upon the centre of her shield shone in deep crimson magic as she stepped closer.

"Is that...?" Maveri gasped.

The figure removed her helm to allow her grey hair to fall over her pale, cracked skin that pulsed with crimson light. "High Warden Tahmaliea it is to you, wizard."

Arcturus' face fell to shock as he struggled, "it can't be!"

She smirked, "oh, but it can."

"Tahmaliea Pythare?!" Maveri's eyes widened.

She smirked. "You know of me? That's sweet. The beings in this realm are so very good at telling each other stories, aren't they? I can imagine they made me some idol and left out the part that after the Great War, I was banished, right? The gods abandoned this realm aeons ago; everything we have worshipped, fought for, or sacrificed was for nothing. Nor'ai has nothing, no gods, no gifts, no worth. So, I believed it was time for her to have a god, it was time for someone to step up and take the throne." She gestured to the surrounding lands. "When I first found Deythron it was nothing, but I had plans to make it great." Raising her sword, she pointed it to the great arched structure in the distance. "I had plans to bring us a god, but they didn't like that."

Wreyth clenched his jaw. "Thousands have died because you have some strange power trip fantasy?"

Tahmaliea tilted her head. "There's no fantasy, child. If Nor'ai were to ever come under assault from demons or hostile gods, who would defend her? No, no, I swore an oath when I became High Warden. I swore to protect this realm no matter what and what better way to protect her than to bring her a god?"

"A god from an outer realm? Do you not see the destruction and carnage you've brought here already?" Aleiá yelled as she pried apart the crimson tendrils.

Tahmaliea chuckled. "What's that old saying? You have to rip something apart before you can truly rebuild it." She smirked. "This is just the beginning, the adjustment period. Once I bring him here, you'll see."

"The crimson will lay ruin to this place and take you with it!" Arcturus hailed out in anger.

Tahmaliea smiled. "I love how passionate you are. You really are my son."

"I am nothing like you! Father would be disappointed and shocked at everything you've done!" Arcturus sneered. "You do not deserve the title of High Warden."

She raised her brow, "and High Warden I no longer am. They will call me the Fallen Sun and from this day forth I will protect this realm the way it needs protecting!" Flashing a sinister smirk, she tilted her head, "your father was the one to banish me! After all those years of fighting side by side for this realm, defending Nor'ai, saving her. All I wanted to do was ensure her safety, but he couldn't see it!" She looked at Maeve. "He wanted to tame me and keep me collared as his lovesick lapdog just like you tried to do with her." Rolling her fingers under Maeve's chin, she grinned. "What is your name, child?"

"Maeve Sel'Tiare; Warden of Light." Maeve locked eyes with Tahmaliea.

Tahmaliea chuckled, "Warden of Light no more. Instead, you will be my

Harbinger of Crimson." She released her and turned to the group. "I will make you all see. One day you will be thanking me for the sacrifices I made for you." Lifting her sword skyward, a great beam of crimson burned down from the shattered skies into her blade. "Join us and we can live in this new world, together."

"Enough!" Maveri linked his hands together to form a blast of azure light dropping the group back to the floor. "We will never join your sick and twisted agenda!"

Tahmaliea frowned, "well that is a shame." She turned to Maeve, "end them, I have a god to welcome." Walking away she whistled and dropped carelessly off the edge of the tower. From the skies, an almighty black and crimson dragon soared down and swooped her up before flying off into the distance.

Crimson light poured from the gem within Karek'Thur's guard down onto the floor like a liquid mist. "This is where your journey ends." Maeve stood tall as her bright crimson eyes glared at Arcturus, "pah, and you call yourself a legionnaire."

Arcturus lifted Aegis, "Maeve Sel'Tiare, you do not have to do this."

The Harbinger's eyes saddened. "I don't have to, but I really want to."

"I am sorry my friend, but she leaves us no choice." Maveri lifted his spellbook.

"No choice at all." Wreyth pulled his hands aside, summoning his ethereal magic.

Arcturus clenched his jaw. "I know."

"Aleiá, to me!" Wreyth called out as the demon turned to ethereal light and plunged into his core. Bolts of ghostly light swirled around the calastain as his skin cracked, exposing a ghastly green magic. He clenched his body as he lifted into the air. In an explosion of ethereal magic, two vast glowing scythe-like demonic wings burst from his back. His arms flung aside as the skin on his forearms and hands turned ghostly. Two curved bone-like horns grew from his forehead. With a manic smile, he glared at Maeve. "This crimson god will never rule this realm!" His voice became entwined with the whispers of claimed souls.

"Then so be it, I'll save Nor'ai from all of you!" Maeve swung her sword releasing bolts of crimson magic at Wreyth. Sweeping his arms apart, Wreyth countered the magic in an ethereal blast of light.

"Maybe we can save you another way," Arcturus launched the image of Aegis at Maeve slamming it into her abdomen.

Maeve chuckled as she slid along the stone, "you cannot save what has already been saved!" She lifted her blade to summon several crimson horrors around her. The creatures dragged their hunched bodies into reality. Their several bony arms clawed at the floor in front of their two horrific, taloned legs. Maeve lifted her shield and rolled her sword's handle over her palm. "Crimson fiends, show them your might!" Now in full view, the beasts circled them, their torn feathered scales rattling as they snorted the air. Twitching and clicking, their featureless faces snapped back to reveal razor-sharp beaks covered in thousands of needled teeth. Snarling in taunting harmonies of terror, they leapt forth. Maveri and Wreyth pulled back as they attempted to rebuff them with their magic. Flashes of crimson, gold, azure and ethereal green beat out into the night skies as they locked in glorious combat.

"Live together, die together; that's what we swore!" Arcturus yelled as he slammed Aegis against Maeve. Pushing away, he weaved through her strikes, ducking and diving before returning blows to her.

Swirls of azure magic surrounded Maveri, "what in my darkest nightmares are these things?!"

"I have no clue and don't want to know! Just kill them!" Wreyth pushed his palm forth and burst ethereal magic through the creatures, tearing them apart.

In a blast of crimson energy, Maeve tossed Arcturus across the room. Controlling his fall, Arcturus flung the image of Aegis. The buckler clouted against Maeve's chest knocking her back. Bracing himself, he slammed against the brimstone floor and dug in the brim of his buckler. The shield ground him to a halt as golden sparks screamed off its ridge. Steadying herself, Maeve smirked and charged at Arcturus.

Azure magic beat through the crimson horrors as they leapt forth. Maveri pulled back his hands, forming erratic azure sparks between his palms then thrust forth to release a beam of pure azure energy. Holding the magic for as long as he could, he watched it eviscerate the charging horrors with ease.

"That's one way to do it, Maveri!" Wreyth grinned as he lifted the remaining horrors into the air before him. "These things have no soul; I truly have no idea what they are." Without a second thought, he ripped them apart with ethereal magic.

Relentlessly attacking, again and again, Maeve pushed for an opening until finally, she broke Arcturus' resolve. She shunted him down and stabbed her sword through his shoulder. Bursts of blood poured from the wound before Arcturus could repel her with Aegis. Stumbling, Maeve watched her Karek'Thur slide gracefully from the legionnaire's shoulder.

Arcturus clutched his wound. "You must resist the crimson, my love!"

Maeve grinned as her skin glowed with crimson light. "I can feel you holding back and that will be your undoing!" Raising her sword, she swung at Arcturus. Bolts of ethereal magic whipped against the crimson harbinger's armour, denying her assault. She glanced over to see Wreyth's almighty demonic form gliding towards her. In a whip of his wrist, Wreyth slung the ethereal image of a great clawed hand. The harbinger pulled back, summoning a crimson dome to block the path of the magic. Her eyes widened as the broken image phased through the barrier with ease. Its haunting guise wrapped around her core and wrenched her through the dome.

"Your magic will not stop mine." Wreyth's eyes stared deep into Maeve's soul.

Maeve smirked, "and yours will not stop mine." She aimed her Karek'Thur at his wing and released an almighty bolt of crimson through it, ripping it apart. Wreyth hailed out in pain as he slammed to the floor releasing his grasp on Maeve. "You are a soul that has chosen to remain tormented by the lands of the living, to remain tormented by your own mortality. How strange…"

"I returned to fight for my kind and to rid the world of threats like you!" Wreyth pulled himself up as Aleiá phased back to reality beside him. "Aleiá?" He glanced over to see the demon lying in a pool of her own blood.

"This really fucking hurts," Aleiá growled.

"I told you; your magic cannot stop mine." Maeve flashed a manic smile. "Demons wish they could harness power like this."

Arcturus pushed himself up and readied Aegis, "Maeve, leave them be!"

The harbinger watched the colour draining from Aleiá's eyes. "And why would I do that?"

"They are obviously no threat to you; they can't beat you. Nor can I." Arcturus clenched his jaw.

"Not alone you can't." Maveri supported the legionnaire. "Wreyth, you need to get her out of here. If she dies, you die, remember?"

Wreyth snarled. "I'm not leaving you here!" He looked at Aleiá, "all you need is a soul to claim, and you'll be okay. I think it's time we claimed hers!"

"Then we give it everything we've got!" Aleiá panted.

"One last shot!" Grabbing his spellbook from the ground, Maveri pulled his hands back. "If you can reclaim her soul then maybe we can save her." His eyes locked back on to Wreyth, "once you have it, we leave, deal?" His spellbook glided around him as astonishing azure runes sparked to life.

Wreyth released a manic grin, "perfect." Raising his hand, sparks of ethereal magic beat against the harbinger's chest. He lifted her to the centre of the room as his body started to shatter with ethereal light. The spectral image of Maeve's soul slowly ripped from her core, drifting into the air.

Arcturus closed his eyes, "we will save you, my love!"

Maeve squirmed and writhed in pain as soul magic lashed against her skin. "No! I will not let you take me!" She dragged her blade to face Wreyth, "release me!" A bright beam of crimson light sundered towards the calastain. Arcturus leapt before him and primed Aegis, releasing its golden barrier. The crimson poured around the barrier, forcing the legionnaire to his knees.

"Do it now, take her soul!" Arcturus tensed as the golden barrier slowly began to crack.

"I'm trying to!" An almighty pulse of soul magic surged through the room as Wreyth's physical form exploded to leave only a glowing ethereal soul. Aleiá raised her hand and poured her last ounce of magic into Wreyth's soul as Maeve's soul steadily phased toward the group.

Arcturus felt his muscles spasming. His wound seared as the crimson started ripping through his golden barrier. "I can't hold it much longer!"

"You must hold on!" Maveri pointed his palms at the golden barrier as the azure runes formed a circle before his body. Casting every remaining ounce of his magic, he began reinforcing Arcturus' barrier. Maeve's armour cracked as the crimson magic surged deeper through her core. She clenched her grasp around Karek'Thur as the beam screamed against Aegis.

"Almost there, I almost have it!" Wreyth's form waivered as his soul burned brighter and brighter. They watched as Maeve's soul reached out her hand to Arcturus.

Please, my love, bring me back to you!

"I'm trying my best." A tear rolled down Arcturus' cheek as the final ounce of his strength waivered. Aegis slowly creaked and bent out of shape as its magic began to flicker out of existence, allowing sparks of crimson to seep through. The magic lashed against his armour and exposed wounds, engulfing him in searing agony. "I can't...hold...on..." He bared his teeth attempting to hold the magic a moment longer. Out of the corner of his eye, he saw the arched claws spark to life. Within their centre, reality tore open to form a deep crimson pool-like portal. Reels of corruption poured from their core, rippling and contorting before them. Horrific screams and roars cried out as swirls of nightmarish images tainted the group's vision while a wave of crimson magic rolled over the land.

Maeve smiled as the magic poured into her core. "Finally, our salvation has come." Lifting Karek'Thur to the skies, she summoned an almighty thunderous bolt of crimson. "Crimson hear me!" As the bolt made impact, Aegis shattered, releasing shards of blazing hot metal. The pieces flew like hailstones towards the group, slicing through the air. Diving aside, they were barely able to dodge the debris. Aleiá's magic fell silent as a shard carved her skull in two, killing her instantly.

"Aleiá?!" Wreyth called out as his soul spasmed.

Maveri stepped back as his magic dispersed, "Wreyth!"

"Fuck, no! Not now, not like this!" Wreyth clawed at his chest as several shadows dragged him into the ethereal darkness.

Maveri's jaw fell agape in disbelief. "I can't believe it; we were so close." His spellbook slammed to the ground as he fell to his knees.

"So close yet so far." Maeve pulled her soul back into her body.

Arcturus reeled in agony as he dropped to the ground. "Is this it then? Is this our end?"

Maeve strolled over and placed her blade to his throat. "Not yet. I want you to watch." She bound the pair in a reel of crimson chains and dragged them to the outer edge of the tower. "We can welcome in our new god, together." Arcturus watched as the distant silhouette of Tahmaliea's dragon hovered before the portal. The vast beast was absolutely dwarfed by the tremendous size of the structure.

"Nor'ai's gods will not allow this," Arcturus muttered.

"They don't have a choice." Maeve glanced down. "This is our new beginning."

Maveri closed his eyes as he fumbled subtly in his pockets, "you can't just bring a new god here and expect it to go swimmingly."

"I'm going to miss your nonsense when all is said and done." Maeve stared on with glee.

Maveri leaned over to Arcturus, "we need to leave, use your crystal if you can reach it."

"What's the point?" Arcturus whispered in return.

Maveri glanced up, "what's the point? The point is so we can fight again another day. We can muster an army and come back here to end this once and for all. We will save them all."

"How will we ever defeat a god?" Arcturus snarled.

"Nor'ai has magic even we can't fathom. With help, we will find a way." Maveri smirked as he felt his crystal. "This will not be our end, don't be such a defeatist."

"Silence!" Maeve slammed her sword to the brimstone. "He is here." The ground throughout Deythron rumbled as a pair of almighty, towering, armoured hooves appeared through the portal. They slammed into the brimstone stairs, cracking them as hulking tri-clawed hands grasped the edges of the portal. Its flesh shimmered as crimson pulsed over its terrifying structure. Its burnished muscular chest pulled through the crimson pool, burning brightly with crimson magic down to its scarred abdomen. Cascading crimson flames formed a loincloth flowing down to its knees dripping onto the ground below the beast. Corrupted magic burned up from its neck as the horrific structure of its skeleton-like face materialized. Four vast menacing horns arched from the sides of its head while its haunting crimson eyes burst to life. Snarling, the creature opened its nightmarishly fanged jaw as the cracks within its entire body ignited in crimson light. Inhaling a long deep breath, it tensed its great maw as shrouds of corrupt magic poured from within. Its soul-tearing glare locked onto Arcturus.

Maeve audibly gasped. "He is wondrous."

"That is no god." Maveri rolled his crystal in his fingertips, "that is the ender of realms. I read about him many moons ago, but I believed it to just be legend."

The legionnaire froze in disbelief. "Maeve, can you truly not see it? Can you not see that this creature will lay Nor'ai to ruin?" He stared hopelessly into her glowing crimson eyes.

"This creature is our salvation. This will birth a new age in this godforsaken realm!" She turned to the pair of them. "He is our god."

"No, he will be our end," Maveri grunted.

Maeve chuckled, "you know nothing of gods, wizard. You learn magic from a book because Nor'ai didn't want to gift it to you."

"What do you know? Your magic was given to you through birth. You may learn to hone and control your magic, but you know not of its history or origins!" Maveri retorted.

Maeve glared at the wizard, "hold your tongue! Do not speak of what you know nothing about!"

"I know that your magic is a gift from Nor'ai herself. I also know that by doing what you're doing with this false god, you will wipe this realm from existence!" Maveri shuffled to look her directly in the eyes. "You are killing the realm that birthed you, that gave you life, that gave you magic, the realm that gave you a purpose."

"And this will be my gift back to the realm! This *is* my purpose as Nor'ai's protector!" Maeve clenched her fist. "This is what Nor'ai has asked of me."

Arcturus bowed his head, "we were Nor'ai's protectors, but this magic has wiped out practically every legionnaire I have known! Eradicating the ones who fought to protect something is not protecting it!"

"You and your false values are blind! Without this crimson we are weak! I had hoped I could make you see that, but I was wrong. This is what Nor'ai and her people need!" Raising her sword, Maeve primed her crimson magic. "And I will not have you trying to deny that!" She pointed Karek'Thur at Arcturus. "Nor'ai will engulf herself if we don't intervene. We swore an oath to protect with any means necessary. This is the only option we have left."

"There will always be another option." Arcturus pushed against the blade. "Especially when the option you have chosen is world domination and death."

Maeve smiled, "you act like you aren't the one who brought me here."

Arcturus frowned, "I thought I was saving you."

"You were, and you have in turn saved the realm." She tilted her head, "but now your use has run out. Consider this the end of your duty, legionnaire."

"Arcturus, do it, now!" Maveri crushed his crystal. Pristine streams of azure magic engulfed him and swept him into a fleeting portal.

Arcturus slid his crystal from his pocket and rolled it to his palm. "I love you." But before he could crush the crystal his eyes ignited in golden light.

If ever your fortress falls, you will find safety in mine.

A surging, unknown power forced him to stand. His bindings dissipated in golden light as the voice resonated through the skies.

Please accept this favour as a gift.

"No, this can't be!" Maeve recoiled in shock. She pulled back her blade and swung it at the legionnaire.

Arcturus gripped the weapon. "I will come back to save you, my love."

Maeve snarled. "No, you will die here and now!" Surging more power behind Karek'Thur, she released a beam of crimson light. Arcturus pushed the weapon aside, forcing the beam to soar into the skies. He looked over the beautiful sparks of gold twirling around him in mesmerizing patterns.

You have done all you can here, legionnaire.

The glorious voice birthed a slight smile on Arcturus' lips. "Grant me the power to do more." He looked to Maeve, "I will come back for you."

"No!" Maeve swung Karek'Thur at this throat but before the weapon could make contact, Arcturus pulled her close. They locked eyes for a moment as their lips lingered but a breath's kiss apart. Two great beams of crimson and gold struck the tower causing an explosion that tore through the structure of the citadel. The blast forced them apart in a hail of rubble and magic. Time seemed to slow as Arcturus watched Maeve fly further away from his grasp. Sparks of gold and crimson magic whipped around them in erratic whisps of lightning as they fell from the tower's spire.

Arcturus welcomed the soft touch of the winds as he fell. Rolling the warp crystal in his palm, he gazed over its now sparkling gold texture. "Take me away from this place. I accept your favour." He crushed it allowing the pristine golden portal to engulf him. Its welcoming embrace warmed his soul and cleansed his wounds as he spiralled into glorious nothingness. Its embrace felt like safety, like home. Absorbing this moment of peace and silence, he closed his eyes drifting weightlessly amongst the turbulent sparks of light. Images of Krytiare bloomed in his mind, allowing him to almost see life walking its streets once again. Memories of his allies, his friends and his home all flooded back to him as he thought back to that fateful night. "One day," he thought, "one day I will see that again."

With this favour, I grant you a second chance. Arcturus, this is only your beginning...

ABOUT THE AUTHOR

Blessed with ADHD and dyslexia, Jamie is an author from the Midlands, UK. He is a dog dad to two wonderful pooches named Jess and Luna, and in his spare time is an avid gamer, actor, singer and airsofter. In his current day job, he runs a successful salon named JAG Hair Studios, but ever since he was a child he has loved being creative, especially with fantasy. Jamie became an author because he found a love for books at a young age, but being neurodivergent, he found reading very taxing. He decided he wanted to create his own world and his own stories for anyone and everyone to enjoy. Thus, The Legends Of Nor'ai was born!